WHAT YOU
ALWAYS WANTED

WHAT YOU ALWAYS WANTED

An IF ONLY *novel*

Kristin Rae

BLOOMSBURY

NEW YORK   LONDON   OXFORD   NEW DELHI   SYDNEY

First published in the United States of America in March 2016
by Bloomsbury Children's Books
www.bloomsbury.com

Bloomsbury is a registered trademark of Bloomsbury Publishing Plc

For information about permission to reproduce selections from this book, write to
Permissions, Bloomsbury Children's Books, 1385 Broadway, New York, New York 10018
Bloomsbury books may be purchased for business or promotional use. For information on bulk
purchases please contact Macmillan Corporate and Premium Sales Department at
specialmarkets@macmillan.com

Library of Congress Cataloging-in-Publication Data
Rae, Kristin.
What you always wanted : an If only novel / by Kristin Rae.
pages   cm
Summary: Maddie's dream guy has to live up to the grace and romance of classic Hollywood
heartthrobs, especially the song-and-dance man Gene Kelly, so does Jesse Morales, her charming
new neighbor and star pitcher of the high school baseball team, have a chance?
ISBN 978-1-61963-345-2 (paperback) • ISBN 978-1-61963-821-1 (hardcover)
ISBN 978-1-61963-822-8 (e-book)
[1. Love—Fiction. 2. Friendship—Fiction. 3. Theater—Fiction. 4. Baseball—Fiction. 5. High
schools—Fiction. 6. Schools—Fiction.] I. Title.
PZ7.R12313Wh 2016   [Fic]—dc23   2015010339

Book design by Amanda Bartlett
Typeset by Newgen Knowledge Works (P) Ltd., Chennai, India
Printed and bound in the U.S.A. by Berryville Graphics Inc., Berryville, Virginia
2 4 6 8 10 9 7 5 3 1 (paperback)
2 4 6 8 10 9 7 5 3 1 (hardcover)

All papers used by Bloomsbury Publishing, Inc., are natural, recyclable products
made from wood grown in well-managed forests. The manufacturing processes
conform to the environmental regulations of the country of origin.

For Gene Kelly

CHAPTER ONE

Contrary to popular belief, Texas is not all tumbleweeds, cacti, and horses. I haven't seen a desert yet, and the people in Houston mostly look the same as people from back home, but with the occasional set of cowboy boots. And the restaurants we've tried so far aren't too bad, though they cook everything in butter. Then cover it with gravy.

Apparently there's zero public transportation in my new north-side community except for some little trolley thing to take you between the mall, the grocery store, and the library. But it's more cute than useful, especially since I live down a dirt road even farther north from everything. People here seem to favor driving their own pickup trucks. I can probably count on one hand the number of times I've ridden in a truck, but now I feel like I must have one too. Or at least something with four wheels. And soon.

We've lived here exactly six days. School starts in three. School, as in, my new school. As in, I get to start all over for my junior year, minus everyone I know. Minus every*thing* I know.

And it's hot here. The melt-your-face-off kind of hot. Our mailbox is way out at the street next to the driveway, not up by the door like I'm used to. So here I am in my new Southern life, forced to walk the acre-long driveway in the scorching August sun because the really good classic movies are only available to rent on disc. I shake my fist in the air at the hypothetical Netflix gods before opening the rusted contraption.

Perfect. Mail's not even here yet. I wouldn't mind so much if I didn't feel like I had to take a shower every time I came in from outside. I smell like a wet dog that just rolled in grass clippings.

I turn to head back to the house and hear gravel crunch under tires as a vehicle pulls out of the driveway across the street. It doesn't drive off, so I toss a curious glance at the cherry-red Tahoe. The window glides down, revealing a woman around my parents' age with highlighted hair in a wedge cut and a chunky turquoise necklace that might possibly be choking her.

"How's the move-in going?" she calls out to me.

I shrug and relax my eyes as a cloud passes over. If I told her the whole truth, I'd sound like a huge whiner. "We'll be living out of boxes for a while. The house needs to be fixed up. A *lot.*" I take a few steps closer as she cuts off the engine.

She nods and gives a little snicker. "Yeah, the last people that lived there were a little . . . grubby. I'm Sherri Morales," she says. "Where did y'all move from?"

"Maddie Brooks. We're from Chicago."

"Really? I'm from Michigan. Well, haven't lived there in twenty years, but I grew up there." She glances at her fancy silver watch. "Are you starting school on Monday?"

"Yes," I say through a frown. "I'll be a junior."

"Aw, why the sour face? I'm sure you'll be just fine. My daughter Angela is a sophomore, but she'd love to show you the ropes. And I'll be there too since I'm the theatre teacher. I also help run the Fernwood Community Playhouse in town."

My jaw drops. "You're kidding me. You're the theatre teacher? I'm signed up for your class, then!" I rush to her and grip the door at the window opening, putting us face-to-face. "What productions are we doing this year? Can you give me a heads-up?"

She doesn't look shocked by my burst of enthusiasm. "Oh, I'm still finalizing the calendar. Got the acting bug, do you?"

"More like a disease."

She smiles, eyes wide. "Well, show me what you've got."

Without missing a beat, I look her dead in the eye and recite one of my favorite bits from *Barefoot in the Park*.

I inwardly celebrate my delivery. I'd worked on memorizing the script last spring for an audition I missed because of the move. At least I'm getting some use out of it.

Mrs. Morales cocks her head to the side and surprises me with the next line of dialogue.

Boosted with confidence, I say what's next and we go back and forth in an impromptu performance in the middle of the street until she says, "If you always perform that well, you'll have no problem keeping up with my core team."

"Thank you!" I resist the urge to jump up and down.

She gazes out the windshield. "I haven't thought about that play in a really long time. Most kids your age haven't even heard of it—the play or the movie."

"Oh, I adore the movie," I sigh, placing a hand over my heart. "Robert Redford. So hot."

"Are you sure you're in high school?" Mrs. Morales rests her head against the seat back and laughs. "Well, I can't tell you how refreshing this conversation is, Maddie Brooks." She checks her watch again and reaches for the keys in the ignition. "You don't happen to have plans tonight, do you?"

Thinking she's about to ask me to accompany her to a play or to dinner so we can discuss my future on Broadway, I shake my head. "No friends here yet."

No friends anywhere.

"Would you mind watching my five-year-old, Elise, for a couple hours? Angela may not speak to me for a week if I make her stay home another Friday night."

I deflate. That's nowhere near as fun. I've always avoided babysitting like the dentist. Snotty noses, whining, all the questions. Makes me shudder.

"I'll give you fifty bucks."

On the other hand, babysitting can be quite lucrative. The little darling shall love me.

Around six o'clock, I start the marathon down their driveway. The house isn't visible from the road, so I have no idea what to expect—if it's small and rundown like my new house or . . . a freaking mansion.

The two-story stucco house spreads wide across the clearing of tall pines and oak trees. Obviously, the Morales family has a lot more land than we do.

A robin's-egg-blue Dodge truck that looks older than my parents' rests off to the side, next to a newer, bright yellow Beetle. I don't see Mrs. Morales's Tahoe anywhere.

I knock on the huge wooden door, and a few seconds later a girl near my age but a couple inches taller than me opens it. She looks exactly like her mother, but only in body frame and facial features—same green eyes and full lips. Her shoulder-length hair is almost black and she has that pretty olive skin tone that makes me jealous.

"Maddie, right?" she asks.

"Angela, right?"

"Come on in," she says, turning and waddling back into the house, her shiny red toes separated with foam.

I follow her past a grand wooden staircase to the kitchen. She plops down at a round dining table and works on her fingernails. Her left hand looks pretty good, but the right is sloppy with paint all over her skin.

"That looks terrible," I say.

She grunts and turns her head back the way we came. "Elise! Your sitter's here!"

There's stomping overhead and a little voice shouts, "I'm staying in my room!"

I spot two twenty-dollar bills on the counter by the phone. "Did your mom leave that for me?"

She nods, then yells, "Elise, get down here and meet her before I leave."

More thumping from upstairs. "No! I have chalk hands. Mom said I can't go downstairs with chalk hands."

Fantastic.

"Then wash them! Don't make me count!" Angela swipes at her pinky nail but the brush hits more of her skin than the actual nail. "Chalk hands," she mutters.

"And you have nail polish hands," I say, pocketing the twenties. I notice a ten-dollar bill under a set of keys on the kitchen island. Pretty sure that's supposed to be mine too.

Angela douses a cotton ball with remover and attacks her fingers. "I can't do this. I'll never get it."

"Whoa, whoa, you're going to mess up your good hand." I sit next to her and wet a new cotton ball. "Here, let me."

"Elise!" she calls again. "I swear, that girl. She's like a little kid or something."

We laugh as I carefully paint her nails. This feels so normal, like any other Friday night, me and my friends painting each other's trouble hands. But I've been here for two minutes. All I know about this girl is that she can yell really loudly and she thinks she's putting one over on me.

"So," I begin, "about that ten dollars over there . . ."

She covers her mouth with her other hand and groans. "She told you how much she was giving you?"

"Uh, yeah." I blow on her fingertips out of habit, then stop myself because really, I wouldn't want a stranger blowing on my hand.

"I'm sorry." Her forehead falls to the table with a little thud. "She never gives me any money, not even when I watch Elise. But she'll pay *you* to do it." She snaps her head up to look at me. "No offense."

I shrug, wondering if Rider ever went through any of this with me when we were younger. Not that he's that much older than me—just a couple of years—but it must be a pain having to watch a sibling. So glad I don't have to deal with that.

"I didn't even have any real plans besides trying to get my friend Tiffany to go to the mall with me. There's this cute guy who works at the candy apple kiosk," Angela explains. "I mean, how lame is it to hang out on the weekend with a five-year-old? No offense there either."

"Hey, I have an excuse. I don't know anyone yet."

Once we moved, I sort of made this plan to be a mopey introvert. I was going to act so alone and depressed that my parents would have to send me back to Chicago and I'd find a way into my old social circle—even though they distanced themselves after my dad lost his job and moved us to Texas, so admittedly, not the most genuine group of girls. But that's not exactly a realistic scheme, and I really want to be accepted here. I'm too needy to give up friends entirely.

Angela inspects her nails before blowing on them. "Thanks. They look great." She sighs, leaning back in her chair.

"Well," I begin, "if you really don't have anything to do tonight, what if we split the money and watch Elise together?"

She hesitates and instantly I feel like an idiot. This girl is a grade below me. I'm guessing she's the one who drives the Beetle the color of sunshine that begs to be seen on the road, and I'm asking her to stay in on a Friday night. Look how desperate I am to make a friend. I'm bribing her with money that she already stole.

"I could paint your nails," she finally says.

I try to tone down my eagerness. "Sure!"

After she does a decent job of turning my nails a shimmery pink, Angela leads me up the staircase to meet Elise. Her bedroom is a purple explosion of pillows and stuffed animals, with three lilac walls and one black with chalkboard paint covered in doodles. A girl in jean shorts and a blue shirt turns her back on her masterpiece to face us, three fat sticks of chalk in her hands. I'm surprised to find that her hair's nearly blond.

"Lookit!" Elise points to a drawing of a pink house among flowers the size of trees.

"It's beautiful!" Angela picks up a few stray pieces of chalk from the floor and puts all but one into a bucket near the wall. "You're a true artist. Don't you think so, Maddie?"

Elise looks at me shyly out of the corner of her eye. I'm not used to little kids, so I'm not really sure how to interact with them. But I'm getting paid for this, so I might as well make an effort.

"I think you're fantastic," I begin. "Best flower-drawer I've ever seen!"

This wins her over. She smiles and shows me a huge patch of chalk flowers in the corner by her dresser, going up as high as she can reach. "They're my favorite! Big ole daisies."

Angela writes ELISE in yellow block letters in the blank space above the house.

"Hey, that's my name!" Elise giggles then turns to me. "What's your name look like?"

I make sure my nails are dry before taking the stick of chalk from Angela, and I spell out my name next to hers, drawing a little daisy as the dot over the *I*. Elise claps and I smile back at her, strangely pleased that I've just been approved by a five-year-old.

Angela wipes her hands on a towel hanging over the edge of the chalk bucket. "Maddie and I are going to play with you tonight, how does that sound?"

"Okay," Elise says, also wiping off her hands. "Can we have egg rolls? And white rice?"

"That sounds like a yummy idea," Angela says. "Go wash your hands and pick out a movie to watch, and I'll order."

After we decide on sesame chicken to go with our egg rolls, Angela points me to the TV room at the end of the hall—a living area with a gigantic screen, a couple brown leather couches, and a built-in bookcase along the entire back wall. As long as I don't look up too high, I can ignore the deer heads mounted above the window. I wander to the bookcase to look at the collection of family photos, and learn there are a total of three children. Elise is the youngest, Angela's the middle child, and whoever *that* gorgeousness is had better be in my class come Monday. He's a little taller than Angela with spiky, near-black hair and the same green eyes. Man, their parents make some pretty kids.

"That's Jesse," Angela says, startling me.

"Cool." If I were a blusher, I'd probably go tomato-faced. Nothing like getting caught drooling over a picture of someone's hot brother.

"Meh. He's pretty cool as far as brothers go, I guess." She plops down on the love seat and hollers, "Elise, come pick out a movie!"

"Is Jesse here somewhere? I'm guessing that's his blue truck in the driveway."

"It is, but he's out with friends. His popularity level is annoying."

Because I can't help myself, I glance at Jesse's image one more time before sitting on the other couch. "Popularity with girls, you mean?" As if that needed clarification.

"Everyone, but yes, girls especially." She wrinkles her nose in the sisterly way I know all too well.

"Don't worry," I say, feeling suddenly guilty for finding him attractive. I put my hand over my chest in hopes of making her laugh. "My heart belongs to another."

This seems to satisfy her, for now.

Anyway, I'm pretty sure no one's brother will ever be able to compare to the man of my dreams.

CHAPTER TWO

"Ma! Where's my backpack?" I shout, practically upside down in a moving box. I've sifted through all of these at least three times this morning. No backpack.

I walk across the hallway to my parents' room. "Ma?"

The toilet flushes and she emerges from the bathroom, red-faced and watery-eyed. "Didn't I ask you to get your stuff ready yesterday?"

"Are you sick?" I take a step back and pull the collar of my emerald-green shirt over my mouth. "I can't get sick the first week of school."

She clears her throat. "I'm sure it's just something I ate. I feel better already."

"Do you have a fever?" I reach up to touch her forehead, but she swats me away.

"I'm fine," she says in a clipped voice. "Let's get you to school."

"Angela's coming to get me in, like, five minutes. You really don't know where my backpack is?"

"She's old enough to drive? I thought you said she was in tenth grade."

"She turned sixteen in July."

"Well, isn't that comforting?" Ma's face somehow falls even more. "I always take you to school the first day."

"Oh. Well, Angela offered to bring me there early and show me around, so I said yes. You wanted me to make friends here, right?" I don't wait for her to answer. "I'll need you to pick me up, though, since she has volleyball practice after school. I get out at 2:35." I offer a concerned smile in an attempt to smooth things over. "Maybe you should drink some orange juice and go back to bed."

"You're awfully sweet to worry about me, but there's too much to do. Wallpaper that needs to come down, carpet to order, paint to buy. This place is a mess." She sighs and disappears into her closet.

I refrain from asking, "Whose fault is that?" She already knows how I feel about our situation.

Land, my parents said before we moved. *We're going to have land!*

Land shmand. Land has bugs. Namely, mosquitoes. And everything's bigger in Texas, they say. Except our house. Well, it's smaller than our old house. And it's a foreclosure so it was cheap. Translation: a wreck. Ma's little project to keep her busy. Whatever. I got to pick out my room and that door is closed to her color samples and fabric swatches. I have my own vision for it that involves a fresh coat of paint, twinkle lights, and every classic movie poster I can get my hands on.

"Well, just don't go climbing ladders or anything when nobody else is home," I call to her before turning for the hallway.

"How did you get so paranoid?"

Ignoring her, I rush to my bathroom and add the finishing touches to my makeup, which include drawing a beauty mark on the top corner of my cheek near my left eye. A tiny star, just like the one Jean Hagen wore in *Singin' in the Rain* for the silent film parts. I've been practicing all weekend to get the look just right. You only get one chance to make a first impression.

Spraying my loose curls—I battled with the styling wand for nearly an hour—and scanning my wardrobe one more time, I approve my combo of casual and dressy. I grab my purse and a thick six-subject spiral notebook from my room and shout a good-bye to Ma, snatch my lunch box, and run out the door before she can stop me and get all sentimental. I slip into Angela's Beetle and resist the urge to change my outfit. She's wearing jeans the same yellow as her car, red flats, and a bright blue top with flowy sleeves, and her raven hair is half up, half down. Giant sunglasses cover half her face, so her deep red lips are the focal point. She'll definitely turn some heads today.

"I'm not sure if I should be going to school with you," I say as she expertly backs out of my driveway. "Your paparazzi might run me over."

"Please," she says with a laugh. "You're the hot one with all those curls. Just so you know, I almost shut the door on you

Friday night as soon as I looked at you." She peeks at me as she shifts into drive. "Did you join a gang since the last time I saw you?"

"What?" I ask, clicking my seat belt and smiling at the blood-red rose stuck in the bud vase near the steering wheel. Matches her lips and shoes.

She taps her cheek. "Star-face."

I laugh and check in the visor mirror to make sure it hasn't gotten smeared. "Have you seen *Singin' in the Rain*?"

"Oh, you like the really old movies." She throws her head back and snores. "My mom's going to want to adopt you."

I sink into my seat in relief. My old theatre teacher and I didn't always see eye to eye. I pushed for musicals while he preferred the straight plays—not that I discriminate. It's just looking like this year I might have a chance to really learn something that's more in line with what I want to do.

"Well," I say, crossing my arms, "the star stays."

"Hey, I wasn't telling you to take it off." Angela's silent for a few seconds before she asks, "Do I get one too?"

Fernwood High School is a beautiful two-story giant of red brick and cream-colored stone. It looks quite prestigious with a grand entrance of archways, tall windows, and an inset clock overhead that reminds me of the movie *Back to the Future*, which depresses me because time machines aren't real. If they were, I'd zap myself to 1930 and rewrite Hollywood history, with me in it.

Angela's a saint and walks me through my schedule, dropping

me off at my homeroom with just enough time for her and her own star-face to make it to hers. Papers are passed out, rules are recited, lockers are assigned, much yawning occurs. Things are pretty uneventful until third period English. Just like I do in any classroom or theatre, I look for an open seat in the middle of the middle.

And I see him.

Tanned skin, green eyes, thick black hair perfectly spiked forward with a slight lean to the left. Angela's brother. It has to be. And there's an empty desk next to him. Maybe I should take it. I mean, I practically already know him.

"Jesse, my man." A thick guy with blond hair does a hand-shake finger-snap thing with Jesse before plopping down right where I was considering.

"What's up, Red?" Jesse's voice is smooth, no hint of excitement.

I wonder if maybe they aren't friends at all, or if he's relaxed about everything. I also wonder if the guy's name is actually Red, or if I misunderstood. I thought that was a nickname for redheads.

Before I make a spectacle of myself, standing in the middle of the classroom staring at the boys, I sit at the empty desk in front of Red. Soon all the seats are filled as students trickle in, followed by an older man in a worn gray suit and glasses nearly as big as his face. The name at the top of the dry-erase board tells me this is Mr. McCaffey.

There are still a few minutes before class starts, but Mr. McCaffey scans the room and says, "Mr. Lyle and Mr. Morales, you seem to think I've forgotten about last year already. I won't have you two talking baseball strategies over my lessons."

Baseball? Gag.

"One of you needs to relocate before the bell."

Red lets out a shocked puff of air. "But Mr. Mc—"

"I'm going to get my coffee," Mr. McCaffey says. "When I come back, you should be sitting somewhere else."

He leaves and I relax in my seat as if I were the one who was just scolded. My teachers have been pretty okay so far, so I guess I was bound to get a persnickety one in the mix.

Red makes a bunch of noise gathering his things, and I hear his requests repeatedly denied to change desks with people farther back. Before I realize what's happening, I'm staring at the hem of his blue-and-white-striped shirt.

"Um . . . can I help you?" My eyes travel the rest of the way up, delaying a second on each of his biceps before meeting his eyes, which are a light blue.

"You can if you trade desks with me."

I turn to look at his desk. It does have a view out the window, while mine is next to a book-cover poster of *To Kill a Mockingbird*. And it's next to the brother of the only friend I have in Texas, so why not? With a nod, I reach for my purse and scoop up my notebook.

"Thanks," he says. "I'm Curtis, by the way."

I open my mouth to introduce myself but remember there's a slight chance Angela may have mentioned me to them as Maddie. I'd rather see how they act around me as someone they know nothing about.

"I'm Madison."

I slide into my new seat, accidentally slapping my notebook on top of the desk with too much force, and it thuds to the floor. I hurry to retrieve it but see that it landed on a pair of boots.

"Eeek! I'm sorry, Jesse," I say in a hurry, bending down to grab it.

He beats me to it and I pause, hunched over, arm extended, as he hands it to me. We both raise our heads until our eyes find each other's. The green of his irises transitions to amber near the pupil, as though they couldn't decide on being green or brown.

"Steel toes. Didn't even feel it."

We sit upright and I busy myself by opening my notebook to the next blank section and writing the date on the top. I want to die. My very own meet-cute. Well, the way we just met might not really be that cute, but *he* sure is.

"So you've heard of me?" he asks, resting his elbows on his desk and leaning toward me. "Been to any of my games, or have we had a class together before?"

Great. He's one of those.

Pressing my eyebrows together in an attempt to look distressed, I say, "We've had at least one class together every year since we were eight."

He sinks into his seat. "What?"

I blink, not ready to break just yet. I want to see if he'll pretend to recognize me or tell the truth even if it makes him look like a jerk.

"I—I'm sorry." He shrugs, looking genuinely confused. Maybe even a little embarrassed. "I don't remember."

Good boy.

"I'm kidding. I'm new. I heard your name when he came in." I motion toward Curtis or Red or whatever his name is. "Jesse, my man," I say, imitating him and offering my hand.

I hold my breath and watch Jesse instinctively take my hand. He smiles when I finish out the handshake with a snap using both of our thumbs, just like the guys did. I may or may not have just initiated myself into some sort of guys club.

Which is fine, I guess, but I have to admit I'm disappointed our touch failed to cue fireworks. No one burst into song. This is just another first day of school, like every other year before.

Reality has a lot to learn from the movies.

CHAPTER THREE

There are four lunch periods over a two-hour span, but Angela and I have the same one. It's typically my policy not to eat cafeteria food, so I'm halfway through my ham and cheese before Angela and a girl sporting a super-high ponytail get their food and sit across from me.

"Maddie, this is Tiffany. One of my friends from volleyball."

"Hey." Tiffany smiles and wastes no time digging into her meal.

"Good to meet you," I say, but honestly my mind's swirling with all the new people I've met. Tiffany should be easy enough to remember, given my love of *Breakfast at Tiffany's*. Though this girl is far from an Audrey Hepburn type.

Angela scoops her mashed potatoes with a chicken tender. "Tiffany's a sophomore like me, but she already plays varsity.

And she's been looked at by a few colleges, including Duke. How crazy is that?"

"Gee, thanks. You're leading with *that* now?" Tiffany's accent is definitely Texan.

"Impressive," I say, sipping on my bottled water.

Pulling a shoulder toward her ear, she says, "I eat, sleep, and breathe volleyball. Momma's orders." She doesn't completely close her mouth when she chews, and it makes me cringe inside.

"When Tiffany was little," Angela adds, "her mom went to the Olympics for volleyball. They got bronze, can you believe that? Her mom medaled in the freaking Olympics!"

"Wow. Is that a goal of yours too?" I ask Tiffany. "To go to the Olympics?"

"I dunno." She tears out the middle of her wheat roll and shapes it into a cube with her fingers. "Momma would love it, but . . ."

"But?" Angela prods.

Tiffany shrugs again. "I'm not sure yet. Let me make it through high school first." She laughs. "One thing at a time."

"One day at a time," Angela adds, raising her can of pop in the air like a toast.

Tiffany rushes to lift her Gatorade bottle, and after they tap them together, they take a swig. I don't ask.

"You're from Chicago, huh?" Tiffany asks after a few minutes of silence. "I went there once. It was freezing."

"Yeah, it gets pretty cold back home." *Home.* I stifle a whimper and shove the remains of my sandwich back in my lunch box, appetite stolen from me. "I don't suppose it snows this far south?" I brace myself for the answer. I love my snow.

"Maybe once every couple of years, but it doesn't stick," Angela says.

"That's so depressing."

"I'll tell you what's depressing," Tiffany says, wiping her mouth with the back of her hand. "That no one told me we were wearing stars on our cheeks today. Who's got the marker?"

A smile spreads over my face as I reach into my purse for my liquid eyeliner pen. I think I just made my second friend.

The school's theatre is massive. Not just the stage, which is complete with state-of-the-art lighting and sound equipment, but the seating too. It must seat over five hundred people. Back at my old school, the theatre was cramped and way past its prime. It reeked of mildew, sweaty costumes, and the teacher's stinky old-man cologne.

A circle of black folding chairs takes center stage and some kids are already seated, a few of them getting a head start on their homework load. There's nothing signifying the teacher's seat, so I sit among a group of empty chairs and take a quick survey of faces. I recognize one girl from Spanish class, but I only know her by the name she picked out for herself: Anita. Now that I see she's into acting, I wonder if she named herself after the character in *West Side Story*. I chose Manuela, Judy Garland's character from *The Pirate*.

Two boys the only ones in class? slip in just before the bell rings, and Mrs. Morales appears from backstage, taking the seat to my left. My heart soars. I *am* the teacher's pet already!

I fight to rein in the pride. That's exactly the type of thought that precedes a major ego-kick, and I don't want any of that. No. It's only a coincidence.

"Another school year," Mrs. Morales begins. "There's something promising about a fresh start, isn't there?"

Murmurs come from the class, which seems worn down from a very long first day.

"And most of you are upperclassmen this year, one step closer to breaking free, setting out on your own, and leaving your mark on the world."

"Anita" sits taller at this, the corner of her mouth hitched, eagerness in her eyes. Oh, yeah. She definitely got her name for Spanish class from *West Side Story.*

"I'm Mrs. Morales, for those of you who don't know me, and this"—she spreads her arms wide as if to encompass all her surroundings—"is the big stage. I like to begin the year here, but we'll meet in the black box theatre starting tomorrow. While most of you are familiar with one another, we're adding some new talent to the group this year."

Several of the girls across the circle exchange nervous glances.

"But don't worry, they're all transferring highly recommended from their former programs, and I'm confident everyone will get along famously. This is going to be the best dramatic year Fernwood High has ever seen."

The boys let out a whoop and the girls nearest them giggle. Seriously, there should be more guys in here. These two don't look to be very promising romantic counterparts, with their graphic T-shirts and bright-colored sneakers.

Mrs. Morales reviews some of the highlights from last year, then outlines what's to come this semester, as well as what she's considering. She even mentions *Barefoot in the Park* and I squeal inside, wondering if I had anything to do with that idea until she winks at me. Now I adjust to sit a little taller too.

"So let's play an icebreaker game with the few minutes left of class, shall we?" she says. "Any suggestions?"

A couple game titles are tossed around halfheartedly before Mrs. Morales thankfully skips over "Truth or Dare" in favor of "Two Truths and a Lie."

"Sarah," she says to the stocky girl with light brown hair on her left. "Would you start us off?"

"Um . . . I spent the summer in San Francisco." She clears her throat. "I'm on the tennis team. I'm allergic to strawberries."

"Okay, everyone," Mrs. Morales says, crossing her feet at the ankles. "Which is the lie?"

A few of the girls shoot up their hands, but the one I know as Anita speaks first. "You spent the summer in your own room," she says like a zinger. "Grounded." No, that's the zingy part. "Everyone knows you already play tennis, and who can forget what happened with the straw—"

"How about you go next then, Rica?" Mrs. Morales jumps in. "Since you're so keen on sharing."

I keep my outward reaction to a minimum—clearly any weakness is fair game for exploitation in here—but I inwardly wince and I'm forced to look at Rica with a different lens. Sarah may not have a good handle on how to play, but I feel terrible she got slammed on the first day. She's gripping the seat of her chair like it might try to run away. Or maybe to keep herself from running.

Rica combs her fingers through her clearly dyed ink-black hair, which rests just above her shoulders, the silver charm bracelet jingling on her wrist. She leans forward, making eye contact with everyone in the circle as if she's about to divulge a state secret. "I went to New York City over the summer. I have a verbal offer from an art school there. My grandparents are buying me a brand-new BMW convertible for my birthday."

Crickets. The gears are turning. Nearly everyone in this room is no doubt used to what this girl dishes out, and they're all lip-zipped like she owns them. Are they afraid to guess wrong? This one's so easy even I know the answer.

Come on. What would Lauren Bacall do?

I give a little flick of my hair to show I'm in the game, and say, "They're all truths." My voice echoes unexpectedly through the theatre. It sounds *good* out there. I'm filled with the power to continue my conclusion. "You probably spent a week in New York touring schools, rubbing elbows, eating cheese, and pretending to drink wine. You even got significant interest from a school because you actually do have some talent, but it's a school so far down your list you won't tell us which. You'll wait to see if all your other choices fall through before you claim that was the one you really wanted to attend all your life. And considering the jewelry and the legit Kate Spade purse you're rockin' on the first day of school, I'd say you even got to pick out the color of your shiny new beamer."

All eyes shift from me to Rica. Her jaw is slack and she's doing a marvelous job testing her ability to blush. I think she got the message: this class is no longer hers.

One of the boys stands on his chair and stretches a hand out toward me. " 'O Captain! my Captain!' "

The guy next to him pops right up without missing a beat. " 'O Captain! my Captain!' "

The room explodes into laughter and I steal a glance at Mrs. Morales, and even she's struggling to keep a straight face. Rica's the only one unamused. She stares at the floor with narrowed eyes, probably already calculating when and where she can strike, which makes me itchy. " 'Thank you, boys,' " I manage once things finally settle, and they hop down.

Sarah catches eyes with me, smiling, and it's not until that exact moment that I feel like my outburst was completely necessary. Not everyone knows how to defend themselves in situations like this. Sometimes you have to reroute a fire with an even bigger fire before everyone gets burned.

"Yes, thank you, boys," Mrs. Morales says before she turns to me. "Maddie, how about you go next?"

I close my eyes to gather my thoughts and lift my face toward the warmth from the can lights. *You got this.*

"I don't have a car. I've taken tap dance since I was nine." I pause, setting up for the one that will really get them. "The only man I've ever loved is dead."

CHAPTER FOUR

As I reach my locker to retrieve the books I need tonight—have to read the first chapter in nearly all of them—a voice calls out behind me.

"That was so cool, what you did back there. With Rica."

I turn to find Sarah and the boys who called me their captain.

"Seriously, it was awesome," the guy with bushy, nut-colored hair says. "No one's ever had the stones to put her in her place like that."

"Yeah, not even us, and we actually have stones," the thicker one says. "Real ones."

I shrug. "The words just came to my head at the right time instead of ten minutes later, when they're not useful anymore."

"Well, I appreciated it." Sarah moves the book she's carrying to the other arm and extends her right hand. "We wanted to introduce ourselves. I'm Sarah."

"Maddie." I take her hand, and each of the boys offers his too. It all feels very adult. I may have just found my people.

"I'm Ryan."

"Brian."

An eyebrow raised, I look from one to the other. "Wait. Your name's Ryan and yours is Brian?" They nod. "Are you related?"

Brian rolls his eyes. "Why does everyone ask that? Do we look alike? No. He's fat, I'm thin. I'm tall, he's short. The rhyming thing is just a coincidence."

Ryan whacks him in the chest. "I am *not* short and fat. You're barely an inch taller than me and maybe ten pounds less. Stop trying to impress the new girl."

"Ignore them. We all do." Sarah laughs, then leans in a little closer. "So, about your truths . . ."

"Was that for real . . . ?" Brian lets his voice trail off.

The solemn expression on their faces lets on that they have heart. They're not chomping at the bit for a meaty piece of gossip. I believe they're actually concerned. Of course, they *are* actors.

"The tap dancing really was the lie. I only started about six months ago."

"Then the only guy you've ever loved really did die?" Sarah clasps one of my hands in her stubby ones, a gesture I thought only friends would take the liberty to do. "Oh, how awful, I'm so sorry." She encircles me with her arms and pulls me against her short frame briefly before pulling away. "Do you need to talk about it?"

I shake my head. "I can't." And I can't imagine how cryptic all of this sounds, but I'm not explaining it yet. Let them create their own romanticized versions of my love life.

No one knows what else to say until Ryan finally tugs gently on Sarah's shoulder. "Well, it was nice to meet you, Maddie. We'll see you tomorrow."

As I watch the trio move away, the boys on either side of her like bodyguards, my phone buzzes in my back pocket. A text message.

Ma: So sorry I'm running late. At store getting paint mixed. Be there in 10.

I consider waiting for her in the nice air-conditioned hallway, but the place clears out quickly and there's a major creep factor in an empty, massive school I'm not familiar with yet. I shudder.

A door slams near the end of the hallway, possibly by the theatre. I glance at the approaching figure in between piling books into my arms, and as he gets closer, I realize it's Jesse. He's heading this way, boots clomping down the hallway, sounding not unlike high heels.

I play it cool like I wasn't just looking right at him, nose in my locker, book stack getting out of control. I shift my arm to make room for one more, but the hardback on the bottom pinches the skin near my elbow and I nearly cry out. The books lose their balance and I let all of them tumble to the floor, some clanging like thunder against the lockers on the way down.

"Gravity pulling pranks on you today?"

"Huh?" I take a step back and survey the damage.

"First your notebook in class"—he peeks inside my empty locker—"now everything else you own."

"My backpack is still in a box somewhere," I mutter, bending to pick up my mess.

"So you really are new, then? Like, just-moved-to-town new?" He adjusts his backpack so it's strapped to both shoulders, then squats and helps me collect the books.

"Just-moved-to-Texas new. Just-moved-from-the-city-to-the-country new."

He laughs. "Fernwood is straight-up burbs. The country is a little farther north."

"Well, a week ago I lived within spitting distance of my neighbors, and now all I see out my bedroom window are millions of squirrels in what looks like a forest, so . . . feels like the country to me." I don't mean for it to come out quite so whiny, so I quickly try to make up for it. "But it's nice."

Jesse makes a half-laughing, half–throat-clearing sound. "Yeah, sounds like you *love* it here."

I'm not about to pretend that I do, but I don't want to dump all my gripes on him about how my friends dropped me before I left, or how I missed the chance to audition for a play I was really excited about. "It's just going to take some getting used to."

He stands with nearly all my books, and a few veins rise down the length of his arm. He does have rather nice arms.

"Where are we headed with these?" he asks. "Which side did you park on?"

He's carrying my books! I die.

"Oh, um . . . just going to the curb out front. My mom's picking me up." I grab my notebook and the last book left on the floor. "So this is what a Southern gentleman looks like? You really don't have to carry them for me. I'm sure you're busy."

He frowns. "Are you one of those girls who has to do everything herself?"

"What?" I hug the books I'm holding to my chest. "I just don't like to make anyone go out of their way for me."

The corner of his mouth hitches up. "It's not out of my way."

Jesse heads for the main entrance and I follow him out into the midday heat. Moisture beads up along my hairline almost immediately. So attractive.

"Do you see her car in line? I can put them in the backseat."

I scan the queue. "No." I check my phone and see I missed another text.

Ma: 10 more minutes. I'm so sorry!

"Ten more minutes, she says. Just set them down. I'll toss them in when she gets here."

He squints up at the sky and three deep vertical lines appear between his eyebrows. "How about I just take you home?"

This could be interesting. He still doesn't know I live across the street from him, or that I know his sister and his mom.

I bite my lip. "How do I know you're not a psycho?"

Surprise colors his expression. "I promise I'm not a psycho. Plus, I'm the captain of the baseball team. Do you think I could afford to kidnap someone? That wouldn't be the best career move."

"So you're, like, the star?"

"Well—" He cuts himself off with a shrug and directs his gaze just below my left eye. "Speaking of stars, you seem to have a thing for them."

I'm glad to hear my beauty mark survived the day intact. I was a little worried it would end up smeared across half my face.

"It's true," I say. "I like stars. Though typically not of the sports variety."

"No?" He tilts his head to the side and his eyes dart down the length of my body, slow enough that it's clear he definitely wants me to notice the action. "Well, you may change your mind one day."

I roll my eyes. *Never.*

"You really don't mind taking me home?"

"Nah, it's cool. I don't have to be at work until four thirty."

I give Ma a call as I walk with Jesse through the parking lot. She apologizes profusely and promises to make something spectacular for dinner. She'll even pick up a cake to celebrate completing my first day at a new school. I love what a guilty conscience can do.

His truck doesn't have a backseat, so we dump all the books onto the floorboard and I climb in the passenger side.

"So where do you live?" he asks, starting the engine, which gives a nice long screech before it finally idles right.

"Twin Oaks Circle." I look out the window and focus on the other kids getting in their cars, even though I desperately want to see his reaction.

This is just like in *Sabrina* when David brings a newly made-over Sabrina home, having no clue she is the same girl who lives above his family's garage with her chauffeur father. Except I don't live above his family's garage—just across the street.

"Huh. What are the odds? That's the same road I live on."

"Well, that's convenient." I press my lips together to keep from smiling and continue to stare out the window as we merge into traffic.

Jesse runs through the same questions I've grown sick of answering today, about where I'm from and whether I'm a Cubs or a White Sox fan (I tell him the Cubbies, but only because Dad and Rider root for them—I don't watch televised sports. Or live sports . . .). He asks if I have any siblings, and I tell him about my older brother, Rider, who moved off to Texas State University. Not only does it have a reputation for being a party school, but also it was supposed to be super far from his family. So what do we do? We relocate within a few hours' drive of him.

I'm sort of glad, though. We were just starting to get close again when he moved. Not that I have a car to visit him with. I really need to look for a job.

His phone dings a few times in a row.

"Want me to see who it is?" I offer.

"No. I'm sure it's just my dad," he says. "Which house is yours?"

I study our surroundings. "Um . . . I think it's on the right after this curve." My stomach clenches. He's going to see how small and gross my house is. I should have thought this through.

"You're kidding." He turns down my driveway, the rocks crunching together under the tires. "My house is just across from yours."

"Huh. What are the odds?" It's probably not a great idea dragging it out this long. I'm going to have to tell him I met his mom and sisters days ago.

I slide out of the truck and we haul my homework load up to the house. I pause at the top of the porch steps when I realize I'm missing a rather important metal object.

"What is it?" Jesse asks.

"I don't have a key."

"How do you not have a key to your house?" He sighs and sets the books down by the door.

I stifle my annoyance. It's a legit question, one I probably would have asked too. "For one, no car equals no key ring. Two, we haven't even changed the locks yet after the previous owners, so we haven't made copies. Three . . . well, there is no three. Those are all my excuses."

"You really should change your locks. Those people were . . . shady."

"Great," I laugh. First they're grubby, now shady. Where the bleep did we move? "I'll remind my dad when he gets home tonight."

We don't have any outdoor furniture on the porch, so Jesse sits on the concrete, his long legs sloping down the steps.

"What are you doing?"

"Waiting with you for your mom," he says without looking back at me.

I sit on the top step and lean my back against the post. "You don't have to do that, you know."

"It would be pretty shiesty of me to just dump you off on the porch and leave." He taps the toes of his boots together. "I would say we could wait in the truck, but she overheats sometimes. I don't like to push her. We could go to my house, if you want."

I pull my phone out of my purse and check the time. "By the time we got over there, you'd probably have to just bring me home again. Really, I don't mind waiting alone. I'm sure you have to get ready for work."

He stretches back and rests on his palms as if to say he's not going anywhere.

"Where do you work, anyway?"

He groans. "Maria Tortilla," he says with an unexpected accent. I wait for him to elaborate. "A Mexican restaurant off the highway."

"That bad, huh? Are you a busboy or something? Dishwasher?"

"Food runner. It's not too awful. Just a little embarrassing."

"Why?"

"Well, my dad sort of pushed the job on me. Thought it would help my Spanish."

I eye him curiously. "You need help with your Spanish?"

"Don't *you*?" he shoots back.

"Uh, yeah, but—"

"But?"

I hesitate before telling him what I'm thinking. "You look like you'd be fluent already."

He laughs from his gut. "The language doesn't come from the look. My mom doesn't speak Spanish so my dad doesn't speak it much at home. I understand most of what I hear, but my pronunciation is off a bit. He wanted me to work somewhere I'd be around fluent speakers."

"Well, that's smart, I guess," I say.

"I don't really see the point. Everyone speaks English here. It's not like I'm gonna move to Mexico."

Now it's my turn to laugh. "Well, I wouldn't mind learning French, and I highly doubt I'll be moving to France at any point in my life."

Jesse closes his eyes and inhales deeply, only a slight smile left. And I feel the strong pull of a subject change mixed with self-consciousness about my living situation.

"I'm sorry there's no porch swing or anything." *Or money for said porch swing.* "It's sort of a transitional home as we get used to the area. Dad wants to flip it." I hope he can't tell how much I'm stretching the truth. "I'm not sure how long we'll be here." Translation: I hope Dad's new job works out so we can get out of this dump.

Ma's car pulls up the drive. She veers around Jesse's truck and parks in front of it.

"I'm so sorry, hon," she says as she climbs out. She looks exhausted, dark circles under her eyes. I knew she should have gone back to bed instead of running errands all day for this stupid house.

She pops the trunk and pulls out a few bags. Jesse rushes over to her, taking the rest of the sacks and a couple gallons of paint. I'm watching it happen, and I don't even understand how he's carrying it all.

"Ma, this is Jesse. He lives across the street." I take the keys from her.

"Ma'am," he says.

Her smile spreads, and we file into the house. I cringe at the sight of boxes stacked high along the walls. What's left of our life back home. Everything that could fetch a price was sold before the move. Nothing like seeing your inheritance spread among your friends whose families still get to be rich.

I pray Jesse doesn't look too closely. I don't think the carpets have been cleaned. Ever.

"Jesse," Ma says, "thank you so much for bringing her home. I was running so late. My whole day just got off schedule."

"Where's the cake?" I ask, investigating the bags when we set everything on the kitchen counter.

She claps a hand over her mouth. "I can't believe I forgot. I even walked right through the bakery section to get to the produce. I'm so sorry."

"Is today your birthday or something?" Jesse asks.

He directed the question to me, but Ma starts rambling in a voice that's much higher pitched than normal. "She loves cake. Yellow cake with chocolate icing. I usually make it for special occasions. Like today. The first day of a new school year." She drops down on a bar stool, looking so upset with herself I'm pretty sure she's about to cry.

Jesse takes a few steps back, eyes widened. "I'm gonna get your books from the porch," he says before disappearing to the front room.

I turn to Ma and flip my acting switch so she doesn't know I'm disappointed.

"It's fine, really. I have so much reading to do, I'm just going to eat a bowl of cereal in my room and blaze through it all. Why don't you go rest? Take a nap or something."

"I think I need to. Just for a little while." She wraps her arms around me and squeezes tight before setting the bag with the cold items in the fridge and heading to her room.

Jesse comes back then. "I put them on the dining table."

My shoulders relax as I exhale. I'm so tired, I don't even filter my words. "You're sort of wonderful."

He laughs, and I walk him outside.

"Thanks for the ride." *And for carrying my books like we're
going steady.*

"Need a lift to school in the morning?" he asks, scratching
his chin, which I don't understand because he has zero facial
hair. There should be no itching.

"Thanks, but I already have a carpool set up."

He cocks his head to the side. "Who with?"

"Angela." I back into the door opening and reach for the
knob. "Your sister." I start to close the door to avoid questions.
"I'll see you tomorrow."

He shakes his head and smiles. "See you tomorrow, Maddie
Brooks."

Brooks? How do you know my . . . ?

He winks and lets that sink in before I watch him saunter to
his truck. Jesse Morales knew who I was all along.

CHAPTER FIVE

After Economics, I head straight to English without stopping at my locker. Only a few people make it before me, so I slip into the same desk by the window that I had yesterday and skim over last night's reading in case I end up having to answer questions about it.

A handful of kids filter in, and I spot Jesse among them, backpack slung over one shoulder, the sleeves of his black shirt rolled up to the elbows. He takes the seat next to me again.

As I debate whether to say hello or let him say it first, he beats me to it. "Maddie Brooks."

"Jesse Morales."

"Guess what I ate last night."

Eyebrow raised, I slap my literature book closed and twist my body toward him. I search the outer reaches of my brain for anything that might have attained significance in our twenty-four-hour relationship.

No.

"If you say cake I'm going to kick you."

"Cake." He laughs. "But you can't injure me. I'm important. I accept verbal assault only."

"Ugh, no fair. *I* was promised cake." I face forward and flip through my book without focusing on anything.

Curtis slips in just in the nick of time, does his handshake thing with Jesse—who again calls him Red—and sits in front of me. Mr. McCaffey walks in and shuffles some papers on his desk. The bell's going to ring any second.

I face Jesse and speak low. "Do you think I could catch a ride home again today after school?" Ma's planning another day of errands, so I'd like to have something lined up just in case. Plus, he's already seen where I live and he's still talking to me.

"Can't." Jesse opens his notebook and clicks his pen. "Baseball meeting."

"Oh, that's fine. I'll figure something out."

I thought it would be a simple solution to my car-less plight to go to school every morning with Angela and ride home every afternoon with Jesse. Doesn't look like that will happen.

"I can tomorrow, though," he adds.

"I'll bring you home today." Curtis turns to me, the tips of his cheeks pink.

Jesse laughs. "What? The meeting involves you too, genius."

"I can come back. How important could it be? Baseball doesn't even start for real until, like, January." He looks at me. "I can take you. No problem."

"Oh, um—"

"Coach isn't gonna let you skip, Red," Jesse says, kicking the leg of Curtis's chair with a boot. "Not if you're serious about preseason tournaments."

"I'm confused," I say. "Is his name Curtis or Red?"

"*He* is sitting right here. My name is Curtis. Friends call me Red."

Jesse looks at me. "You can call him Red too."

"But where did that come from?" I ask. "He's almost blond."

"Still right here," Red says, shaking his head. "And it's a story you won't be hearing until I get to know you better. Like during lunch. Sit with me."

Jesse grunts.

"Oh," I begin slowly. "I didn't realize we had the same lunch period."

"We do. I saw you yesterday." He smiles as if this should please me. "I'll find you."

I rub at my eyebrows, wishing I'd thought of a way out of this. Nothing makes me itchy more than giving someone the wrong idea. I'm possibly the pickiest girl on the planet. My standards are sky-high. No one I've ever met has lived up to them.

I watch Red as he rolls his pen back and forth, and notice the way he sort of hunches to fit in the desk. He's a big guy, at least six feet tall, and very thick with muscles. Solid. Looks more like a football player than baseball. The desk might possibly break away from under him. You can tell just by looking at him that there's not an ounce of graceful ability in his body. Which, assuming he weren't a jock, would knock him out of the running all by itself. I need someone who can dance.

Like I said, my standards are up in the stars.

"Why's Babe Ruth headed this way?" Tiffany asks at lunch between bites of taco salad.

Here comes Red, as promised.

"Oh, no," Angela says. "He's gonna sit over here."

"What do you mean, *oh, no*?" Tiffany smooths her bangs so they swoop over her forehead.

He takes the empty seat across from me and next to Tiffany, who straightens and shifts to get closer to him. Angela drops her eyes to her plate, pushing at a tomato wedge with her fork.

"You're off the hook, Red," I tell him before he has a chance to say anything. "My mom's picking me up after school. Thanks for the offer, though."

"Sure, whatever." He shrugs and pulls a slice of cold pizza from a camouflage lunch box with a deer-head silhouette on it. "I was gonna tell you I couldn't anyway. I really need to go to that baseball meeting." Before taking a bite, he looks to Angela. "Hey, kid."

Tiffany catches eyes with me. "He was going to take you home? Wait. Baseball meeting? Are y'all ordering this year's uniforms? Will there be modeling?" She spins her entire body on the little circle seat to face him. "I will make out with you right here if you let me help pick them out."

Red swallows and wipes at his chin with a napkin, as if he doesn't even hear her. Then he catches eyes with me, the corner of his mouth hitching up, and he slowly angles toward Tiffany. Closer. Closer. She leans toward him, cheeks pink, but no sign of backing down. He glides one of his giant hands along her jawbone and cups the back of her head, just under the base of her ponytail. A surprisingly graceful move.

I can't look away. This sort of thing doesn't happen in real life.

Angela mutters, "I've got some homework to finish." She grabs her tray of mostly uneaten food and disappears.

Red's lips are maybe three inches from Tiffany's. Closer. She's not even breathing now. Closer. I still can't look away.

"Tempting," he says before he pulls back and resumes eating his pizza. "But no."

"Holy whoa," I think I hear her say through an exhale. I can't tell if she's disappointed or relieved. "Just please go with lighter-color pants. Like gray or white. That's all I ask. The tighter, the better."

"So," I jump in, "why do they call you Red? What's the big secret?"

"Oh, everybody knows that!" Tiffany has magically recovered. "He got totally trashed one night at a pool party, and—"

Red smacks the table with an open palm and I jump. "Tiffany, Tiffany, Tiffany Barrett. Gossip doesn't look good on you."

"But you—"

"Sssshhhh." He presses a finger to his lips. "It's not your story to tell. It's mine. And she's not ready."

I clear my throat. "You fell asleep drunk at a party, woke up naked the next day, your butt got burned." So classy.

"Who told?" His mouth hangs open in surprise before he shoves in another slice of pizza.

I munch on a tortilla chip and tap my temple. "No one had to."

"Go to homecoming with me," he blurts out.

"What?" Tiffany and I ask together.

"Not you," he says to her before looking back at me. "Madison."

"It's Maddie."

"You said your name was Madison."

"And you said your name was Curtis."

"Go with me. To the dance." He sits taller. "I won't be available long."

"Who could refuse such an offer?"

"No one?" he says as a question, which gives me hope that I've shaken his confidence.

Tiffany's eyes have been darting back and forth between us like she's watching a tennis match. She mouths "No one" to me.

"I can." I break a chip into pieces and crumbs fly all over the table.

"What?" Tiffany is the one to ask. "Why not?" She leans forward as if Red can't hear and whispers, "Don't you know who he is?"

I mirror her posture and whisper back, "Hello. It's my second day here. I don't know who anyone is."

"Answer her question." Red crosses his arms. "Why not?"

I stash the empty plastic baggie from my sandwich in my lunch box, zip it closed, and lock eyes with him. "You don't even know me, for one. And all I know about you is that you play baseball and you think an awful lot of yourself." I count off each point on my fingers. "Secondly, you act like you're going to kiss Tiffany right in front of me, and you turn around and ask *me* to homecoming. That's just—there isn't even a word for it. Third, this is the second day of school. I don't even know when homecoming is."

Tiffany pipes up. "It's in a month. The theme is Sherwood Forest."

I smile at her but let it dissolve when I look back at Red. "Lastly, you don't ask a girl to escort you to the first homecoming dance at her new high school, mouth full of cold pizza in the middle of a cafeteria. You go to her house. You bring her flowers. You look her father in the eye when you shake hands with him. You gush about how wonderful she is. You're charming."

Both of them gape at me.

"Good luck finding a guy who does that." Tiffany stands and picks up her tray.

I close my eyes and release a long breath. There's the man of my dreams, standing on my porch with a handful of daisies.

The table shifts under me as Red grabs his lunch box. "Sounds like you watch too many movies."

CHAPTER SIX

It may be true I watch too many movies, but what I said to Red obviously made an impression. By Friday, a cheerleader named Colene is hanging all over him, and the story spreads about how he brought her flowers and introduced himself to her stepdad. And, of course, he asked her to homecoming.

The idea catches on like a virus, and throughout the next two weeks, I keep hearing talk of similar acts of romantic spontaneity. Homecoming dates go like candy. Here are all these girls benefiting from one of my fantasies, and they don't even know it. Angela gets a volleyball with *Homecoming?* written on it tossed to her in the hallway between classes. And Tiffany's asked in person by a guy on the football team, which is a huge deal, apparently—Texans love their football. Even Jesse asks someone—Gabby something. She doesn't go to our school, but I hear she's pretty and Latina. So they have that in common.

I don't fret about getting asked again.

I'm gradually learning the rhythm of my new school, so by the end of the third week, it feels almost normal to be here. It's Friday night and I finally have plans that don't involve homework or babysitting Elise, which I've done once in a while. After dinner with the parentals, I'm spending the night at Angela's.

I scarf down my food in hopes of going over early. Dad piles our dirty dishes next to the sink and then opens the fridge, pulling out a cake with chocolate frosting and placing it on the table in front of me.

"Cake! What's this for?" I ask, rushing to the cabinet for clean plates and forks for the three of us.

Ma rests her head in a hand, elbow on the table. "I felt bad about not getting you one on your first day of school, so today I made it happen."

"We're so proud of you for jumping in and making new friends," Dad says. "I know starting over isn't easy."

I focus on cutting three pieces from the cake. "I mean, you already know I'm not totally happy about the whole thing, but you guys didn't want to move either. It's one of those things, right? You don't want to do it, but you have to." I refrain from listing off the movies that share this common theme. Let them think I reached the conclusion to tough it out with class by myself.

Dad turns toward Ma and they share a look. I like to think of it as the *We have such a great kid, why can't everyone be more like her?* look.

"Which is why," Ma continues, "we know you can handle what we're about to tell you."

Panic. I drop my fork. "We're not moving *again*."

The faces of everyone I've met the past couple of weeks flash through my mind. Angela, Jesse, Tiffany, Sarah, Brian, Ryan, Red, and even Rica. I can't do this all over again somewhere else, with new faces. Maybe I didn't audibly complain enough through this whole process. It's just that I can't stand whiners; therefore, I try not to *be* a whiner.

"No," Dad says without humor. "I'm sure you've noticed how your mom hasn't been feeling well lately."

I look to her, my eyebrows tense. "What's wrong?"

"I went to the doctor earlier this week—"

A thought occurs to me, and I can't hold it back. "West Nile? Do you have West Nile?" My heart races. "They keep talking about it at school, how people are dying from it, right here in Texas even. From mosquito bites. There's a senior who's missed the past week and rumors are flying about either mono or West—"

Dad raises his hand to cut me off. "She's fine. Nothing's wrong."

I relax, sinking into my chair. "Then what?"

Ma takes a deep breath. "I'm having a baby."

I blink, waiting for one of them to bust out laughing, because it has to be a joke. It has to be.

They stare at me expectantly, bracing themselves for my reaction. It takes a lot of power to keep from blurting all the questions coming to mind. *How long have you been keeping this from me? Do you realize how old you are? Who's the father?*

I start counting to three, like Alonzo tries to do in *Meet Me in St. Louis* when he needs to cool off so he doesn't raise his voice at his kids. It didn't exactly work for him, but I can't give some kind of response until I collect my thoughts. I don't even make it to three before my eyes well up. I tear away from the table without a word and sprint to my room.

Rider. Does he know?

Locking the door behind me, I grab my cell phone and fling myself onto my bed. I call Rider's number but it goes straight to voice mail. It's the weekend. He'll probably be unreachable by sisterly types until Monday, when he's sobered up. I text him to call me anyway, just in case.

I spot the overnight bag I packed earlier by the closet and lunge for it, slinging it over my shoulder. I stomp back into the dining area and they're still at the table, Dad picking at his cake and Ma nearly finished with hers.

They eye me curiously but don't say anything. They still need my reaction. Well, other than me fleeing the scene.

Too bad I don't have a good one yet.

"I'm going to Angela's," I say, looking between them and turning for the front door.

As I grip the knob, I hear one of their chairs scoot against the tile floor. Shutting my eyes tight and wiping away the single tear that finally decided to fall, I head back to face them one more time. Ma's standing behind her chair, a hand on Dad's shoulder.

I can do this. I'm the good kid.

"Congratulations." I test out a smile but a sob escapes.

I turn to leave again, but at the last second I pivot, snatching the plate with the remainder of the double-layered cake and walking out the front door with it. I sure hope they have milk at Angela's house.

*　*　*

I walk the winding driveway to the Moraleses' house, the sinking sun filtering through the trees overhead like long fingers ready to seize me and carry me up to the sky. I wish they would.

A baby. A sister. Or another brother, ugh. It's too much to process. It's like in *Yours, Mine and Ours* with Lucille Ball and Henry Fonda when their two already huge, widowed families are joined, and the oldest boy just enlisting in the military finds out his new stepmother's pregnant. He gets blood drawn for the health exam and tells the doctor to take it all. I get it now.

A baby. An infant. A toddler. Child. Adolescent. Adult. They're going to have to go through every stage all over again. And I'm going to have to help. I'm going to be one of those seventeen-year-old girls who have to watch a baby sister and not get paid for it. If I take her anywhere, people will think she's mine. That my mother's just helping me out because I got myself into trouble. Little do they know I don't even let guys kiss me offstage.

This better not interfere with my life after high school. I'm going places. College, where I'll study my craft with other kids just as serious about theatre as I am, then on to traveling shows—the dream is at least one traveling Broadway show, but I know how stiff the competition will be. I have to be at my absolute best. The window of opportunity is very small for making it anywhere significant. You can't be too young and inexperienced, and you can't be too old, because of the physical demands. The human body has such a short prime of life. And mine's almost here.

The overnight bag slips off my shoulder to my elbow, but I'm gripping the cake plate with both hands. When I reach the porch, I have to poke at the doorbell with my elbow. The dead bolt unclicks and it's Tiffany who appears. When Angela said *slumber party*, I didn't realize that involved more than me and her. I need a good venting session with carbs, not an actual party. That's not going to help my mood.

About the only thing that might perk me up is the possibility of glimpsing Jesse in whatever he wears to sleep.

Tiffany looks me over. "What happened to you? And what's with the cake?" She takes it from me when I hold it out to her.

I shake my head as I follow her inside, not yet ready to speak. Cool, pizza-scented air slaps me in the face, prompting my eyes to water all over again. I drop my bag at the bottom of the stairs on the way to the kitchen. Angela's at the dining table cutting a slice of pizza into smaller bites for Elise to eat with a fork—she doesn't like to touch her food with her hands.

"Maddie's here, Maddie's here!" Elise squeals, hopping out of her seat.

She rushes to me and hugs my legs. My body tenses at her touch for an instant, but I make myself relax. This is Elise. I adore Elise. She won me over the very first night I was here, dragging me all over her room to show me her drawings. She has nothing to do with my parents. It wouldn't be right to take out my shock on her.

"I made you a picture!" She runs back to where she was sitting and grabs a black sheet of paper with colorful chalk scratches all over it. She points to the boxy figure in the center, then to a smaller one next to it. "That's you and that's me. And my balloon." A bright red ball floats above her chalk head.

The smile I've been holding back wins. It's the balloon I gave her earlier this week. They were passing them out at school to promote some club I don't remember the name of, and I took one for her. I don't even know what made me do it. I just thought she'd like it.

I look into Elise's eyes, so big and green and innocent. They whisper, *Wouldn't you like to have a baby sister like me? Wouldn't you love her?*

And I realize I would love her. Or him. It won't be the kid's fault I'll be seventeen years older, about to really start my own life. Or that by the time the kid's seventeen, I could have children of my own. Eventually, I'll get used to the idea. But I don't have to be happy about it at this moment.

Or talk to my parents for a long time.

Angela puts Elise to bed—Mrs. Morales is at the playhouse, helping with a production, and Mr. Morales is visiting family in Mexico—and then the three of us polish off the rest of the cake. After two thick slices and a tall glass of iced milk, I find myself loosening up and spilling my secret.

"Maybe it was an immaculate conception," Tiffany says. "Like Mary when she got pregnant with Jesus."

Angela smacks her on the arm. "Don't make jokes. She's upset. How'd you like to be reminded that your parents . . . ?" Her voice trails off and she shudders.

"Please," Tiffany says. "How do you think *you* got here? How did any of us get here? It's what happens." She raises her cup. "To nature . . . and all that implies." No one clinks glasses with her so she guzzles the last bit of milk and wipes her mouth with the back of her hand.

"What does your brother think?" Angela asks, stacking our paper plates and tossing them into the trash under the sink.

"Hold up," Tiffany says. "You have a brother?"

"Rider. He goes to Texas State. He's a freshman." I pull out my phone to check for missed messages. Nothing. "I haven't talked to him yet."

"Texas State? In San Marcos? Partaaay! Let's go see him." Her expression brightens. "Next weekend! It's not far. Is he hot? If he looks like you, he must be."

Angela returns to the table, frowning. "She won't think her own brother's hot. That's sick."

"Like you don't know yours is hot," Tiffany shoots back, looking to me for support.

I shrug and look at Angela. "He isn't even close to my type, but he's not exactly terrible to look at."

Angela and Tiffany both go silent, looking over my head with wide eyes. Tiffany bites her lip.

A soft laugh rings out just behind me. "Thanks? I think."

CHAPTER SEVEN

I can't bring myself to look at him. *Improvise. Improvise.* I stand and go to rinse our empty glasses. "Don't you wish I was talking about you."

"Weren't you?" Tiffany has to open her stupid mouth. "Because I don't have a brother."

I slide the glasses onto the top rack of the dishwasher and risk a glance at Jesse. He leans his shoulder casually against the wall, untucked black collared shirt, hands in the pockets of his black slacks. Bare feet. He smirks like he just beat me at a game. I can't believe I just added to his clearly large ego.

"I knew you had a thing for stars, *mi reina*," he says, tapping the top of his cheek.

I'm pretty sure he just called me his queen, but I don't give him the satisfaction of a response. I reach up to touch my cheek, and realize I didn't wear my star today.

"Get over yourself. You must have missed the part where she said you aren't her type," Angela says to him as she switches on the washer. "He always comes home in Spanish mode *después del trabajo*."

"Well, that's why he works there, right?" I clarify. "To learn Spanish? It's good he's using it."

Tiffany snorts as she tries to contain a laugh, and Angela's jaw slacks. I glance at each of them, confused. Jesse's eyes widen in surprise, staring me down before he retreats into the darkness behind him. My stomach full of cake feels heavy.

"What did I say?" I ask Angela once I'm sure he's out of earshot.

She shakes her head. "I can't believe he told you that's why he works there."

"I didn't know he couldn't speak Spanish," Tiffany says. "I assumed he was just as good at it as you are, Ange."

Oh, no. I totally forgot he said it was embarrassing. He told me that in confidence, which I didn't realize until this very second.

"I actually try, though. I *want* to be fluent." Angela finishes cleaning up the mess on the table, folding the empty pizza box and clearing away crumbs from the cake. "If I'm bilingual, I'll have so many more opportunities, like for scholarships, jobs, whatever. I'd be dumb to let all that go."

Tiffany stands at the window watching Mrs. Morales pull up the drive. "Yeah, but you're such a daddy's girl. He wants his children to go to UT; you're probably the only one who will do it. He wants you to marry a Latino, and you probably will."

"I'm already the doomed middle child; I've gotta do something right."

"The doomed middle child. No, no, no." I drop into a chair and lay my upper body on the table, head down. I can't believe for a whole five minutes I actually forgot. "I'm not going to be the baby of the family anymore. There'll be a newer version, a better version. She'll grow up like an only child, too, because she won't understand that her siblings can be adults. Yes, I said 'she' because I refuse to accept another brother." We laugh, but mine comes out a little delirious. All that sugar I ingested is hitting me and I can't stop. "To her, we'll just be like the cool aunt and uncle who swoop in with presents on holidays and birthdays. But I'll always know. I'll always feel like the middle child from here on out. I can't believe this is happening to me."

"Oh, no. Are you *crying?*" Tiffany asks, and I can feel her eyes roll.

"Rude," Angela says to her from behind me. She squeezes my shoulders. "It's not all bad. There's a little more freedom, since all the attention goes to the little one. Well, unless you're babysitting. There's no freedom in that. But you'll be in college soon enough, so really you won't even notice." She taps me on top of the head and I look up at her through blurry eyes. "I hate to say this, but you may love it. The whole thing. I was upset when Elise was born, but look at her. How could I stay mad? Now I don't even remember what it was like without her around."

Mrs. Morales enters the kitchen, dropping a stack of mail and her purse on the counter. "Hey, girls. Everything okay?"

You'd think I could improvise in front of my theatre teacher, but I've got nothing, and I'm worried what Angela and Tiffany might say. I'm not ready for anyone to know, especially an adult. Too mortifying.

"Maddie doesn't have a date to homecoming yet," Tiffany supplies, and it happens to be the truth. "We're discussing potentials." That's not the truth, but it can be remedied. "Hey, what about Jesse?"

"Dad suggested he take his friend's daughter Gabby, remember?" Angela catches eyes with her mom, who shrugs. "So that's a done deal."

"Well"—Mrs. Morales leans in close, talking low—"I may have overheard something I'm not supposed to know." The girls perk up. "But I won't ruin the surprise for Maddie."

Now I perk up too.

"Mom, you have to spill now," Angela whines. "Is someone going to ask her?"

She pulls her lips in and tilts her head. "All I can say is you shouldn't pout. You don't want to get wrinkles prematurely. Trust me." She stretches out the skin around her eyes. " 'Stay gold, Ponyboy.' " And with that, she hums the tune from the credits of *The Outsiders* and sneaks off to the dark part of the house.

I have the coolest teacher in the world. A smile takes over my face, but quickly fades at the realization that someone is making it known that he wants me as a date to the dance. What are the chances he'll ask me in some epically memorable way? Why am I already preparing how I'm going to say no?

"Should we watch a movie or something?" Angela asks.

I shake my head wildly in a figure eight. "I have too much energy. I could run a marathon."

"The pool feels like a bathtub, but we could swim. Might not be too bad now that the sun's down."

"Or we could jump it out," Tiffany suggests.

"Yes!" I turn to Angela. "To the trampoline!"

Every Christmas and birthday for as long as I can remember, I've asked for one. But no, they're too dangerous. It's not like I was asking for a Red Ryder BB gun I might accidentally shoot my eye out with.

We run past the pool and outdoor kitchen in our bare feet, through a patch of tall, cool grass, and crawl over the springs of the trampoline through the slit in the protective netting. Keeping my feet on the taut black fabric, I bounce a few times to get the feel of it. It's been years since I've been on one of these. Every time I've come over here, I've eyed it with jealousy, but I've always been afraid to ask Angela if we could play on it. I mean, we *are* nearly adults.

Angela and Tiffany are already flying high into the air, and I work up the nerve to join them, allowing myself to go higher and higher. With each jump, I get looser, throwing my arms wide and arching my back, face to the sky. Freer and freer.

Right now, I'm nobody's sister, nobody's daughter. Nobody's potential homecoming date. I'm just me, working to tear away from gravity and failing, but loving every second of it.

We challenge each other to a toe-touch competition, which Tiffany wins with her gift for all things athletic, and promptly collapse on the bounce mat on our backs. We lie in silence save for our ragged breathing, heads together in the middle, legs stretched out like a pinwheel. I notice a light turn on in a room upstairs and my eyes automatically shift toward it.

Jesse's silhouette is framed by the window. He pulls his shirt over his head and lets it drop to the floor, then ruffles his hair with his hands, no idea we're out here. Tiffany must not see because she wouldn't be quiet about it. I'm sure not going to tell her. This show is for me. I deserve this. Though it's doing the opposite of lifting my spirits.

After the way he looked at me tonight when I unknowingly revealed one of his secrets, I'll be lucky if he speaks to me at all when he brings me home from school next week, assuming he even continues doing that. He may be afraid to tell me anything ever again.

I may have permanently stunted our friendship.

Jesse and I are at school by my locker, and he offers to carry my stack of books. Then suddenly we're riding in his truck, except the seats are beanbag chairs and he can hardly see over the steering wheel. The sun sets at the snap of his fingers, and it begins to rain. The windshield wipers don't work, so he pulls over. Then the rain turns into a blizzard, trapping us inside without a heater because he says the engine might overheat if he turns it on. I'm shivering so hard my teeth clank together, and he squeezes next to me on my beanbag chair, running his hands down my arms to warm me. I tell him I'm scared we'll never get out, and he sings softly to me in Spanish. The most beautiful voice I've ever heard in a language I don't understand. The most beautiful voice . . .

The high-pitched *whir* of a motor jolts me awake. I blink in the bright sunlight and roll over, my body rising and falling.

I'm on a water bed. I open my eyes fully and see Jesse wielding a Weed Eater around the flagstone of the pool. Not a water bed. I'm still on the trampoline. And he was the last thing I saw before I closed my eyes.

Which would explain my completely wacky and unwelcome dream.

A groan sounds next to me and I realize all three of us must have fallen asleep after our jumping spree, and after our sugar crash. An all-night buffet for mosquitoes with their West Nile virus. I see a couple bites on my arms and at least one on my leg, and feel around on my face in a panic. I need a mirror.

"I can't believe we slept out here all night," Tiffany says, rubbing her neck. "How stupid. I feel so stiff. And I have a game this afternoon. Unless it is afternoon and I slept through it."

"Jesse and Red like to do the yard early in the morning before it gets hot," Angela says as we come down the three-rung ladder and step into the dew-covered grass. "It's probably, like, eight."

"It's seven thirty," calls a man's voice from the table by the pool. "Did y'all get banished from the castle last night or something?"

"Dad!" Angela rushes to him for a hug. "When did you get home?"

"This morning. I brought breakfast." Mr. Morales motions to a white box with a red stripe that says Shipley Do-Nuts. I don't know about Shipley, but just the sight of the pastries makes my mouth water for the goodness that comes from the orange-and-pink box that is Dunkin' Donuts. Apparently they aren't very common around here.

"Thanks, Mr. M." Tiffany high-fives him before snatching a glazed and pulling out a chair.

"Help yourself." Mr. Morales smiles at her, then looks at me. "Maddie, how are you and your family settling in?"

I've met him once before, briefly, but I'm surprised he remembers my name. Maybe Angela talks about me.

"Slowly," I say. "Mom's tearing apart the house to fix it up."

"Been there," he says through a sympathetic laugh. "Sherri and I want to have y'all over for dinner sometime. I'll have her call your mom."

"That's so nice, thank you." I brave a smile, but all I can think is that my parents should wait for Ma's barfing stage to be over before making new friends.

"Boys!" Mr. Morales shouts over the string trimmer. "Donuts!"

Jesse abandons his task as Red finishes filling the lawn mower with gas, and they join us by the pool. I hear Angela quietly suck in a slow breath like through a straw, and I turn just in time to see her gaze linger on Red's arms. In his sleeveless white shirt, his muscles are more massive than I thought. He could probably lift either of us with a pinkie.

Red shakes hands with Mr. Morales before sitting and snatching two donuts, sliding the extra one onto his thumb.

"Hey, Dad." Jesse brushes off his hands on his shirt. "The Weed Eater's acting—"

"I'm sure you can fix it," Mr. Morales dismisses, nudging Jesse's shoulder with a fist. "So, since I'm finally home this weekend, I can work with you on your curveball." He selects a donut at random for Jesse, who puts it back and takes a different kind.

"I've *been* working on my curveball, Dad." Jesse's eyes dart to mine for a second. "Can we talk about this later?"

I glance at Tiffany as she shifts in her seat and bites her lip. Red continues chomping on his breakfast, unaffected by the conversation going on around him.

"All I'm saying is, we need to get it consistent before the pre-season games start. It's not too soon to get in some extra practice." He waits for a response, but doesn't get more than a nod.

I expect Jesse to give me one of those annoyed eye rolls that says *Parents*, but he keeps himself from looking at me again, and returns to his yard work without another word.

"Well, come find me when you're done. I'll catch for you," Mr. Morales calls to him before turning to Red. "I pay you to sit on the mower, not a chair," he teases. "Get back to it."

Angela asks her dad about his trip to see her grandmother, and he answers in Spanish, the two of them chatting as she follows him inside the house. Tiffany snatches a second donut— chocolate-iced—and watches Red unashamedly as he climbs onto the mower.

Using the band around my wrist, I pile my hair up into a loopy bun to get it off my neck. "So you're just gonna sit here eating donuts, watching the guys work in the yard?" I ask Tiffany.

"Uh, yeah," she says, like I'm stupid for asking.

The trimmer makes a strangled sound and I find Jesse attacking a thick patch of grass creeping into a flower bed. I've never seen him dressed so casually before—blue shirt with ripped-off sleeves and bright red athletic shorts that cling to his legs. His muscular, tan legs. If I didn't know any better, I'd think they were dancers' legs.

And now I'm staring. I reach for a donut and take a bite, officially joining the sport of spectating. Still struggling with the trimmer, Jesse smacks the end of it against the ground to get it to spin again. He looks in our direction as if to check to see if he has an audience, and holds my gaze with an unreadable expression and no hint of a smile.

Then he decapitates the seedpod of a weed, and I can't help thinking he imagined that it was me.

CHAPTER EIGHT

I wish I could say Rica was forced to see the light after that first day, but she's just mean. People like her shouldn't be allowed to be talented. She can outperform almost everyone in class. And I've heard her sing-humming to herself in a disgustingly pretty tone. If she can dance too, she'll have me beat. And that simply won't do.

I need to sign up with a dance studio ASAP before I lose all my groove ability.

Sarah is Rica's opposite, which is probably why I get along with her so well. We gravitate toward each other, performing a lot of the in-class exercises together. And where Sarah goes, Ryan follows, with Brian close behind. But Brian's never sat next to me before today.

"Nervous about auditions on Monday?" he asks.

We're doing *Barefoot in the Park* mid-December. Part of me feels like I already had my audition, in the middle of the street, no less. And it *was* basically my idea to do this play in the first place. I mean, if I hadn't started reciting lines from it that day, we'd probably be doing something else. Something less awesome.

I shake my head. "Trying not to be."

"I'm sure you'll be amazing," he says, smiling. "It's like that part was written for you, even though it was probably written before our parents were even born." We laugh.

Not one to discourage a compliment, I ask, "You really think so?"

"Oh, yeah. You've got that same spunk. Quick wit."

It's too bad I don't blush. He's working really hard for it.

Offering a smile, I tilt my head to the side and study Brian's face. He has a few freckles on the ridge of his nose and the tips of his cheeks. At first glance, his hair looks about the same brown as mine, but there's a coppery undertone to it that gives it a zing of personality. He's not unattractive, but, well, I haven't really thought about him that way before. I'm not sure if that says more about me or him.

"I've officially decided you shall be Corie and therefore I must be Paul."

"Oh, are we a package deal now?"

"Yes!" Brian leans in close like he's about to hug me. "Maddie." He swallows. "Let's audition together."

The gears in my head automatically start turning. I've never done a scene with him in class, but I've seen him. He's a natural. The type of acting where you can't really tell if he's reciting lines or making them up. And in real life he's relatively funny and quick-witted himself. This could work. We could practice to perfection and completely blow the casting directors away. They'd have no choice but to cast us both. Assuming we have chemistry. Chemistry is key. The movie wouldn't have been quite so memorable without the perfect pairing of Robert Redford and Jane Fonda.

I raise an eyebrow and see Brian's confidence shrink. "You have to audition for that."

"For what?"

"To be my audition partner. You have to audition for me first. We need to make sure we have chemistry."

"Shoot, Maddie, I got this," he says, relaxing into his chair, his legs stretching out long in front of him. "When and where?"

"Hold up." I raise my hand, signaling for him to stop. "We need to find out if we're even allowed to do this. Monologues are the norm, you know, as in, performed by one person."

"Already asked. We're approved."

I smile at his determination. "Okay, we should get started right away, then." I take out my phone and text my address to him. I won't be nearly as embarrassed now that we have new flooring and all the boxes are stowed out of sight in the garage. The house itself is still tiny, but I can't do anything about that.

"Come over after school, and we—"

"What are you two talking about?" Rica drops into the seat next to Brian.

He rolls his eyes so only I can see before twisting to look at her. "Nothing that concerns you."

"That's funny, because it sounded like you were talking about the auditions," she says, spinning the silver bracelet around her wrist, charms clinking together. "And since the part of Corie is mine, I'd say it concerns me. I overheard you asking to audition with a partner." She slides closer to him on her chair. "If you want to be Paul so bad, you should read with me."

"You can't have the lead in everything, Rica," Brian says loudly, so that everyone in class is now turning to look. "And Maddie is just as good as you, if not better."

As flattered as I am by his words, I don't need help making her hate me.

Rica's cheeks redden and she stares me down. "We'll see."

Since Jesse did such a great job of ignoring me in English— not that I tried to speak to him either—I'm surprised when he appears at my locker after school.

"Ready to go?"

I nod, attempting to shove one last book in my backpack, but it won't fit. He takes it from me, tucking it under his arm, and starts for the parking lot. The clouds overhead are dark, and a soft rumble echoes off the building behind us. The wind kicks up dust and we move a little faster to get inside his truck.

"I'm sorry about Friday night, what I said," I tell him as I buckle the seat belt and he takes off.

"It's fine, really." He scratches his arm near the elbow and then lets his hand rest there, steering with one hand.

"You just seemed so open about everything, I didn't—"

"I'm not sure why I told you all of that. I don't usually . . . talk so much."

Drops of rain splatter against the windshield and Jesse clicks on the wipers, which I'm relieved to see actually work. And the rain won't turn to snow. And we won't be trapped in here. It was just a stupid, sugar-induced dream.

"So," I say, breaking the silence. "Why aren't you involved in theatre? Angela told me she didn't have the patience for it, learning lines and stuff, but what about you?"

"That's what she said? That's not why she quit." He laughs. "Angela's just a terrible actress."

My protectiveness comes out with a gasp. "What an awful thing to say about your own sister!"

"Even if it's the truth?"

"What's your truth? Are you terrible too?"

He shakes his head. "Of course I'm not terrible."

"So . . . ," I prompt him to elaborate.

He shoots me a quick glance with playfully narrowed eyes. "Are you trying to get me to say too much again? Going to spread pretty little rumors about me all over school?"

"Me?" I ask innocently, a hand on my chest. "Anything you say to me from now on gets locked in the vault." I pretend to zip my lips.

Nothing but a smirk. This is going to be like pulling teeth.

"So you're a good actor, then? Do you dance?" My heart flutters at the thought. I let my eyes fall to his legs, remembering how muscular they looked when he was working in the yard, but his jeans hide them now. Even though it's wishful thinking, I continue, "If you sing too, you'd be a triple threat."

If only I could find a triple threat . . .

"Oh, I'm a triple threat, all right, *mi reina*." He winks.

There's no way. He's probably just messing with me. "Sing something." I hold my breath and stare at him.

He turns down our street. "Nope."

"Come on, it's just me. Let me hear what you got."

"Nope."

"What are you afraid of?" I huff.

Jesse's jaw sets in a hard line. "Just drop it, Madison."

I shrink back into my seat and watch the drizzle outside until we make it to my house. Without even trying, I've become an expert at irritating him.

"You got a key yet?"

I peek up the drive. No one's home. I retrieve my key from the front pocket of my backpack and dangle it so he can see.

The sky rips open with a flash and tear of thunder. The truck gently rocks with the sudden onslaught of heavy rain.

"Great timing," I groan. I hug my backpack close to my chest, ready to bolt.

"Hang on." Jesse unbuckles his seat belt and leans toward me, reaching behind my head for something. My eyes find the strip of tan skin exposed just above his jeans.

I don't look away.

He returns to his seat, clutching an umbrella. I try to take it but he's out his door and opening mine in a matter of seconds. He holds it high over us as I slide off the seat and shut the door. But it doesn't close all the way. I turn, preparing to slam it with my hip, but Jesse extends his free hand, palming the door just next to my head. He pushes hard and it clicks, his arm brushing across the top of my shoulder in the process. I refrain from looking up into his eyes and instead study every detail of this potentially romantic scene.

The darkened sky, the grumble of thunder. Water coming down in sheets around us. The black umbrella. Black with an old-fashioned hook handle. Just like the one from . . . My heart kicks up speed. I look at Jesse just as a stray droplet falls along his temple, and I'm sucked into one of my favorite scenes.

The sky turns to night and I'm standing on the front stoop of an apartment, sporting a bright yellow rain slicker. Jesse's plaid, button-down shirt transforms into a gray suit, and a dark brown hat appears on his head. The taxi in the street waits for him to kiss me good night and then get back in the car.

I lean into him. "Take care of that throat," I say, flipping the collar of his jacket to cover his neck. "You're a big singing star now, remember? This Texas dew is just a little heavier than usual tonight."

"Uh . . ."

Please tell me I didn't say that out loud.

"Why are you looking at me like that?"

My eyes clear and I realize my hand is resting against Jesse's chest. I shake my head and shrink against the truck as much as possible, completely mortified I zoned out right in front of him. This is not *Singin' in the Rain*.

"What's going on *here*?" a voice calls from down the driveway.

The vehicle in my periphery isn't a taxi. It's a little blue car. And Brian.

CHAPTER NINE

Jesse removes his hand from the door and turns toward Brian. "Who's this?"

Brian moves closer to us, hiding a small book under his shirt from the rain and holding a flat paper grocery sack over his head. "Who am I? That's really funny, Jesse."

I glance up at Jesse, curious. "Are you just being funny, or do you really not know Brian? He's in your mom's theatre class with me."

He doesn't laugh. "Just because everyone at school knows who I am doesn't mean I know all of *them*."

If I knew him better, I'd jam my elbow in his side for that.

"But you sure know all the girls, don't you?" Brian sneers. "And you've run through your options, so you've moved on to the new girl."

Now I want to elbow Brian. "What are you talking about? Nothing's—"

"Nice shoes," Jesse scoffs, raising an eyebrow at Brian's obnoxiously bright sneakers.

Behind Brian, a thick bolt of lightning pulses down from the sky, followed by an ear-splitting boom that makes me jump.

"That hit something," Jesse says, nudging my shoulder and leading me toward the house. "We shouldn't be standing out here."

Brian's paper-sack umbrella droops and he runs ahead of us through the front yard, water sloshing up around his feet. By the time he makes it up the steps to the porch, the bottoms of his jeans are soaked.

I unlock the front door and turn to Jesse, who's still standing close to me with the umbrella over his head, even though we're safe on the porch. I have to push back my movie-scene daydream. He's not going to burst into song and start splashing through puddles, no matter how much of a fantasy come true that would be.

Brian pushes open the door and steps inside, treads squeaking on the faux wood in the entryway.

"Let me go get a towel so you don't make tracks on my mom's new flooring. I'd never hear the end of it." I follow him in and hold the door open for Jesse. But he's already halfway across the yard.

"Thanks for the ride," I call out over the rain.

Without looking back at me, he waves his free hand with a slow, careless flick of his wrist.

You just think you're so cool.

I lock the door, though I briefly consider leaving it open like they would have in the olden days, back when it was improper to be in a room with a boy without a chaperone. And here I am riding home with one boy and locking myself in an empty house with another. I was born so far out of time.

"So why's the Baseball King bringing you home?" Brian asks, one hand clutching the dampened script, the other shoved in his pocket.

"He lives across the street." I shrug indifferently as I walk through the house toward the laundry room to grab an old rag. "I don't have a car yet."

"I don't live that far from here. I could bring you home after theatre from now on." He takes the fraying towel from me and stares at it. "If you want."

Suddenly I'm forced to look at him not just as an audition partner, but as a potential beau. That's all it took: three sentences and shifty eyes, and everything's different. There might be interest tied up in this audition hoorah. I'm not sure how I feel about that.

"That's okay. Thanks, though." I leave him to dry off and make room for my backpack on the coffee table. "What part do you want to work on? Did you discuss a particular scene with Mrs. Morales for the audition?"

Brian slips out of his awful alien-green sneakers and joins me on the couch. Too close. "Maybe we should make sure we have chemistry first, like you said."

"Chemistry . . . right," I carefully agree, scooting away from him while reaching for his script. "I know just the scene to test that. The one where—"

"That's not what I mean." Brian laughs, keeping a firm grip on the book and using it to pull my upper body closer. "We have to test out the kissing."

I catch a whiff of spearmint. *You've got to be joking.*

I pull my lips in and bite, shaking my head rapidly.

Brian leans against the back of the couch. "Aw, come on, Maddie. These characters are newlyweds. If we end up doing this play together, we're gonna have to kiss like crazy, you know. I'm just suggesting we get that out of the way first. Like Leo and Kate when they filmed *Titanic.*"

"What are you talking about?"

His cheeks redden. "They, uh, filmed the nude scene first. To break the ice."

Great. Now he's probably picturing the two of us in that scene. And now I am. Gag.

"Well, I'm not stripping down and lying on this couch for you to draw my likeness, and I'm not kissing you. I don't kiss—" *Oh, no, what was I about to confess?*

"You don't kiss? Now what are *you* talking about?" Brian crosses his arms and cocks his head to the side.

Blast.

"I didn't say that," I hedge.

"Yes, you did. You said, 'I don't kiss.' That can't mean anything else." He lets out an amused sound, more from his nose than his throat. That, combined with the sudden spark of mischief in his eyes, and I think I might actually be getting nervous.

"Sure it could."

Smooth. Real smooth, Madison. I could have finished with *"I don't kiss boys in months ending in R,"* anything! But it's way too late to recover now.

"But . . . I thought—before you said . . ." He's tiptoeing around something, but I'm not sure what. "You've had a boy-friend before, right?"

"Of course." Which isn't *exactly* true.

I've gone on plenty of dates, but they've just never inspired me to give up that first kiss. Stage kisses don't count, obviously. Those aren't real. Sure, the emotions you develop for performance night might make it seem real, but it's called *acting*. I'm just one of those girls who's good at keeping my personal and professional lives separate.

"If you've kissed before, kissing me right here, right now, shouldn't be that big a deal." He moves closer. I want to choke him.

I exhale, weighing my options. I want to be in this play. *Need* to be. I'm not going to kiss him for the sake of practicing, but I need him on my side. To commit one hundred percent.

"Brian, you help me land this part, and I'll show you kissing that will change the color of your sneakers."

By the time I get to English class the next day, my name has been whispered to me in the hallway followed by puckering sounds, and I've found notes in my locker from two guys on the theatre tech team asking me to homecoming—one was a check "yes" or "no" type, the other gave a link to a website for me to select my answer.

Preoccupied by the puzzle of my sudden popularity with the male masses, I drop into my seat without immediately noticing a book slide across my desk.

"Helloooo?" Jesse says, waving a hand in front of my face.

Blinking, I realize he gave me my literature book. "Oh, no! Why didn't you tell me you had this last night? I was supposed to read an entire chapter for today!"

"I only saw it in my truck this morning," he says with hands raised in surrender. "If it was so important, why didn't you ask for it back? I don't remember getting any texts from you."

My heart skitters at the thought of sending Jesse a text. He may be my neighbor and carpool driver, but I've been at this school long enough now to see the way everyone acts around him. Like he's a god. And the way the girls look at me when I'm near him, like I'm a stray dog that needs a bath. I couldn't possibly be the instigator of our text conversation, no way. That has to come from him.

"Well, I think it's your responsibility to give me the condensed version of what the reading was about. It's only fair."

He scrunches his eyebrows together and curls up a corner of his mouth. "Like I read it."

Red rushes into the room, and before his butt even touches the chair, he asks, "Have you seriously never been kissed, Maddie?"

"What?" My head snaps up at him, eyes wide, pulse racing. "Who told you that?"

Red clears his throat but Jesse answers, "I heard it from Mike."

I keep my eyes fixed on Red, unable to face Jesse, and try my best to keep my voice down to avoid a scene, though I can't imagine anyone within earshot is missing any of this.

Brian. The little . . .

My jaw clenches as I try to find a way out of this. Denial will only make me look guilty. And I *am* guilty because the rumor's totally true. Owning it is probably the best way to go, even though all the decent guys might think there's something wrong with me, that I'm undesirable.

"Can you believe this hot little thing hasn't been kissed?" Red says to Jesse. "Someone needs to do something about that."

Or maybe someone will want to do something about it. . . . That would explain the notes in my locker this morning. Brian and I are going to have words later. Many words.

I collect my cool, counting to three and filling my lungs with a long, steady breath.

"So, it's true, then?" Red asks, and I can see Jesse direct his gaze toward me. "You're not exactly denying it."

There's nothing wrong with saving my first kiss. I refuse to be teased about it.

Mysterious. Be mysterious. Be attractive, alluring. Desirable.

"Wouldn't you like to know?" I finally say.

Red grunts, facing forward as the teacher walks in. "Such a tease."

"Is it true, what they're saying?" Tiffany asks as she squirts mustard on her cheeseburger.

I groan. Not them too.

"Have you really not kissed anyone before?" Angela fluffs rice and some kind of meat with her fork. Her mom actually attempted a home-cooked meal last night and these are the unfortunate-smelling leftovers.

"Listen to you guys, helping spread rumors." I cluck my tongue and change the subject. "Why don't you help me figure out where I should work instead? My future car isn't going to pay for itself."

Angela leans in and speaks low. "Hey, we're trying to get to the bottom of this thing so we can help put a stop to it. Where did this even come from, anyway?"

I wrinkle my nose. "Brian from theatre." They wait for me to elaborate, so I give them a quick play-by-play of last night's failed attempt at an audition practice.

"So, basically you're saying you've never kissed anyone except in shows?" Tiffany raises her bottle of pop and says, "To the saddest thing I've ever heard," then takes a swig.

Angela ignores her. "What's the holdup, exactly? You like boys, right? Why don't you want to kiss them?"

Can I tell them? Would they understand? Do *I* even understand why I'm still holding on to the dream of perfection? Does it exist anywhere?

I swallow hard. "I just haven't found the right guy yet."

"Well, buy yourself some new lip gloss because you can have your pick of the crop now," Tiffany says. "I overheard a few guys in the lunch line talking about whether you had a date to homecoming yet."

"What guys?" I ask, ears perked.

"I have no idea. I think they're juniors."

I take a bite of my ham sandwich. "Brian asked me."

"What?" they ask at the same time.

"He must have been the one Mrs. M. was talking about," Tiffany finishes. "Did he ask before or after he tried to plant one on you?"

"After. Right before he left." I exhale and toss the remains of my sandwich in my lunch box. "But it was so lame. He just . . . asked me. Red's self-obsessed offer was somehow more appealing. I said I'd think about it, but obviously I'm going to say no."

Silence. Blank stares.

"What *should* he have done?" Angela asks.

Tiffany snorts. "Don't even get her started."

"Ladies," I say, snapping a slice of pear in two, "I think it's time I introduced you to the love of my life."

CHAPTER TEN

After ten minutes at the homecoming game Friday night, one thing is clear: I don't belong in Texas. I've never seen so many cowboy boots and hats outside of the movies in my life. Grown men spit, actually *spit*, anywhere and everywhere. En masse they're a Southern bunch, some with the drawl I expected to hear when I moved down here, all boasting about how their kid is the best. And the moms . . . I can't even.

Every high school girl seems to be here to cheer on the football guys. And their bodies are practically covered in these gigantic, fake white flowers with ribbons and bells and who knows what else hanging from them. They call them mums. I guess it was a Texas tradition back in the day for the boys to give their homecoming date a chrysanthemum flower, and over time it's evolved into a social-status competition. The bigger, the better. Some of the senior girls' mums are so big, they have to wear this special thing over their shoulders to pin them to so their shirts don't rip off. I can't believe the administration allows those noisy things to be worn at school. Between every class today, it was like walking among a herd of dairy cows.

Angela and Tiffany agreed to marathon my choice of movies tonight, with the condition that I attend the homecoming game with them. Well, I'm here, but it doesn't mean I have to sit on these uncomfortable metal benches and watch the whole game.

I talk the girls into a snack just before halftime—I'm in the mood for something cheesy and wonderfully disgusting. We head for the concession stand, but I lose my appetite when I see who's working the register. Brian is not touching anything that goes in my mouth.

"Y'all go ahead," I tell them. "I'll just wait out here."

As I turn around, Brian calls out, "Nachos are only five bucks, Maddie. You know you want some."

Greasy, gooey cheese. I really do. "Only? Five bucks seems a little steep for a bowl of corn chips and neon cheese."

"Worth it," Angela says, digging cash out of her purse.

"Money goes to the drama department tonight. Did you forget?" Brian removes his school-colored hat and scratches his head with the same hand. He's definitely not touching my food. "And we get extra credit working the stand."

I motion to his customers. "Well, carry on, Chef Boyardee."

He fills Angela's nacho order, then disappears behind the wall. We start the walk back toward the bleachers, when suddenly Brian's standing in front of me with a constipated look on his face. Then he drops to one knee. A few nearby kids and a teacher slow to see what's going on.

"Whaaa . . . ?" Angela draws out as Tiffany leans toward me and whispers, "Holy whoa, girl. What's happening?"

"Go to homecoming with me, Maddie," he says, taking my hands in his.

Because I'm in shock, and not because a boy is holding my hands and my brain doesn't know what to do with that information, I don't pull away. But I do have enough wits about me to understand this is still Brian.

"After what you did? You can't be serious."

"I'm sorry about that." His smile fades into regret. "I swear I only told *one* person that you might not have been kissed. You were just so cryptic about it."

My lips curl into a snarl. "You caught me off guard. How was I supposed to know you wanted to jump right into the kissing? Seriously, Brian, you're such a—" I swallow back all the words I'm too classy to say and make a noise of revulsion instead.

"I didn't mean for it to turn into a thing. I really didn't. I *will* make it up to you, I pro ”

A chirp from his pocket prompts him to pull out his phone and glance at it. The smile returns. "Just"—he stands and brushes off his knee—"stay right there. Don't move."

He takes off but I don't turn to look. I'm too busy processing that he was down on one knee, proposing to be my homecoming date. It was almost a full-fledged romantic gesture.

"That was weird," Angela says. "Does he think you're going to change your mind by the time he comes back or something?"

"He may not be the smartest in the bunch," Tiffany says, stealing Angela's food, "but his nachos have an excellent cheese-to-chip ratio."

A country song blasts from somewhere to my right, and I quickly locate the source, as it's heading straight for me. It's Ryan, carrying an iPod in one hand wired to a portable speaker in the other, both of which he sets on the ground at my feet before stepping back and joining hands with Sarah, who has appeared out of nowhere. About ten other girls I don't recognize run to fill the empty space around them, everyone facing me.

What. Is. Going. On?

When the chorus of the song starts, everyone in the group moves their feet simultaneously. They grapevine one way, kick out their heels and clap, then go the other way, kick, clap, more kicking, hopping and twisting, some of them twirling an arm like they've got a lasso or something. When they turn to change direction, a few of the people standing around to watch join in, and soon everyone around me is clapping the beat. It's like a flash-mob line dance.

If I knew the complicated-looking dance, I'd probably join them, but Brian told me not to move, so I have a sinking feeling this all has something to do with me. Thankfully, Angela and Tiffany are still at my side.

When the people turn again and have their backs to me, Brian weaves between them, holding out a gigantor mum in front of him, a sly grin on his face. Suddenly I wish I hadn't so audibly made fun of them with Sarah today in class. But really, I can hear the teeny cowbells ringing over the Grand Ole Opry blasting at my feet.

Moo.

Brian grabs at the blue-and-silver ribbons hanging from the fake white flowers, and there in sparkly silver letters are our names.

"Please, Maddie?" is all he says, his brown eyes watching me expectantly.

"It's like he read your mind," Tiffany says in awe.

I look to Angela for help, and she shrugs. "You won't get much more epic than a choreographed musical number."

I glance back up at the dancers and see Jesse walking slowly alongside them, trailed by a gorgeously tan girl I assume is Gabby, his homecoming date. She stops to take in the scene, but after a quick nod to me, Jesse grabs her hand and keeps moving.

Even Jesse has someone to hold hands with. And dance with.

I want this for me.

Brian wants to dance with me. He organized a miniature flash mob, even spent who knows how much personalizing an extremely tacky homecoming memento to tell me so. A remarkably nice gesture considering I haven't spoken to him outside of rehearsing our lines together after school this week. He probably really didn't mean to spread news of my kissing status to the entire Fernwood High populace. And it would be nice to have an excuse to get all dolled up.

A smile fights my lips until it wins, and I take the awful mum thing from him. I wonder which moving box my dresses are in.

"Popcorn!" Tiffany cries as she bounds into the Moraleses' TV room carrying three bags of popcorn—one for each of us.

"Shut up!" Angela hisses, taking a bag from her. "You'll wake the little monster."

I shut the door behind Tiffany, dim the lights, and clear my throat. "I hereby call this meeting to order, the first of what I hope will be many."

"Meeting?" Angela asks. "I thought we were watching movies."

"Boo!" Tiffany tosses a handful of popcorn at my face. "You promised us hotness!"

"And hotness you shall have." I snatch a piece that landed in my hair and eat it. "Ladies of the newly-formed-just-this-second Teens for Classic Movies Club, I'd like to—"

"Wait." Tiffany throws more popcorn at me. "We're a club now?"

"*Classic* movies?" Angela groans. "How did I forget you haven't seen any movies made in this century? You with the star on your cheek from whatever that movie was. I suppose we're watching that one tonight? Something about it raining?"

"Yes, we'll get to it," I say, trying to keep my tone even. "I'm telling you, the classics are—"

"Like black-and-white grainy movies where people sing and dance every few minutes?" Tiffany asks, preparing to take aim with another handful.

"Some of them are, but not all." My confidence dips, but I hold my head higher. "Look, you wanted to know why my standards are so high, and this is it. Ladies, I'd like you to meet"—I fix them with an expectant stare, and Tiffany gives me a drumroll on her legs—"Mr. Gene Kelly."

Holding my breath, I present them with a crisp printout of Gene, then carefully watch their eyes for any hint of a reaction. Sharing this part of me is not an emotionally simple task, which is why I generally keep the whole truth to myself until absolutely necessary. And I guess it's not to that point just yet, but I feel I've found a pair of girls who won't judge me. Who may even join me in my madness.

I hope.

"Oooooh," Angela purrs, taking the picture from me. "He's handsome."

"Lemme see that," Tiffany says, leaning over Angela's shoulder to take a look before sinking back into the couch. "Meh. He's okay, I guess." She shrugs. "Who else you got?"

I don't answer, and instead sift through the stack of DVDs I brought from home, selecting *Anchors Aweigh* as our starting point.

"Tiffany, I know you're a fan of tight, clingy uniforms, so there will be plenty of eye candy in this one since Gene and Frank Sinatra are in the navy."

"Oh, that sounds nice." Her expression brightens. "Is this your favorite Gene movie?"

"I'm not telling you which one is my favorite. It'll be more fun if you guess after you've seen them all."

"Well, uniforms are good." Angela tucks her legs underneath her and grabs the throw hanging over the back of the sofa. "What else does this movie have to offer for me?"

"Um . . ." I let out a sigh as I slide the disc into the player. "A flash of muscular man-thigh when Gene runs around in his boxers?"

She straightens, fully alert. "I approve. Let's meet your boyfriend."

"And his thighs," Tiffany adds.

The movie is a hit. They laugh and sigh in all the right places, and I'm pretty sure I hear Tiffany "Mmmmmm" every time Frank sings. Next, I introduce them to the ultimate fan favorite, *Singin' in the Rain*. I find myself watching the girls more than the screen, because there's nothing like witnessing someone, for the first time, enjoy films that are close to your heart. That are so much a part of you and who you are.

I nestle deeper under the quilt, using the armrest of the leather couch as a pillow. Despite my efforts to stay awake, my eyelids betray me somewhere between *Summer Stock* and *An American in Paris*, and I drift to my favorite place.

I stand in front of the vanity mirror to stare at my reflection, framed by huge round lights. My long sapphire dress flutters around me as I twist and double-check that everything is in order.

I turn and there he is, my perfect man in a dark blue suit. Gene pulls me close, cheek to cheek, one hand at the small of my back, the other clutching mine. I close my eyes and melt against him as he sing-hums in my ear, nonsensical words and phrases, and we sway to the rhythm of his made-up song.

"Look who I've found," he sings. "Madison . . . what you've done . . ."

The most beautiful voice I've ever heard. The most beautiful voice . . .

"Madison? Are you okay?"

I bolt upright, sections of my hair falling around my face from my bun piled high on top of my head. Blinking a few times at the daylight streaming in through the open door, I become aware of my surroundings. Blankets strewn everywhere, popcorn and DVD cases all over the floor.

And Jesse. Sitting on the couch. At my feet.

My hand flies to my face to clear my eyes and the corners of my mouth of anything that shouldn't be there.

"You were, like, whimpering," Jesse says, his momentary look of concern morphing into pure amusement.

"Oh." I fight back a yawn. "Dream, I guess."

"Must have been a nightmare."

"Hardly," I mutter before stretching my legs out. He *would* have to wake me up right before the kissing part. "Where'd everyone go?"

"I assume they're in bed. I didn't expect you to still be in here."

"They left me. I must have been completely zonked." Another yawn.

"Looks like it was a pretty wild night watching super-old movies," Jesse says, eyeing my DVD collection. "Are all of these yours?"

"Yes. They're only the most swoon-worthy movies ever made." I sigh. "I consider it a tragedy I'll never get to see any of these on the big screen. Your massive TV here is about as close as I'm going to get."

He laughs, tapping the uneven stack of movie cases with his foot. *Anchors Aweigh* and *On the Town* slide toward him. "Someone has a sailor fetish. Wait, do all of these movies have the same people in them?"

"A couple of them do." I change the subject in a hurry. "So, what were you looking for in here?"

That crooked smirk of his creeps out. "I was just gonna watch some sports highlights before mowing the yard." He picks up the remote from the floor, but doesn't press any buttons.

"You don't have a TV in your room?" I thought all rich kids had their own televisions.

"No. Do you?"

"Not anymore," I say quickly, desperate not to dwell on my former lifestyle. "What time is it?"

"Seven."

"Why, why, why are you awake so early on a Saturday?"

"Habit."

Leaning back into the couch, I groan and pull the blanket over my head. If I fall asleep, maybe I can get back to that dream.

Jesse pokes my foot. "So, are you awake now?"

I huff and fling the blanket off, shooting him with my best angry glare.

"Good," he says as he stands. "I want to show you something."

CHAPTER ELEVEN

"You are *so* slow," Jesse says from outside the bathroom door.

"Beauty takes time," I say in singsong, trying to do damage control. There's not one speck of makeup on my face, my hair is a frizzed-out disaster, and pillow lines streak down the side of my cheek.

"Let's go," he says, annoyed.

With as much as he's rushing me, it's a wonder I even had time to change out of my pajamas.

I crack open the door and frown. "You're at least going to let me brush my teeth."

He takes a step back and laughs. "Oh, yeah. Definitely do that."

"Why can't you tell me what we're doing?" I ask as I open the medicine cabinet, locating the pink toothbrush I leave here for sleepovers.

"Because this is the sort of thing you just need to see." He crosses his arms. "And if you don't make it quick, it's going to be too late."

I slow the movement of my brushing and raise an eyebrow at him. His jaw clenches and his eyes narrow. They're so green I can't help but stare back into them, and for a second I forget what I'm supposed to be doing.

"Never mind," he says with a shake of his head, turning down the hall for the stairs.

"Chill out, Jesse. I'm coming." I rinse quickly and rush after him. "I didn't know you were so easily flustered."

Without a word, he leads me out the back, past the pool and across the yard to the shed where the equipment is kept. And grown-up toys. Several four-wheelers are lined up alongside a tractor. Jesse climbs on the dark green one and starts it with the push of a button. The roar echoes loudly against the metal walls and ceiling as he drives it out the main door to where I'm standing, and I refrain from covering my ears. He's been vexed with me enough already this morning.

"What's with the face?" He brings the vehicle to a stop in front of me.

Don't whine, don't whine. I swallow back a wave of fear. "Am I . . . driving one of these? Because I don't even have a ca—"

He pats the small space on the seat just behind him. Emphasis on *small*. There would be touching if I sat there. Lots of touching.

"Oh." I take a step back toward the shed. "Where are the helmets?"

Laughter is not the answer I expect, but it's the one I get.

"Why is that funny?" I scold. "Are you afraid to mess up your perfect hair for the sake of safety? I'm not afraid to wear one." I raise my head higher to prove that I'm above such vanity.

Of course, he laughs even harder. "Maddie. We aren't racing. We won't be hitting any jumps, I won't pop any wheelies. We're not even going to leave the property."

I bite at my bottom lip, considering his assurances.

"You can trust me." His mouth forms that whisper of a smirk I'm beginning to think of as his signature expression.

"Trust you with my unhelmeted head? I'm still getting to know you," I say as I sit behind him, cringing as my legs press against his hips. And now I'm staring at his thighs, his athletic shorts riding up and exposing more of his skin than I've seen. Those quad muscles are just unbelievable. My stupid weakness for strong legs.

"You know enough."

Jesse pushes on the throttle, and my body gets thrown backward. Reflexively, I reach for him to steady myself. He straightens as my fingers dig into his sides.

"You can retract the claws." With the hand that's not controlling the gas, he adjusts my death grip a bit lower. Closer to the thighs. "You're not gonna fall off."

Past the lush, manicured lawn of the backyard, he steers through a patch of overgrown weeds, some of them rising high above our heads. Something pokey reaches out from the ground and scrapes at my shin, and a group of winged, mothy things escape our path.

I open my mouth to ask him why he didn't warn me to wear long pants, but I already know the answer. He's a boy.

We hit a dip and my jaw decides to snap shut, the inside of my cheek producing a lovely *crunch* sound between my teeth. I'm so busy waiting to taste the blood, I don't consciously clamp my hands back where they were before, but there they are.

"Seriously," he says, swatting them away as if they're insects. "Verbal abuse only, remember?"

And of course, because he asked for it, I've got no comeback. I lean back and away from him, finding a metal rack to grab on to instead. A sneeze overtakes me so suddenly I barely have time to cover my nose and mouth. It's quickly followed by two more, complete with watery eyes.

"You better not be sneezing on me," Jesse calls over his shoulder, giving the beast more gas instead of waiting for my reply.

"Where are we going, anyway?" I ask with a little more grouch than I prefer.

"I thought your attitude toward the *country* needed a positive boost." He emphasizes *country* with one-handed air quotes.

"And riding on this thing is going to improve my outlook how?"

"Just shut up," he says, rolling his head back in annoyance since I can't see his eyes.

We burst through another patch of giant weeds before turning onto a trail that weaves between spindly pines. My body slides a bit closer to Jesse, a sign that we're headed down a slope. The trees get bigger, and the sky seems farther away the deeper into the woods we venture. How much land do they have?

I cover my face for another sneeze and rub at my eyes. My eyelids. Something is very wrong with my eyelids. They're thicker than usual . . .

Another sneeze. I can't stop massaging my eyes. *What's happening?*

"Jesse," I say between sneezes, "I think something's—"

"Shhh!" He stops and cuts the engine, motioning for me to get off.

With a sniffle and a soothing palm smashed against one of my eyes, I follow him down the trail. He crouches low, leaning his upper body forward and bending his knees as he walks like he's sneaking up on someone. I instinctively mimic the awkward position, doing my best not to make any noise. But then I sneeze and Jesse ducks his head at the sound.

"I. Can't. Help. It!" I whisper. "I think I'm—"

He turns to shush me again, pressing a finger to his lips before pointing down the hill and continuing to creep along. Irritated, I walk at a normal height, one hand on my hip, the other scratching at my eyes.

After a few minutes of stepping over twigs and fighting back sneezes, we come to a clearing with a nearly dry creek dribbling through the middle of it. He points across the water to the grassy bank. At first I don't see anything important, but a slight movement causes me to look closer.

"It's a baby deer thing!" I whisper, hoping it won't hear me and run. Make that *they.* "Two of them! And mommy! How adorable!"

Two little brown babies with light spots are curled up in the grass next to an adult deer, relaxing in the shade alongside the water like they do this every Saturday morning.

Jesse bites his lip to keep from laughing, and his body shakes. "A baby deer *thing*?"

Too overwhelmed by the cuteness to glare at him, I step closer to get a better look.

"I think this is the biggest smile I've seen from you," he says from beside me.

So of course my smile widens.

"Have you ever seen a deer this close?" he asks.

I shake my head. "I don't think I've even seen one in person at all."

My eyes pool with tears, but it's not an emotional response. Sneezing is imminent.

I swallow, sniffle, and rub my eyelids in an effort to distract my sinuses. "They're amazing. How'd you know they were here?"

"That was luck. I saw the little ones hopping around close by last week. Thought you'd like to see them. Sorry for rushing you earlier. I wanted to get out here before the feeder went off."

"Feeder?"

"Yeah, we feed them corn. Keeps them around during hunting season."

The thought of Jesse shooting one of those babies in a few short years sends a quiver from the back of my neck down to my toes. And I sneeze.

All three deer crane their necks in our direction, then hold still as stone, like their lives depend on it. Someone needs to teach them that a moving target is harder to kill.

"I think I just became a vegetarian," I say, wiggling my nose to prevent another sneeze that's coming on.

Jesse tilts his head to the side and takes a step toward me. It's my turn to freeze like a statue. His eyes search mine, brows pulling together.

"What's wrong with your face?" he says just above a whisper.

Exactly what a girl wants to hear from arguably the most attractive guy at school while alone with him in the woods. It's like he was born without a romantic instinct.

"What do you mean?" I back away from him. "What's *wrong* with my face?"

The already apprehensive deer take the opportunity to make a break for it. I wish I could run away right now too. I also wish I had a mirror or that I could look at my reflection in the surface of the water like you see in shows, if that really even works.

"Your eyes are all red and . . . puffy. Are you crying?"

"No, it's the pressure in my forehead!" I massage between my eyes. Cue another sneeze. "I don't feel so good."

"You don't look so good."

"Yes, we've established that." My eyes and nose may be malfunctioning, but I know my scowl works.

"Allergies?"

"No. I mean, I've never had to deal with allergies before." I'd certainly remember this sort of facial failure if I had.

"Well, we have a different set of trees and weeds than you do up North," he explains, starting to climb the hill toward the four-wheeler. "I'll take you home. You need meds."

Home. With *my* trees. *My* life. So very far away.

"It's not my home," I bite. "It's just where I'm living at this moment in time." I pivot and march behind him.

Jesse's arm catches on a branch, which flies back and smacks me in the head. He doesn't notice. And I sneeze three more times before he starts the engine.

There aren't enough spotted baby creatures in the world to get me to find favor with this much nature. Texas officially hates me.

CHAPTER TWELVE

With the help of some hot-pink miracle pill my dad rushed to get from the store, my eyes shrank to their normal size and thankfully stopped itching. My voice still sounds a bit scratchy and nasally, like a perpetual whiner, but the sneezing stopped just in time for the homecoming dance.

And I look gorgeous.

At least that's what Brian said when he picked me up. Well, actually I think he used the word "good" but I upgraded.

"I like your star," he says once we're en route, having survived the obligatory pose-in-front-of-the-fireplace-and-look-awkward pictures. Thankfully, my mom's pregnancy isn't really showing too much, so *that* topic gets to be avoided a little longer.

I smile, pleased I decided to add glitter to the star on my cheek tonight. A dance is a special occasion, after all. And I feel all kinds of glam in my 1950s-inspired halter-neck dress. The red polka dots pop against the black, and the thick red belt around my waist really completes the look.

"You're not afraid to stand out, are you?" Brian asks.

The elastic strap on my wrist corsage itches, so I take it off and hold it, examining the arrangement of apple-green orchids. My dress is not green. But he didn't try to match my dress, oh no. It makes so much more sense for the flowers to match the boy's shoes.

And he thinks *I* stand out? "Neither are you, I'd say."

He turns the Camry onto the main street toward the school. "Well, I don't really see the point of holding back just because of what someone else might think. I mean, if something about me is a friendship deal breaker, who needs 'em?"

I twist in my seat to look at him. "Seriously, I think you may be the only person I've met here who would ever say that."

It's refreshing, but I'm not sure how attached to this guy I want to get. Let's see how he does at Monday's audition first.

"It might also be why I don't have that many friends." He laughs and waves a hand dismissively.

I laugh with him, smoothing out my dress under the seat belt. "You're good people, Brian. Even if you inadvertently told the whole school I've never been kissed."

"Hey, you know how sorry I am for that. I shouldn't have said anything to anyone," he says as he pulls into the parking lot. "Good thing you're not afraid to stand out, right?"

Doesn't mean I need the misconception flying around that I don't *want* to be kissed. I most certainly do. Everything just has to line up . . . perfectly.

We make our entrance into the school common area, and it's like I'm stepping back into the woods from this morning, but at night. The overhead fluorescents are off, but can lights throw sparkling blues and greens against giant papier-mâché trees stretching overhead. The cafeteria tables that usually occupy the space are out of sight, replaced by a DJ presiding over the dance floor, blasting some country song from the speakers.

Two sets of arms grab me, stealing me away from Brian, who finds a cluster of guys to chat with.

"Maddie, you've ruined me," Angela says dreamily.

"What do you mean, I ruined you?" I ask, observing her floor-length aqua knockout and Tiffany's strapless green number. All three of us have our hair down in curls. *Look out, boys.*

"I've got all those stupid old songs in my head now," she explains. "And I *like* it."

My heart flies.

"We stayed up all night watching your ancient movies," Tiffany adds. "All night. And I'm completely shocked with myself to be admitting this, but they weren't terrible."

"You watched *all* of the movies I brought over?"

Angela nods. "Well, we watched one while we were getting ready for the dance too. And we have guesses for your favorite. *Summer Stock.* It has to be *Summer Stock.* The way your boyfriend looks at her even though they're both dating someone else. Whoa."

Is it possible? Do they *get* me?

"No, it's *Singin' in the Rain*, yo." Tiffany crosses her arms and chatters a hundred miles an hour. "She's even wearing the star on her cheek right now, just like that Lina woman.

Personally, I'm partial to *Anchors Aweigh* because of the little guy with the tight pants and the voice, if that was even him singing for real."

My heart. It's swelling. So. Happy.

"Of course it was. Even I've heard of Frank Sinatra before." Angela rolls her eyes. "Anyway, I get it now, Maddie. No wonder you've got a thing for legs. The dancing is pretty hot."

"Meh, the dancing doesn't do it for me as much as the singing," Tiffany says. "But I'll bet Jesse could have been that good if he hadn't stopped."

What? My breath catches. "Jesse? As in Angela's brother? A dancer?"

"Oh, yeah," Tiffany continues. "He used to be all about it. Because of his mom, you know? Musicals, plays, everything."

"He was really good," Angela agrees. "Mom was ticked when he quit. She thought he was going to be her Broadway golden boy."

Mind. Blown. My personal driver, the Baseball King of high school, was a dancer? There's no way.

"You guys are messing with me," I say with a hand on my stomach and one at my temple. "What *kind* of dancing?"

If she says tap, I'm going to collapse. I glance at the floor to see what I'd land on, just in case.

Angela steps closer to me and speaks low. "Keep it down, Maddie. He doesn't like to talk about it."

I turn to her but don't decrease my volume. "For someone who likes attention from girls so much, I'd think he'd be all over it."

"Mmm," Tiffany ponders. "Sports are the name of the game. The theatre stuff isn't all that popular here." Angela's eyes narrow so Tiffany quickly amends, "Though it's gotten better since your mom took over last year. I'm just saying it's hard to get too many guys involved in it when sports are the bigger draw. More notoriety, more money in the future. I mean, unless you're good enough for Hollywood or something."

"But," I begin, struggling to form a coherent sentence, "I just don't see how sports are hotter than a man who can dance like that. And who doesn't think singing is hot?"

"Maddie," Angela says, a hand on my shoulder. "As much as I wish it was different for your sake, your reality is skewed. This is high school. When most of us want to see a guy sing and dance, we ask daddy for tickets to a concert, not a high school production of *Newsies*. This is Texas, which is synonymous with football and baseball."

"What's wrong with *News*—"

"Then there's the name calling," Tiffany cuts in. "What did the guys call him?"

"No," Angela defends. "He wants to forget all of it, so let him. Baseball's his thing now, and he's really good at that too."

And just like that, I deflate. So close. I knew Jesse had dancers' legs, I just knew it. What a waste to use them standing on a pitcher's mound. I have to figure out a way to talk to him about it.

"I don't know about y'all," Tiffany says, rising up on her toes and bouncing a few times, "but I came here to dance. Let's warm up before our dates steal us."

I link arms with Angela as we hit the dance floor. "*Summer Stock* is my favorite Gene movie ever."

"I knew it!" she exclaims.

As we start to dance, she sings a few lines of "You Wonderful You," terribly off tune.

"Okay, leave the singing to Frank," Tiffany says, "and let's dance!"

We giggle and the three of us move to the center of the dance floor, throwing our hands in the air and letting loose. I feel so free, so exhilarated. *Understood* for maybe the first time ever.

And I can't stop thinking about Jesse. I need to see what he can do.

Brian isn't a dreadful dancer, but he does like to step on my feet. By the third time, I pretend I'm thirsty and ask him to get me a pop.

"You want a what?" he asks, brows scrunched together.

"Pop, like a Sprite or something."

"Oh, you want a Coke." He smiles like he gets it, but he clearly doesn't.

"No, I don't like brown pops," I explain. "I want something fruity, like a Sprite."

"Yeah. Right. Pop." He shrugs as he turns for the drink table.

As soon as I'm left alone, a guy I vaguely recognize from Spanish approaches and clears his throat. His lips part to unveil a set of jacked-up teeth, desperate for braces. I offer him a sympathetic smile.

"Maddie, right?" he says, hands deep in his pockets.

I pick at the flowers on my wrist. "Uh . . . Juan?"

"Francisco." He laughs and lifts a shoulder. "Gregory, r-really."

"Ah, Greg," I say, twisting at my waist to watch my skirt spread out. I wish they'd play some swing music so it could get some real action. And I wish there were a boy at this school who knew how to swing dance. . . .

I glance around, following the flashes of light across the dark room in hopes of glimpsing Jesse's face. I haven't seen him yet tonight.

The crowd parts. A figure steps into the spotlight. Black slacks, white shirt with sleeves rolled up to the elbows, suspenders. So. Adorable.

The band starts a slower swing number, something from the Glenn Miller catalog, but I can never remember the names of songs with no lyrics.

He makes his way to me one pronounced step at a time, with each beat, fingers snapping. That perfect smile comes into view, and the scar on his left cheek creates its own little shadow, proof he was once a child prone to accidents. But now he's so far from a child. And he's here. With me.

I lean in and kiss the indentation, feeling his smile widen under my lips.

His hand slides around my belt like it's a pathway, coming to rest against my lower back. We sway cheek to cheek for a moment before the music kicks into high gear and we clasp each other's hands, step-step-rock-stepping to the rhythm. In a swift movement, he grabs my waist and—

"It's j-just Gregory."

"Oh." I startle, having forgotten he was there. "Okay, Gregory then."

He smiles again. The teeth. They're so unfortunate. I can't look away. And they're getting closer. The teeth are getting bigger. *What is happening?*

I look up to his eyes and find him looking at *my* teeth, or mouth. My *mouth*!

Just before he crosses the point of no return, I take a step back and shove him away at the same time.

"What do you think you're doing, *Greg*?"

"I was j-just . . . I wanted to be th-the first . . ." His face goes tomato, and sweat beads along his little set of sideburns. He's still way too close.

"See you in class, Francisco." I twirl around, hoping my dress smacks against him in a dramatic exit, but I run right into a thick body.

"Need some saving?" Red asks, steadying me, eyes examining me closely and lingering a little too long in the chest area. "Well, check you out."

Jesse stands next to him, sleek in a black suit and tie. Now that I know he's a former dancer, it's like he's glowing, shining. All those secrets up in his head. The steps he must still have memorized, the melodies his mouth could sing at a moment's notice. All of it, waiting for me to discover, to witness for myself. Because a part of me can't believe it until I see it.

"No, I don't need saving," I say, fluffing my curls and bringing some in front of my shoulders. "He was just—"

"Trying to stick his tongue down your throat?" Red says.

I cringe.

"Yeah. We saw that," Jesse chimes in.

"You sure were slow to push him away. Wonder why that is? Got a little something for the younger boys, do you?" Red throws an arm around my shoulders. "Because that's what he was. A boy. What you need is a man. Someone strong. Someone athletic. Like a baseball player."

Or maybe just a dance with a particular baseball player.

"*Please*, Red," I say, shrugging out of his hold. "Not. Interested."

He crosses his arms. "Fine, fine. Have fun twirling with the other children." With that, he stalks toward the drink table.

I expect Jesse to follow but he's still standing there, looking at me, eyes extra green from the mood lighting splashed across his face.

"You look really nice," he says.

At least, I *think* that's what he says. He's not exactly projecting his voice appropriately for the noise level in here.

"Thanks." I'm about to return the compliment when my eye catches on a mark. The lights are hitting him just so, making a shadow on his left cheek. There's a tiny round indentation. A scar.

I'm about to ask what happened, but an overeager voice calls out from behind him.

"Okay, I'm all freshened up! I think this lipstick is a better shade for me, don't you?"

Gabby stands next to him to join our conversation, I assume, but instead Jesse takes her hand and leads her away. I'm left alone, struggling to stand straight in the wake of Jesse's blatant and inexcusable snubbing. And just after he said I looked nice. How do I not warrant an introduction? Am I ranked that low on his social scale that I can't even meet his homecoming date?

Well, I don't want to dance with someone that rude, anyway.

I scan the room to find Brian—who's taking an awfully long time getting me something to drink—and spot him clutching two cups, chatting with Sarah and Ryan. Sarah looks so pretty in a blood-red, knee-length dress. And the flowers on her wrist actually match, along with Ryan's tie. Good boyfriend.

Joining them and taking a cup from Brian, I down it before I figure out it's one of the brown pops. Ugh.

"So, I was practically mauled by someone from my Spanish class," I tell them. "Is this what happens at dances in Texas? Do people get freakishly horny or what?"

"First of all, that was my Coke," Brian says, exchanging the now-empty cup for the other. "Second, I think I know what's going on with the horniness. And I think it's my fault."

My stomach drops. I feel the need to brace myself, but there's nothing close by to hold on to.

He exhales, eyes heavy with apology. "Apparently there are a couple creeps making bets on who can kiss you first."

CHAPTER THIRTEEN

After a million more apologies from Brian for having the ability to speak and unintentionally starting a kissing bet, we spend
all day Sunday practicing for auditions. I sound like I'm on the
verge of crying the entire time, even with the help of my magic
pink allergy pill, but we're able to get some serious work done.
If I didn't have such a good feeling about our chances of getting
cast together, I would have abandoned him to perform his own
monologue. But a strong acting partner trumps any personal
issues I may have against him. I know he didn't mean for any of
it to go that far.

By Monday morning, after my daily dose of meds kicks in,
I'm ready to face the casting directors. Too bad auditions are
after school.

And too bad I sit next to Jesse in English class. I'm still
not totally clear on what happened at the dance, why I wasn't

good enough to meet his friend. I half expect him to ignore me, but I sneeze when he takes his seat, which serves as an invitation.

"Bless you," he says.

"Thanks."

"Allergies still bothering you?"

"A little."

"Need a tissue?"

I clench my teeth at his helpfulness and sniffle. "Nope."

"Need a ride home after school?"

Without looking at him, I shake my head.

"Oh, right," he says, slouching and stretching his legs out. "Auditions today."

He waits for me to confirm, but I pretend to read "The Yellow Wallpaper" in my lit book.

"Mom says you have it 'in the bag.'" I can see the air quotes in my periphery. "She doesn't usually talk about school at home. You must be pretty good."

My confidence swells, but I'm unable to bask in it. I've been tortured by too many questions this weekend to hold all of them in.

I turn on him. "And I hear you're a pretty good dancer. What's up with that?"

He slides down farther in his seat. "I told you to drop it before, and I'm telling you again now."

"I thought you were just acting cool, like you could do anything, but according to Tiffany and your sister, you're a regular—" I stop myself from saying Gene Kelly or Fred Astaire. "Broadway star."

Red drops into his chair with a nod to Jesse and a lesser nod to me, Monday clearly beating him down.

"That's not me anymore," Jesse mutters.

"I just don't believe a love for something like that can leave you so easily," I say quietly to avoid a scene. "Especially with the level of talent you apparently have."

Jesse's jaw hardens. "What makes you think I loved it? Just because you're good at something doesn't mean that it's what you should be doing."

I let his words sink in along with the tone in which he delivered them. There's plenty of "Just shut up" in there, but I sense a hint of something else too. Maybe he misses it.

Maybe I'm the one who needs to give that part of his life back to him.

Auditions are on the main stage, even though Mrs. Morales says the show itself will be in the smaller black box theatre where we have class. She said school plays like these don't draw that big a crowd, which is a shame. I really wanted to stand up there in front of a full house, surrounded by all the fancy technical sparklies this place is equipped with.

I find Brian and we sign ourselves in with Sarah, who was elected to be the student director for *Barefoot in the Park*, then take a seat among the other hopefuls to wait until our number is called. Brian and I have a high number, but I'm determined not to get nervous watching so many others go before us. If any of them blows me away, I'll have to do that much better. Motivation.

My surprise sneeze echoes all around us, amplified. It's quickly followed by two more.

Brian turns to me, eyes wide. "Do I need to be worried about this?"

"No, it's fine. My medicine is just wearing off."

Rica drops into the row in front of us. "Aww. Feeling sick? That's too bad."

I can tell it bothers her *so much*. "Maybe I'm just allergic to you," I say jokingly. Sort of.

I search through the front pouch of my backpack, locating my meds and pulling out my bottled water.

"You're supposed to leave that stuff with the nurse," Rica says like a know-it-all.

"Well, I didn't." Truthfully, I hadn't thought about it. I'm unfamiliar with this allergy medicine dependency. "Are you going to tell on me or something?"

She straightens, lifting her chin. "Like I care what you do."

"Might as well read through my lines while we wait," Brian says as he stands. "I'm gonna grab our script out of my locker before they start. Be right back."

He leaves and I nod, swallowing the medicine and hoping it kicks in sooner rather than later. My eyes are already itching and my sinuses are beginning to close up. Next will be the pressure between the eyes. The last thing I need in the middle of an audition.

"My mom takes those for her allergies," Rica says casually, flipping through her index cards. "If you take two, it works twice as fast."

I stare at the plastic-and-foil sheet with individually enclosed pills. The box is at home so I can't read the directions, but what she says sounds plausible.

Another sneeze sparks the pressure. I just became desperate. I rip open a second one and swallow it as Brian takes his seat.

He snatches the pill pack from me and stares at it. "How many of these did you take?"

The panic in his voice raises my eyebrows in alarm. "Two?" It comes out as a question. I feel like I'm getting in trouble.

Brian closes his eyes and inhales deeply. "Didn't you notice they come in ones, not twos? You're not supposed to take two . . ." Now I really am being scolded.

"But Rica said . . ." My voice trails off as I lock eyes with her. She's grinning like a villain who just came up with a foul plot.

Brian looks at her. "What did you tell her?"

She only shrugs and moves to sit closer to the casting directors.

"She said it would work twice as fast," I explain after another sneeze.

"That's just stupid." He crosses his arms. "Rule number one of theatre at Fernwood High: Never assume Rica's telling you the truth. About anything."

"Look," I defend myself, "I feel like trash. Something has to happen before we get up there. I can hardly breathe!"

"Whatever. Just don't be surprised if you start to feel . . . funny."

My heart races. "What do you mean, 'funny'? What's wrong with taking two?"

He holds up a hand for me to calm down, but how can I when he's acting like I just overdosed?

"Maybe nothing," he says, lowering his voice. "But you weigh what? Like, just over a hundred pounds?" He pauses and I smile at his very wrong, complimentary guess. "Just warn me if you start to feel different."

Twenty-three minutes. That's how long it takes. At twenty-six minutes, everything is sunshine, rainbows, and glitter. And hilarious!

I'm not usually one to audibly judge someone else's performance, but when one of the guys auditioning for Mr. Velasco starts up a wretchedly unidentifiable accent, I lose it. I bend over to hide from onlookers, burying my face in my folded arms across my legs. Brian pats my back hard like I'm choking, and it temporarily snaps me out of it.

This must be taken seriously. Auditioning is serious. It's life or death! I will die if I don't get to play Corie, die!

The giggles. I can't stop them.

"Maddie?" Brian says, a hand still on my shaking body.

I bite the inside of my cheek as I look up at him. "I feel 'funny' now."

"Ya think?" He rakes a hand through his hair and tugs on it. "They just called our number. Are you going to be able to handle this?"

"Pssshhhaw." I stand and straighten the ugly yellow sweater I stole from Ma's closet. "It's in the bag."

Ignoring the dizzy, head-swimming thing, I link arms with Brian and lean on him as we climb the stairs on the edge of the stage. Brian announces our names and the scene we've chosen. It's one of the more intense moments of the play, when Corie tells Paul she wants a divorce.

And I'm still laughing.

No, this is not funny. I want a divorce. Divorce is not funny. Neither are dead puppies. Or dead baby deer things. Or—aww, baby deer things!

And now I see Jesse. Not the mean Jesse who ignores me, but the sweet version who shows me cute animals and offers me rides and tissues. A dancing Jesse, on this very stage. I take notice of the abundance of scuff marks on the floor. *Did he make any of those?*

Why do I feel like I'm floating around the room? I know I'm standing still, but I'm also . . . everywhere.

I snap my head up and find that I'm next to Brian, who looks legit angry. He's staring at me like . . . like it's my line. I'm in the middle of my audition. What's wrong with me? Why am I so tired?

What's my line?

I say the first one that comes to mind, but it's oozing with sarcasm.

Get a hold of yourself, Maddie.

Brian adjusts the tone of his next line to fit, and through sheer determination, I finally get into the swing of my character by midscene. I am *angry.* I want a *divorce*!

I also really want to be done with this so I can go to sleep.

But Brian keeps giving me "the look" that one expects to precede a beating. He's angry too, but at me. The real me, not my character.

We finish to weak applause from those still in the audience, and as Brian helps me down the steps, I catch eyes with Mrs. Morales standing offstage by the curtain, chewing her thumbnail. Concerned. Confused. Disappointed.

It's only then that I fully understand I may have just blown an audition for the first time ever.

CHAPTER FOURTEEN

"What happened?" Ma asks when Brian passes me off to her just inside the front door of my house.

The funny has long since died, and I'm so tired and upset that it feels like I'm crying. I swipe at my eyes and allow Ma to wrap her arms around me. I've given my parents a bit of the silent treatment since they told me I'd be getting another sibling, but I can't keep that up right now.

"She's having a really weird reaction to the allergy medicine."

Brian quickly relates the afternoon's events before he excuses himself. Ma brings me to my room and helps me change without a word. By the time I slip under the quilt, I burst into sobs.

"Oh, hon," Ma says, climbing onto the bed next to me.

I fall against her and bury my face in her shoulder. She hugs me close and gently massages my head with her fingertips, like when she used to tuck me in at night. I don't even remember when she stopped doing it regularly, but now I realize how much I miss it. How much I miss this, just being held. Comforted.

"I ruined it, Ma. I totally blew the audition." My body's shaking, but I'm able to speak without gasping for air between every word. "I can't believe she tricked me into taking two of those pills."

"If I'd known you'd react so strongly to them, I never would have let you take them with you to school." She adjusts to lay her head on a pillow, and I curl up alongside her.

"Trust me, if I'd known it would turn me into a crazy person, I wouldn't have. The side effects were worse than my sinus junk. I was laughing at someone else's audition. *Laughing.* I never do that. It's rude and unprofessional." I suck in a deep, calming breath and release it slowly. "And rude."

"Yes, you said that." She sounds tired. Exhausted tired, not drug-induced tired like I am. "Can you audition again tomorrow? Do you want me to talk to someone about it?"

My selfishness smacks me between the eyes, which is worse than the residual sinus pressure. Here I've been *rude* to her basically since we moved to Texas, and she's still asking what she can do to help me. Maybe it's my exaggerated emotions, but I don't think I deserve a second chance even if it were possible.

I cling to her tighter, hoping she senses my apology. There's no way I could verbalize one right now.

"No," I say, shaking my head. "It's done. I'm ready to accept my fate."

She laughs. "Always so dramatic."

Reaching between the rods of my headboard, she grabs the cord to my paper-lantern craft experiment and switches it on. A soft glow leaks through tissue paper images of Gene, Frank, Cary Grant, Jimmy Stewart, Rock Hudson, Grace Kelly, Judy Garland, and Katharine Hepburn—a collection of my favorite classic stars. The plan is to make a few more to cluster above my bed, but I just haven't gotten to it yet.

"Your room's really coming along," Ma says, glancing around at my newly painted blue-gray walls.

It's been a while since she's seen my room. I haven't allowed her in here lately because of the paint fumes and all, but now it smells like fresh laundry. I've pinned up a couple movie posters already—*Summer Stock* and *An Affair to Remember*—and I plan on ordering more. And when the boxes of white string Christmas lights get a price reduction after the holidays, I'm buying them up to border all my posters, and I might swag a few strands from the ceiling. Haven't decided yet.

"I'm proud of you, you know," she says.

I swallow the lump that forms in my throat, unable to think of any reason for her to be proud.

"You've settled in here," she continues. "You've made friends, gotten involved. Invested in what's happening at school. It's nice to see. I know it's been hard for you, breaking ties with your old friends and leaving behind everything you worked so hard for these last two years of high school, only to start over."

"I know it hasn't been easy for you either," I manage, bottom lip threatening to quiver. "With this disaster of a house and . . . everything."

She laughs. "I think our lifestyle was too easy before. So what if our house is smaller and demands attention? We needed to get our hands dirty, change our perspective. It might be harder and we're doing without some of the things we're used to, but what's important to me is that we're here together, you know?"

"Minus Rider," I point out. He's been nearly impossible to keep tabs on with his thrilling college life. Heaven forbid he check in on his little sister. I still don't even know how he feels about the baby, and it seems weird that I don't know this.

"Speaking of," Ma says, clicking the lantern off again. "He's coming home in a couple of weeks."

All of us together. Just the four of us, while we still can. That's what's important.

A smile spreads across my face. "It's about time."

Sarah staples the cast list to the message board of the common area during lunch on Wednesday. All the hopefuls crowd around her to learn their role or assignment in the production. I expected my name to be missing, but none of us could have foreseen this pairing:

PAUL BRATTER: Ryan Hodges

CORIE BRATTER: Rica Castro

Rica wedges herself between Brian and me to snap a picture of the list with her phone. Then she turns on me with the same vindictive smirk that she had while watching me overdose on allergy meds and pave her road to stardom.

"I was really hoping you'd get the part of the mother. You've got the loopy thing mastered."

I'd really like to punch her pretty little face, but I refrain from all forms of comebacks. She nailed the audition, and I didn't. There's nothing I can do about it now, even if it was largely her fault.

"And not even an understudy," she continues. "Well, I'm sure you could help with makeup or something. You seem to have a flair for"—she motions toward the star on my cheek— "theatrical application." She takes my stunned silence as an opportunity to keep piling it on. "That upset, huh? Maybe you should go cry about it to your boyfriend." A hand flies up to her mouth as if she surprised herself. "Oh, that's right. He's dead."

Gasps sound off all around me like a tidal wave, one of them my own, even though I have no clue what she's talking about. It just *sounds* mean. More than mean. *Malicious.*

I feel a hand clasp mine and look over to find Sarah's face twisted in concern. Then it clicks. The first day of school. Two truths and a lie. I called Rica out in front of everyone, and now she gets to put me in my place in front of even more everyones.

The spark in her eyes is unnerving. She truly believes she just stuck a dagger in my heart, and she's thriving on it. The idea that someone I go to school with can be so hateful is pretty debilitating. I've got nothing. No defense, no words at all.

Sarah's hand squeezes mine tighter, and Brian gently touches my shoulder.

But I do have friends.

Brian takes a step forward to put himself between me and Rica. "At least Maddie's capable of loving someone other than herself."

Burn. Major burn. Below-the-belt burn.

I grab his hand with my free one and tug on it, signaling that I want him to stop. This isn't the way. I mean, what Rica said was inexcusable, but I don't want my friends to turn into her for my sake. The phrase "kill them with kindness" pops into my mind, and I suddenly know what I need to do to get her off my back, at least for now.

I lift my eyes to meet Rica's and conjure a weak smile, keeping my tone as genuine as possible. I am, after all, a great actress. "Congratulations on getting the lead. I know you'll do an awesome job."

Bingo.

She doesn't give me the gasp I was hoping for, but her cheeks redden and the spark in her eyes is doused. We maintain eye contact until I'm certain she sees me as a big, watery blur. There's real emotion somewhere under that witchy exterior, and I just tapped it.

Still holding hands with Sarah and Brian, I turn and lead us down the hallway. None of us says a word until we round a corner, out of sight and earshot from our impromptu audience.

"You guys," I begin, nervousness buzzing in my ears. "I have to clear something up, now that I feel mostly confident you won't think I'm completely insane."

Brian laughs. "Well, we already do, so . . ."

"Funny." I fake a smile. "Really, though, when I said the only guy I've ever loved is dead—"

"That was a lie, too?" Sarah asks, crossing her arms.

"Technically, no." I pause. "It's just . . . I don't want you guys to go on thinking my boyfriend died or something. The guy I'm hung up on . . . I've never actually met. He died before I was born." I bite my lip and wait for a reaction.

They both stare at me for a moment, then Brian laughs. "So what if we do think you're completely insane?"

"It's not that insane." Sarah jabs him in the arm. "He's a movie star, isn't he?"

Brian's eyes widen. "Ohhhhh. That actually makes a lot of sense."

"Was that sarcasm?" I ask.

"No, for real. I couldn't quite wrap my head around you having been in love but never kissing anyone."

"Right. That."

So I divulge my big secret. I tell them about Gene Kelly. How I've seen all his movies so many times I know them by heart. How he's ruined me because I don't just want to be randomly kissed, I want it to be epically romantic.

They stare at me again. I shift my weight from one leg to the other.

"Yep." Brian breaks the silence. "Insane."

"I think it's adorable," Sarah says before patting the top of my head. "And maybe a little sad."

"Well, real-life boyfriend or no, what Rica just did was reprehensible," Brian says.

"Ugh. I can't believe Ryan has to kiss that serpent," Sarah says, taking out her ponytail to redo it. She yanks her hair with such fury, the elastic band snaps and drops to the floor. "Not only do I have to watch it happen, but then I'll be thinking about it when he kisses me! With the same lips! What if her poison is contagious?"

"You should buy him some Listerine or something," I say, attempting to lighten the mood, and glad we're done talking about me. " 'Congratulations on landing the male lead, babe. Now go sterilize your mouth.' "

"It's not like he's gonna make out with her," Brian offers. He shoots me a pointed look. "Stage kisses don't count as real kisses, do they?"

"Maybe not to the actors, but it doesn't make it any easier to watch when it's your boyfriend." Sarah grabs a wooden pencil from her bag and uses it to secure her hair up from her neck. "Ugh, why is it so hot in here?"

Brian and I exchange pity glances.

"You're the student director," Brian says, leaning against a locker. "Take out the kissing bits. Problem solved."

"Like the other directors would ever go for that," Sarah huffs. "Besides, who's going to believe a play with non-kissing newlyweds?"

Now I cut Brian a look warning him to let go of whatever remark his brain is working on. He bites his lip and drops to tie his shoelace. Today his sneakers are the color of traffic cones. Not my favorite.

"Well, I'm gonna go eat before lunch is over," Brian says, standing and adjusting his backpack. "Y'all coming?"

Sarah shakes her head. "I can't eat now. I need consoling. I'm gonna see if Ryan can get out of his advisory period."

I open my mouth to respond, but my name is called from behind me. It's Mrs. Morales. Usually I'd be happy to chat with her, but since my failure of an audition, the plan has been to get to class just before I'm considered late and leave as soon as the bell rings to avoid the possibility of an *I'm so disappointed* speech.

"Can you walk with me for a minute?" she asks.

"Um, sure." I wave to Sarah and Ryan as they go their separate ways, leaving me to face the lecture alone.

She sets the pace slowly through the empty hallway. Every second she waits to speak, the worse I imagine what it is she's preparing to say.

"How's your tap dancing?" she finally asks.

I study her face in an effort to gauge her sincerity, sure at any second she'll say, *"I'm just kidding. I really wanted to tell you how much you tanked your chance to play Corie. Get out of my theatre program."*

"My tap dancing?" I repeat, mostly to stall. My tap dancing is elementary, at best, and I know that's not the answer she's looking for. "I've taken some classes back home, and I'm definitely interested in learning more. I found a dance studio close by, but they said I couldn't start until the first of the year."

She moves her clipboard from one hand to the other and hugs it against her chest. "Well, next month we're going to hold auditions for *Crazy for You* at the playhouse. Have you seen it?" I shake my head and she continues, "It's a fairly tap-heavy musical, so we're looking for people who either have experience or can catch on easily."

My heart flutters. She's not chewing me out; she's asking me to audition for a *real* musical production at the community playhouse!

"I'm confident I can catch on to anything if I practice it enough." I keep myself from skipping the rest of the way down the hall.

"I believe you could." She smiles. "I know Monday was hard for you, and—"

"I'm *so* sorry about Monday," I dare to interrupt. She just *has* to know. "I took too much allergy medicine and it knocked me out. I feel like a dope."

Mrs. Morales raises a hand to stop me from explaining. "Angela told me all about it. And you would have made a great Corie, but you know what? I think you'll like being a part of the musical more."

"*Would* I?" A musical! My mind races with audition preparation. So much to do!

"Maybe things aren't so bad after all?" She winks and I want to hug her.

"Things are almost perfect," I say, grinning like a fool.

"Oh, I nearly forgot." She grips the door handle to the black box theatre and twists to face me before opening it. "Angela told me you're looking for a job. I've got one for you if you want it."

CHAPTER FIFTEEN

My very first job! And it's at a theatre!

I'm now *the* office girl of the Fernwood Community Playhouse, handling online ticket sales, coming up with new marketing ideas, making sure the rooms are clean and tidy, checking inventory of toilet paper, and doing a variety of other things I have no clue how to do yet. But I love it. I love the people, the atmosphere. The buzz that comes from the creation of entertainment that works itself into the carpet and the walls and the very foundation of the building. You can't help but be energized and inspired by this place.

After a few weeks of learning the ropes, I come to realize something: Mrs. Morales practically lives here. No wonder they're always ordering takeout. Jesse's at the playhouse more than I knew, too—he helps design and build the sets, in addition to being the resident handyman. I hoped to learn more about him, like his performance history, but it's like some huge secret I don't understand. Over a month of hitching rides from him and I've learned nothing concrete aside from the stats of his favorite Major League players. I'm itching to see him dance or hear him sing. Anything. I want a glimpse at just one little morsel of talent. He would be a million times hotter. Why doesn't he get that?

The playhouse itself is a combination of vintage and modern. It was actually a house once upon a time—more like a mansion—and was converted to a theatre in the 1950s. Dark burgundy upholstered walls, ornate chandeliers, a one-person ticket booth, and a concession area take patrons back in time the moment they cross the threshold. Thankfully, the expansion in the 1990s left the original charms but added a much bigger stage footprint, more seating, and a series of rooms in the back and along one of the building's sides, which are now used for rehearsals, meeting spaces, storage, and prop-making.

Mrs. Morales lets me use whichever room is empty to practice my tap dancing after work and has promised to have someone show me some new steps soon. Considering auditions for the upcoming musical are in a couple weeks, I wish this help would come sooner rather than later. I don't generally get nervous about auditions, but after that disaster at school, I need to work my tail off to make up for it. There are no guarantees.

Grabbing my tap shoes from the bag I keep in the closet like space off Mrs. Morales's office, I search the hall for a room with an open door. There's always some group or other having a meeting, or a dancer renting out one of the mirrored rooms. I have to be careful not to burst in on anyone.

As I pass one of the closed doors, I hear music playing—a song I don't recognize—and intricate tap work following the rhythm in perfect sync. The song is stopped and starts over, and the taps continue, intense and dizzyingly complicated. Even if I knew all the names, I wouldn't be able to pick anything out, as one sound multiplies into a waterfall of flowing steps. Whoever's in there tapping like that needs to be my teacher. I would work here for free in exchange for learning how to dance so well. But that wouldn't be smart. I still need a car.

I grip the handle to crack open the door but it's locked. Blast. I consider knocking, but how rude to interrupt what sounds like choreography brainstorming.

My phone chirps from my pocket.

Ma: Rider just made it in. We want to go somewhere to eat. Will pick you up on the way if you're done.

I almost forgot my brother was coming this weekend. I hope he brought something to wear to the Halloween party tomorrow night, because I fully intend to drag him along.

I text Ma back that I'm ready to go, and with one more jiggle of the handle in a vain effort to meet my future best friend, I return my shoes and gather my things. I make myself useful dusting the lobby as I wait for my family to show up, keeping an eye on the hallway that leads to the back rooms, but I leave before she comes out.

There's a twenty-minute wait at Maria Tortilla, and Rider and I busy ourselves catching up. I think he looks taller. He says he hasn't grown since I saw him last, which was over the summer, but there's no way. He's wiry and his light brown hair has gotten shaggy, along with his facial hair. I guess that's what happens when boys go to college. They wear pajamas to class and only brush their teeth if there's a chance of making out with a girl. So this is what I have to look forward to when I get to college. Even less hygiene.

"I think you've gotten taller, though," Rider says to me just before we're finally seated in a booth.

I told them Jesse's working tonight, and I think Rider believes Jesse's a girl, because he seems a little too excited to meet one of my school friends.

"No, I haven't gotten taller," I say, sitting across from him and Dad. "I forbid it."

"I forbid it, too," Ma says, sliding in next to me. "I'm already freaking out enough about the fact that it won't be too much longer before both of my babies are legal adults. It's just not possible."

A stocky man with a handlebar mustache brings us a basket of tortilla chips and two bowls of salsa, then disappears as quickly as he came.

"For real," Dad adds when the man walks away. "Where did the years go?"

Ma reaches across the table and pokes the skin around his eyes. "They went right there."

"Hey, now," he laughs, swatting her hand away. Usually, this would be the time for him to playfully toss some sort of insult right back in her face, but lately it's been too dangerous. The hormones are all over the place.

"Don't worry. Now you get to do it all over again," Rider throws out there, scooping at the chunky salsa with a chip. "Anything you wish you'd done differently with us, you can."

His cheerful tone takes everyone off guard, mostly because there's a hint of a jab that's uncommon with him. He's generally chill. I assumed that his not reaching out to me to talk about the situation meant he was totally cool about it.

I'm too scared to turn and look at Ma's face, but Dad takes it in stride. "Yeah, let's hope it's another girl, because we obviously don't know what we're doing with boys."

Rider tries to play like he's shocked and appalled, but we all laugh together, and it feels right. It's hard to imagine a fifth person throwing us off balance, so for now I push away the thought and focus on the here and now. My comfort zone.

Enter Jesse, my uncomfortable zone as of late.

"I thought I recognized y'all over here," Jesse says, approaching us with a surprised smile. "Mr. and Mrs. Brooks." He shakes hands with my dad, does the head nod thing to Rider, even though they haven't met yet, then looks my way. "Maddie."

"Jesse."

My eyes dart to Rider. His expression clearly shows disappointment in Jesse's lack of female parts. I snicker to myself.

"How are y'all tonight?" Jesse asks.

"Fine, fine." Ma folds her hands together on top of the table. "I don't think I'll ever get used to your manners, Jesse. It's so nice to hear."

"Speaking of manners," Rider says. "It seems like I'm the only one who doesn't know the waiter."

I kick him under the table but he doesn't react, besides jutting his hand out for Jesse to shake. "Rider Brooks. Son to these two old people, and brother to this one," he says, tilting his head toward me.

"Jesse Morales," he says, taking his hand, the veins along Jesse's forearm bumping up from the strain of the manliest-handshake contest. I wish I didn't like it when his sleeves are rolled up to his elbows. "Neighbor, and carpool driver to that one," he says, indicating me too.

Rider's eyes meet mine and I can already see the questions forming. No, no, and no.

"And I'm not the waiter, just a food runner until I'm eighteen." He glances at the table. "But I can get your drink order in."

Ma asks for water with lemon, Dad orders a Dr Pepper, and Rider tries to order a beer but Jesse puts a stop to that by asking to see his ID. He settles for sweet tea.

Jesse looks to me. "Maddie? A fruity *pop*?"

I'm not sure how he knows that, but I allow the corner of my mouth to hitch up, mirroring him. "Yeah."

Rider's foot makes harsh contact with my shin, but I ignore it until Jesse disappears.

"Don't even," I tell him as soon as our parents get wrapped up in their own discussion about the menu.

"He likes you."

I keep my expression blank. "That's ridiculous."

"Denial is the surest sign."

"That would only count if I was denying that *I* like *him*. Moron." I reach for a chip and dunk it in the green salsa.

"So you're not denying that you like him. Interesting."

I clench my teeth. "You're impossible."

"Impossibly brilliant, you mean." He moves a handful of chips to a small plate and sprinkles more salt on them. "I know things, Maddie. There's something going on there."

I consider this for a moment so I don't appear too defensive, but I just don't see it. Besides, what possible future could I have with a guy who's so different from me? "We're friends, Rider, that's all. And if you say something to embarrass me, I swear—"

"What could you do to me that would even be a threat? I don't live in the same house anymore."

"Rider, please," I say, working up the pouty face I've mastered through the years. He's never been able to go against it.

"Okay." His shoulders fall. "But soon I'm going to be saying 'I told you so.' At least he had a strong handshake. He can't be too bad."

"Oh, is that the measure of a good man? If he can nearly break your hand when you meet him?"

"Of course it is. And you don't need to be dating a wussy who can't protect you."

I cross my arms over my chest and lean against the seat. "He's not even close to my type."

"What type is that?" Rider laughs, balling a fist under his chin and holding his head high and proper-like. "A *thesssspian*?"

Before I can kick him again, Jesse returns with our drinks. As soon as he's finished passing them out, a man from the booth next to us says in a flustered tone, "Excuse me, can we get some service around here?"

Holding the drink tray flat against his side and under an arm, Jesse says, "I'm sorry, sir. I'll go get your server right away."

"Wow!" the man exclaims. "Your English has gotten good."

I can only see half of Jesse's face over the booth, but his eyebrows press together in confusion. My family and I take turns widening eyes with each other, unable to avoid eavesdropping.

Jesse's silence prompts the man to continue. "You're the kid that mowed our lawn last summer."

A hard line appears along Jesse's jaw, then disappears. "No, sir. That was someone else."

I wish I could see this guy. From his congested voice, I picture him fat and balding with a comb-over and thick, bottle-cap glasses that distort the shape of his eyes.

"I cannot get over your perfect English!" The man proceeds to tell Jesse his address. "Remember? We have two giant mimosas in the front yard."

We? This guy actually landed a wife?

"No, sir," Jesse says, maintaining his outward composure. "The only yard I mow is my own. If you'll excuse me, I'll go get your server for you. Have a good night."

His eyes are cast to the ground as he passes us and walks out of sight.

"Could have sworn it was him," the man continues, talking to someone else at his table. "Looked the same."

"And now you told him where we live, so he's gonna bring his gang friends over in the middle of the night to rob us," a woman's voice replies.

We all straighten in our seats, including Rider, looking at each other like, *Did that really just happen?*

My dad's face darkens as he stares into the basket of chips. His best friend growing up was from Chile, and apparently my grandfather never approved of the friendship. Dad's pretty sensitive about it, even still, and I can tell he's contemplating if it's his place to say something. But what can he do, really? Asking someone to apologize doesn't create genuine regret.

Our waiter comes by to take our order, and recommends we share a couple pounds of mixed fajitas with all the fixings, their signature entrée. And when Jesse delivers the sizzling tray to us ten minutes later, it's obvious his mood has been dimmed by the ignorance at the next table. I make a mental note to talk to him about it when I see him tomorrow night at the costume party, or maybe the next time he brings me home. Though it's probably going to be another one of those things he won't talk about, further proof that what Rider says is so far off base. If you like someone, even just as friends, you share stuff about yourself, open up.

What do I know about Jesse Morales except that his dad wants him to work here to improve his Spanish, he plays baseball, and he drives a truck the color of a bird's egg?

You know that he used to dance.

That settles it, then. Tomorrow night at the party, I'm getting him alone and making him talk.

CHAPTER SIXTEEN

As a rule, I try not to brag, but I'm super proud of my costume for the Halloween party. I found an old pair of cowboy boots at a thrift store, and after several rounds of sanitation, I Mod Podged red glitter all over them. Ruby boots! Add a white shirt with short, puffed sleeves, a blue-and-white checkered dress I found in the costume closet at the playhouse, two braids with ribbons, and *voilà*! Texas Dorothy. I'm even going to carry around my phone and lip gloss and other such necessities in a little basket along with a tiny plush dog. It's about the size of a rat, but it's all I could find.

The party is a big to-do at Red's uncle's ranch, as it has been for years. I'm told parents have their own grown-up party inside the house, complete with a high-stakes costume contest, while the kids play capture the flag in the cow pasture, take hayrides through a haunted trail, and sit around by a bonfire, roasting marshmallows and telling scary stories. It sounds extremely country, but I'm secretly looking forward to it.

Ma's still throwing together a last-minute outfit—she didn't really want to go, but Dad thought it would be a good opportunity to meet people since they haven't done much besides a dinner or two with Angela and Jesse's parents—so Rider and I head out first in his Camaro.

I know nothing about cars, but I do know that his is a sweet ride and I want to be seen getting out of it at the ranch. It's the most beautiful deep blue, with white racing stripes on the cowl. Our parents bought it for him when he turned seventeen, back when we still had money. I'll be seventeen next Valentine's Day, and I've already been told how much I'll be getting toward a car of my own. . . . It's not enough for me to buy a Camaro. I'll be lucky if I end up with something made after I was born.

"So who am I going to meet tonight?" Rider asks as he pulls the car onto the highway. The ranch is about ten miles north, according to the navigation on my phone.

"My friend Sarah and her boyfriend, Ryan, will be there for sure. She won't tell me what they're going as, but she's really excited about it."

"Doesn't do me any good if she has a boyfriend. Next."

I punch his shoulder and the car swerves a little bit, which I'm mostly sure he did on purpose.

"Be nice, I'm driving," he says, sticking out his tongue. "Next? And don't roll your eyes."

"Too late." He knows me well. I clear my throat and continue down the list of people I know will be there. "Well, you'll think

Angela's pretty hot. She's Jesse's sister and the closest thing I have to a best friend. Super tall with nearly black hair, green eyes, naturally tan."

He nods. "Yes, yes, this night just might be worth the price of my Jedi costume."

"But she's a sophomore," I add. "In high school."

"Aw, come on!" Rider groans. "Shouldn't have expected you to know any cool senior girls."

My mouth drops open and I overexaggerate my gasp.

"I only meant because you're still new," he explains, half-heartedly. "So is *Jesse* going to be there?"

"Oh, um . . . maybe."

I asked him back when I first heard about it, but he wasn't sure if he was going to be hunting this weekend. I can't really see Jesse donning a costume, anyway, with his negative attitude toward anything theatrical. If he does come, he'll probably cheat and wear his baseball uniform or something lame.

"Well, it would be nice to know at least one person there," he says.

"You do, idiot." I nudge his arm, carefully this time.

"Plus, I have to make sure his intentions are honorable with my little sister," he says with a devilish snicker.

I know he's just trying to get a rise out of me, but suddenly I want him to turn the car around and take me back home. I never once said anything to him or anyone about liking Jesse—because I don't—and now Rider's gone and made it a huge thing in his head, which is starting to become a thing in *my* head. And this thing is sure to become an even bigger thing the second he opens his mouth at the party, then everyone is going to be talking about the same *thing*. He's going to screw up what I have going here. It's what brothers do best.

We park among the other cars in a front pasture of the ranch just as the sun dips behind the tops of the trees. Rider and I walk toward the action near the giant red barn to the left of the house. One by one, a ghost, Superman, a sexy nurse, a vampire, and a sailor climb up onto a trailer piled with mounds of hay.

Wait. A *sailor*?

I glance around near the bonfire and find a handful of guys, all wearing service dress blues, or "crackerjacks," white hats and all. Boys dressed as sailors! It's one of the hottest sights I've ever seen. The only thing that could top it is if they were actual sailors and not kids from my school.

My feet quicken their pace; I'm anxious to meet these guys with obvious good taste—you can learn a lot about someone's hidden personality on Halloween. My eyes take in all of the gloriousness. The tie, the striped square collar that hangs down over the back, the dark pants that flare at the bottom, tight on the thighs. Those thighs.

I stop abruptly and Rider runs into me. "What?" he asks.

That dark silhouette against the fire. The stance. The posture. The way the hat sits tilted ever so slightly forward on his head. Straight out of the movies.

I think I might hyperventilate. This is the best costume party ever.

The sailor turns to Captain Jack Sparrow next to him and they do a complicated handshake finger-snap thing.

No. No way.

I really am going to hyperventilate.

Rider nudges me forward and before I know it, I'm standing face-to-face with Jesse Morales, in full sailor garb. The golden sunlight splashing on his face combined with the orange glow of the fire reflecting in his eyes. His *legs* in those tight pants. I die.

He's gorgeous.

My brain.

Can't. Look. Away.

So glad he didn't go hunting.

"It's Dorothy," Jesse says, keeping my gaze locked on his with that evil smirk.

Rider shakes his hand before subtly nudging me with his elbow. I blink back to reality. It's just Jesse. I see him every day.

Not dressed like that, you don't.

Red, or Captain Jack, snatches the basket from my hands and pulls out the toy dog. "You call this thing Toto? It's a hamster." He attempts to tie it up within his long dreadlocks.

I take it back and place my fingers over its ears. "Shh. He's sensitive."

Jesse laughs, and I get a tingling sensation down the back of my neck.

But that's just stupid.

I distract myself by turning away from him and introducing Rider to the people around us who I actually know. It doesn't take long for all the girls on the property to smell the presence of a college man. He's whisked away to play horseshoes with four cheerleaders, vampire number two, and Barbie—senior girls I've only passed in the halls at school. I don't expect to see him again until it's time to leave.

Screams followed by laughter echo through the trees from the hayride. I fight against a shiver just as Angela and Tiffany walk up in matching pink poodle skirts and saddle shoes. Tiffany cinches her high ponytail, as she always does, and I tease her for coordinating her costume around her usual hairstyle.

"Holy whoa," Tiffany exclaims, ignoring my remark. "Is Red wearing eyeliner?"

"I thought you were into the Frank Sinatra types now," Angela says, crossing her arms low over her stomach. "We joined the Teens for Classic Movies Club and everything."

My heart leaps, I'm ecstatic they still want to make the club a real thing. We've discussed meeting once or twice a month at the Moraleses' to screen old movies, maybe even advertising it at school to see who else is interested.

"Please. Be realistic. There are no Franks these days." Tiffany keeps her eyes trained on Red, at the other side of the fire, roasting a marshmallow on a stick. "You've seen those pirate movies. You tell me that eyeliner on guys isn't hot." She licks her lips. "You know you want to talk to him."

"It's just Red," Angela huffs. She follows Tiffany's gaze and swallows. "I talk to him all the time."

I clear my throat. "Well, the makeup works in pirate movies, but not for real-life, everyday wear," I say, fixing Tiffany's skirt so the poodle isn't hidden in a fold.

"But this isn't a real day," she protests. "It's Halloween. Anything goes on Halloween."

Red chooses this exact moment to head our way, so Tiffany leans in close to Angela and quickly says, "If you're not going to go for it, I am."

"Do whatever you want," she shoots back.

A few charms dangling from his wig jingle like bells. I'll admit, the dark eyes shadowed under the hat . . . it's not a bad look. Though it doesn't beat a sailor.

"Hey, kid," Red says to Angela, who doesn't return the smile. "And Tiffany Barrett, nice costume."

I refrain from pointing out that Angela is dressed exactly the same.

"Yours is better," Tiffany says, running a hand along the fabric hanging from the belt at Red's waist.

The hayride comes back and everyone climbs down, giggling and making fun of each other for being scared.

Tiffany hooks onto Red's arm, pointing to the trailer pulled by an enormous green truck. "Take me on the hayride?"

He laughs but doesn't push her away. I can't tell in the fading light, but he might be blushing the tiniest bit on the tips of his cheeks.

I'm hyperaware of Angela's tense posture, even as she sits down at the picnic table near the fire.

"Next riders," someone shouts, "load up!"

"Okay, let's go," Red says, leading Tiffany away. "Anyone else coming?" he asks before they get too far.

"You should go," Jesse says, suddenly next to me. The tiny scar on his cheek is the first place my eyes go every time I look at him now. "Mr. Lyle and his neighbors put a lot of work into it. It's cheesy but something to do. You always like the hayrides, Angela."

She grabs a skewer and threads a few marshmallows onto it, then holds them over the fire. "I'll go later."

"Well, I'm not going by myself," I say. "I'll wait."

"Mmmm, just go now." Angela doesn't look up from her dessert, which is now burning. She blows out the flame and pokes at the charred black crust. "I don't know how long I want to stay. I'm tired."

"I'll take you," Jesse says, extending his arm toward me. For a second I think he's waiting for me to take his hand, but he's reaching for my basket to leave it with Angela.

I'm ashamed to say, I'm a little disappointed.

Getting up into the trailer is quite the feat. It's not a flat trailer sensibly lined with rows of neatly packed hay bales; it's a four-sided pit filled with mounds of loose hay. Red helps pull me up over the back gate while Jesse shoves me from behind. And by "behind" I mean my actual behind. His hands are *on* my butt. Well, close enough to freak me out.

When I make it to the top, my glittery boots sink into the hay so I sort of fling myself off to the side, making room for Jesse to climb up after me. I prepare for uncontrollable sneezing, but so far I'm allergy-free tonight. Red plunks down next to Tiffany on the other side of a mound, where I lose visual, and another couple is getting awfully friendly up near the front. I do a double take and realize that it's Sarah and Ryan dressed as Fred and Wilma Flintstone.

I fight a smile and twist my body so I'm facing the back. I won't be able to see what's coming, but this way I can experience the frights after everyone else has already reacted to them, hopefully avoiding looking like a total wimp.

The truck takes off, and the trailer lurches. To keep from sliding, I brace myself with my hands, one of them clutching a wad of hay, the other . . . mostly Jesse's leg.

"Sorry," I say quickly, turning my face from him.

He just laughs, and we're pulled under the dark canopy of pines. The deeper we go into the woods, the more I dread what's coming. Tiffany lets out a yelp at nothing—probably Red—but I jump anyway. Thanks to a string of orange-and-purple lights over our heads, I'm not completely blind, but I still find myself nestling farther into the hay, out of the chill in the breeze, and maybe a smidge closer to Jesse . . . for protection.

No. I scoot away. Rider is in my head. I am not attracted to Jesse like that. He's not what I want.

Even if he is wearing dress blues right this minute. It's like he reached into my brain and extracted the very thing I'd want to see someone in tonight.

The girls behind me scream, and I sit upright, stifling a cry of my own when we pass two figures with wolf heads and claws, snarling and growling in front of a strobe light. More screaming follows and skeletons hang from low branches. Glowing ghosts weave in and out of the trees all around us. Flashing red eyes over there, now over *there*. A howl that may or may not be part of a sound-effects track carries through the air. A raggedy child under a spotlight clutching a teddy bear. Most of it isn't particularly violent, just extremely creepy.

I shut my eyes and the illuminated images are burned into my mind, swirling around all together.

"Are you actually scared?" Jesse asks quietly, breath warm on my neck. "It's cheesy, right?"

"I know," I say, straightening my skirt to cover more of my legs. "But I know how my brain works. It's still spooky enough to get stuck in my head and give me nightmares."

"We don't have to look." He pulls down the white cap behind his head and leans back against the hay.

I copy him, shifting to separate our shoulders, but a dip in the hay keeps the sides of our bodies pressed together. He doesn't move, so I stop trying to adjust. Sarah and Tiffany let out squeals once in a while, but I'm happily ignoring all of it, watching the tiny lightbulbs bob on the strand overhead.

I wanted to get Jesse alone. With the rest of the gang out of earshot on the other side of our mound, this is my chance to grill him.

"So, why didn't you introduce me to your . . . girlfriend?"

He doesn't miss a beat. "What girlfriend might this be?"

"Gabby," I nearly snap. "Don't play dumb with me."

"What makes you think she's my girlfriend? She's not."

I pick at a piece of hay and start tearing it into little pieces. "And I'm still not worth an introduction at the homecoming dance?"

"What are you talking about?"

"You just walked away from me. You grabbed her hand, and you left me standing there when I thought we were in the middle of a conversation."

"That's why you've been so weird lately?" He bends his knees, half crossing one leg over the other at the ankle. "Why the heck did you wait so long to talk to me about it if it was bothering you so bad?"

"What do you mean, I've been *weird*?"

"In class, on the way home from school. You're different. Not as . . . chatty as you used to be."

"I guess I should be glad you actually noticed something about me," I mutter.

He props himself up on an elbow, facing me, so I move to face him. "I notice you."

I lick my lips in preparation to reply, and his eyes slip to my mouth.

"I didn't mean it like that," I say, lying back down to keep from looking at *his* lips. "I just thought we were friends, and sometimes I don't feel like you want that."

Jesse exhales and lies with his arms crossed beneath his head. "I didn't introduce you to Gabby because I didn't think about it. But she doesn't really need to meet my friends, anyway."

"Why?"

"Her parents are close friends with mine. Especially my father," he says with a little bite. "We have nothing in common. She's a spoiled brat, and she thinks she's better than everyone else. I hang out with her sometimes as a favor to my dad. That's all. I'm sorry I didn't think to introduce you, but don't be offended."

"I'm not offended." As it comes out, I realize it's a lie. If I weren't offended, I wouldn't have brought it up in the first place. Wouldn't have let the wound fester for so long. I pick the oddest things to be sensitive about.

"You're totally offended, and you shouldn't be." He rolls up onto his elbow again. "New subject."

"Okay . . ." The sharp ends of the dead grass poke into my skin, but I tough it out to look him in the eye. "Why are you—"

"No, no, no." Jesse lifts a finger toward me as if he might press it against my lips, then lets his hand fall. "It's my turn."

"That's fair," I concede, even though I really want to know why he and his friends are dressed as sailors.

A chain saw revs up just next to the trailer, and Tiffany lets out a bone-chilling scream, which becomes muffled as if she slapped a hand over her mouth. I twitch and instinctively lean closer to Jesse, our faces only inches apart.

"Is it true that you haven't kissed anyone, like, for real?" he asks. "Offstage."

I move back so I don't end up on top of him if we hit a bump. "That's really your lead-in?"

"Why not? I feel like I don't know much about you besides the theatre stuff and your lack of transportation."

"Hey," I say, stabbing at him with a twig I pulled from the hay. "Are you trying to get out of bringing me home from school?"

He swats it away and laughs. "Not yet, but here's your official notice that once baseball season starts, you're gonna need an alternative. You'll have to come to my games if you want to see me at all."

I wrinkle my nose. "I might come to one or two. If you're lucky."

"If *you're* lucky, *mi reina*." He covers his mouth with the back of his hand and yawns. "Now, answer my question."

I think back to what he asked, a little too flattered that he cares enough to get to know me better. Besides the few times he's accidentally revealed too much about himself, our interactions have typically been surface-only. Maybe it's time to come clean.

I swallow, then confess, "Yes, it's true."

Thankfully he doesn't dwell on this, or make fun of me, and he jumps to the next question as if he didn't even register the answer to the last one.

"Do you still talk to your friends from your old school?"

I wish I could get away with lying to him. How much more pathetic can I sound to the hottest guy in school? "Not really." I stay propped up on my side, but my eyes focus on the insignia stitched onto the chest of his uniform.

"Why not?"

I suck in a deep breath. "After my dad lost his job, the girls I'd been hanging out with sort of . . . let me go."

"Let you go?" he asks, genuine curiosity in his tone.

"Well, money got tight, so that was strike one to them." Even though I'm proud I slipped in a baseball reference, I still can't look at his face. I don't want to witness the pity. "And we were moving to another state, so . . . they just stopped talking to me. Phased me out."

And it fully hits me just how wrong those girls were for me. I'm still getting to know Angela, Tiffany, and Sarah, but even in this short amount of time, I know they're different. They wouldn't drop me over differences of money and address.

"But it's fine," I continue. "I actually don't really miss them anymore. I just don't get how I never saw it coming. How I spent years of my life developing false relationships." As the rest of the words come out, I feel a mix of embarrassment and relief.

But he doesn't respond. The hayride's been quiet for a few minutes, the chain saw bit seemingly the grand finale. We should be back at home base soon. I finally risk a glance at Jesse and find him looking at me, his expression blank.

"Regret wanting to know more about me yet?" I ask, not quite a whisper, anxious for his reply.

The corner of his mouth pulls up. "Want to know what I think?" I nod. "I think you're better off here. Angela's happier with you around, Elise really likes you." He pauses. "You fit here with us."

I smile at his unexpected and extremely kind words, and I have to look away from him again. "Thank you for that," I manage, throat tight.

"Even if you do plan on brainwashing everyone with your out-of-date movies."

We both laugh and relax onto our backs, me reveling in the acceptance I've found here. New friends. Real ones. I still have plenty more questions itching to be answered, but there's time. I can't push him too far too fast.

Here on a pile of hay under the soft lights, the gentle swaying of the squeaky trailer underneath us, me dressed as a farm girl and Jesse as a member of the US Navy, I could almost believe I'm back in time. He's about to be shipped out, and this is our last night together for months. We're taking a romantic ride through the park on an autumn evening.

I lace my fingers through his and hum a made-up melody. He joins in, harmonizing, and we just lie next to each other, gazing at the stars and the sliver of a moon between the tree branches.

The ride comes to a stop and the other passengers disappear. It's only the two of us.

I sit up, taking my time to pick the grass out of my hair as he climbs down before me. I don't want to say good-bye. Not yet.

Something clicks and the back gate falls open. My sailor jumps to get out of the way. The pile beneath me gives, and my body starts to slide with it. He rushes to help and grabs my waist, pressing himself against me to slow my momentum, hay falling all around and over me. Over us. I clutch his arms, and my feet stop just short of the ground.

His eyes, a brilliant green with a ring of amber, stare intensely into mine. Slowly, slowly, he tilts his head in close, his breath sweet and warm.

"Do you want me to kiss you?" he whispers.

I lean closer and closer until our lips touch, and a spark races to my toes. A small, perfect kiss to end a perfect night.

But when we separate, I look back into his eyes and find them mirroring everything I'm feeling.

Warmth. Curiosity. Longing.

Suddenly, his lips crush mine. His body pins me against the hay, one hand still at my waist, the other tracing up my side all the way to my face. His fingers tangle in one of my braids, thumb resting along my jawline. My hands continue to grip his sleeves, tugging him closer and closer until—

"Holy. Whoa."

My eyes fly open at the sound of Tiffany's voice, and my heart skitters.

Jesse. Lips half an inch from mine. Hand in my hair. Hand on my waist. Body pressed against body. Hay absolutely everywhere.

Jesse kissed me.

Jesse *kissed* me?

I push him away to get a better look. He cocks his head, jaw slack, eyes unreadable.

A few people nearby holler their approval.

And some idiot says, "Looks like Jesse just won. Everybody pay up."

CHAPTER SEVENTEEN

All of that . . . was real? My pulse pounds in my ears as my brain catches up. I shove Jesse even farther so no part of him is touching me, and my feet finally connect with the ground.

"This was about the bet?" Anger fizzes through me.

His "getting to know me" was all a setup. The sweet words to make me feel accepted. Like I actually belong here.

Lies.

"Maddie, it wasn't—"

"You *stole* my first kiss?" I yell, not caring who hears.

"I didn't steal anything." Jesse looks me dead in the eye and whispers, "You kissed me back, *mi reina.*"

I slap him right across the cheek. Someone who sounds like Red curses through a laugh and a few girls let out high-pitched gasps. My fingers tingle. Sting. I just hit a boy. I just *kissed* a boy. Like, for *real.*

Too many firsts.

I need to get out of here. Too bad I can't move. Too bad my eyes keep darting back to his mouth.

His jaw drops and he touches where I hit him. "You grabbed my hand!" Jesse says, raising his voice to my volume. "What did you want me to think?"

"I . . . I thought—"

I thought it was all in my head.

"What's going on?" Rider breaks through the gathering crowd and is at my side in an instant. "Madison? You okay?"

I nod and he turns to Jesse. "Did you touch her?"

Jesse raises his hands, taking a step back. "Look, man. I didn't do anything wrong."

Red moves to stand next to Jesse, both of them looking at me with eyes that say *You need your big brother for this? Really?*

"I can handle it, Rider. Let's just go."

But I can't move, not yet. I scan the faces around me for Angela, both terrified she saw what just happened and desperate to talk to my friend. But . . . it's her brother and this just got even more awkward. The look on her face is telling me too many conflicting things, while Tiffany's grin says this is the most excitement she's seen all day.

And then there's Brian, inching forward, eyes hidden underneath the sunglasses of his hippie costume. I should slap him too. He's the reason I'm in this mess. Him and his big, punchable mouth. I shoot him a warning glare and he stops. I just need to make an exit before I do or say something I'm going to regret come Monday at school.

Jesse takes another step back and straightens, brushing loose hay off his uniform. That's when I spot her approaching from the direction of the house. Gabby. Something in my chest cracks. After what Jesse said about her, it didn't occur to me that she'd be here. Especially not wearing a super figure-flattering corset thing.

She stops just behind him like she wants to come to his aid but isn't quite sure if it's her place. Then she puts her hand on his shoulder. The claim has been staked.

I situate my braids to rest in front and straighten my checkered dress my last-ditch effort to regain a bit of dignity, at least by appearance. My irritation froths into anger that overflows from my mouth, and I have no control.

"And look who's here, Jesse. Your *not-my-girlfriend* girlfriend." I let my shoulder slam against his as I pass by. "Happy Halloween."

On the way to school Monday morning, Angela doesn't mention my kissing scene, but I feel sure she's thinking about it. She's a more reserved version of herself today—darker clothing, hair in a messy bun, no lipstick, uninterested in conversation—and I wish I knew if it has to do with me or if there's something else on her mind. I'm too chicken to ask her. Which probably makes me a terrible friend, but I'm not in the mood to share the gory details of her brother's tongue in my mouth.

Not that it was gory. At all.

That's what makes me a terrible friend.

I hover outside the door to English until the bell goes off, then sneak in. Red winks at me as I pass, repeatedly tapping the eraser of a pencil against the top of his desk. When I sit, Jesse leans toward me and I hear him inhale as if he's preparing to speak. I don't look at him. I refuse.

He says my name at the same time Mr. McCaffey announces a pop quiz on the reading assignment. The good student in me panics when she can't remember touching her lit book over the weekend. She can't remember doing *any* homework over the weekend.

Quiz papers are passed out and the timer is set for ten minutes. Mr. McCaffey is one of those teachers who likes to make us work under pressure. Good practice for the SAT, he says. Usually, I have no objections to this method, and these pop quizzes are all simple, observational-type questions that anyone who actually read the material should know how to answer. It's only a problem when you spend precious hours of your life staring at the ceiling fan, reliving your first real kiss and trying to decide how you actually feel about it.

A wad of paper makes a soft noise when it lands near me. I know better than to pick up a note during a quiz. I smash it with my heel and keep my eyes trained on the first question, which I'll never have an answer to.

Another ball of paper crashes into my leg and falls to the floor. Jesse clears his throat. I glance at Mr. McCaffey, who's scanning the room carefully, presumably for the cougher. Jesse isn't as observant, and he slides the paper closer to me, his foot hitting mine in the process. I swallow and allow myself to look at the point of contact.

"Jesse and Maddie."

My head snaps up in surprise, more at hearing our names

paired than the negative tone Mr. McCaffey generally reserves for whiners and troublemakers, of which I am neither.

"Turn in your papers, please, and wait for me in the office."

Office?

"Now, please."

"But I didn't—"

"I lack patience for excuses today, Miss Brooks." The corners of his mouth dip down much farther than normal. His voice is tired. "I don't tolerate cheating in any form."

Jesse finally speaks up, calmer than anyone faced with a zero and an office visit should be. "We weren't cheating—"

"Office," he repeats, bending down and scooping up the mystery notes from the floor.

I hold my breath as I wait for him to open and read them to the class. I have no idea what could be written in them—what could possibly be so important Jesse had to write it out and throw it at me during a pop quiz. Idiot. Like I wasn't mad at him enough already.

We follow Mr. McCaffey to the front of the classroom, backpacks slung over our shoulders, feeling other students' eyes burning holes in the backs of our heads. In slow motion, our blank quizzes and the two balls of notebook paper float into the trash. It's like my worst nightmare, next to choking an audition—I now have experience with this—or forgetting lines on opening night.

Jesse and I escape to the empty hallway, the door clicking shut with finality. My locker isn't too far, so I exchange books for my next class, assuming I get to go. I'm not exactly well versed in getting accused of cheating, but I'm fairly confident we can explain that it was all a misunderstanding. Mr. McCaffey clearly just woke up on the side of the bed that makes him irritable and unwilling to listen to students with no priors.

I thought Jesse went ahead without me, so I jump when his voice comes from behind me while I'm digging in my locker.

"You're mad."

Can I get away with ignoring him when we're the only two people in the hall?

"That I kissed you. You're mad."

And you're a genius.

"We should talk."

I grit my teeth and inhale deeply through my nose, eyes closed. Count to three, only make it to one. "In case you haven't noticed, I'm not exactly speaking to you right now."

"That's fine." He opens my locker door wider and leans a shoulder against it, putting us much too close. "Just listen."

I'm afraid to look at his face. I know the first place my eyes will go.

"I lack patience for excuses today, Mr. Morales," I say, copying Mr. McCaffey's words.

He snickers and shoves his hands into his pockets, still leaning against the lockers. I cave and look at him. And there they are, twisted up in a smirk. Now that I know how they feel against my own, I'll never again be able to look at his lips quite the same way.

"I don't have any excuses. I kissed you. The end."

I raise an eyebrow as my heart sinks. Of course it had nothing to do with his attraction to me. He thought I was throwing myself at him. "Easy money for you, right? How much was the payout?"

"I didn't have anything to do with that childish bet."

"Why should I believe you?"

He straightens, and his Adam's apple bobs as he swallows. "Because if you don't, then you're the one being childish. I thought you wanted me to kiss you, so I did. I didn't know you were gonna make such a big thing out of it."

He thought *I* wanted to kiss him. Nothing about *him* wanting to kiss me. Was he just being a guy, interpreting the situation however he wanted? He might have kissed any girl he'd been next to on that hayride. The tiny flicker of hope inside my chest dies. My first real kiss was just as fake as all my stage kisses.

Shutting my locker with a clang, I turn on the balls of my feet and take off down the hallway.

"Maddie," Jesse calls after me and I ignore him. "Madison, stop!"

I whip myself around, eyes narrowed. "Don't yell at me with my proper name like you're bossing around a kid."

"The office is this way," he says, pointing in the opposite direction.

He catches my arm as I try to breeze past, and I glare at his hand until he lets go.

"Look, I don't know what you're so upset about," he says. "You could probably even thank me."

"*Thank* you?" I nearly shout, then lower my voice to a hoarse whisper to keep from getting in further trouble. "You're so full of yourself, I'm shocked there's even room for both of us in this hallway."

"Stop it, I'm being for real. Those other losers will probably leave you alone now that everyone knows your first kiss was with me."

My *stolen* first kiss.

I call upon the strength of all classy women before me and bite down a string of curses. "You're such a cad," I say, shoving past him toward the office to debate my way out of adding "cheater" to my expanding reputation.

Jesse rushes to catch up to me and shifts his backpack from one shoulder to the other. "I don't know what that means," he says before leaning in so close his cheek brushes against my loose curls. "But you're welcome."

CHAPTER EIGHTEEN

"I've decided it doesn't count," I tell Sarah.

We're sprawled out on the floor of the Moraleses' TV room, sorting the DVDs I brought over, killing time while Angela and Tiffany flirt with the pizza-delivery guy downstairs.

"It doesn't work like that," she says, pushing *The Philadelphia Story* toward me. "This one sounds funny."

I add it to the "maybe" pile for tonight's meeting of Teens for Classic Movies.

"Maybe I wasn't Texan enough for you." I clear my throat, conjuring my best Southern drawl. "I ain't countin' it."

Sarah shakes her head and lies on her back with a sigh, folding her hands over her stomach. "You can't just pretend Jesse doesn't exist for a week and magically erase the fact that he kissed you. And you kissed him back," she adds with a cough. "We all saw it."

I think back to the disaster of English class on Monday and shudder. Thankfully, all we got was a warning. "He almost got me sent to detention! There's no way I would engage in a relationship with someone I have zero in common with."

Sarah snorts. "No one said anything about getting engaged to the guy."

"That's not what—"

"And I'm sure you have *something* in common." She sighs again. "There's probably some chemical thing inside both of you, pulling you together. Some sparkly, otherworldly particle you both have buried deep in your hearts. Magic particles. Oooh, *magnetic* particles. Hence the pulling together."

I blink. "Don't get all weird on me."

"I'm just trying to find a pretty way to say maybe what happened wasn't quite the daydreamy accident you claim it to be. Maybe y'all are being brought together by the fates." She rolls onto her side, propping her head up. Her bangs fall in front of her eyes but she leaves them. "He was active in theatre once upon a time, after all. I'd say that's a *thing* you have in common that's not too weird and otherworldly for you," she says with a laugh.

"Doubtful," I dismiss, though my pulse speeds up. "I can't even get him to talk to me about it. He gets all PMS-y every time I bring it up."

I add *That Touch of Mink* to the growing pile and put *Send Me No Flowers* back in my tote bag. I love Doris Day in both of these, but it might be a Cary Grant kind of night.

Sarah skims the synopsis of *How to Marry a Millionaire* and tosses it in for consideration. "This one sounds like it could be useful."

I smile but my mind stays on track. "Was he amazing?"

She doesn't look up from her task of movie-sorting. "I mean, his mom had him in classes all his life. He was bound to be amazing."

"But he quit and never looked back? For sports? I just don't *get* it. Did he get teased that badly about it? Haven't we come further than that? Don't people watch *Glee*?"

She grunts.

"You know, Gene Kelly wanted to quit dancing all the time," I say, straightening. "He got teased and beat up, but he stuck it out, and look what happened. He became one of the most influential dancers of his time. He revolutionized the way movies filmed their musical numbers. He played the lead in one of the most beloved musicals next to *The Wizard of Oz*. He'll be remembered and loved for, well, *forever*."

"Hey, now don't you go gettin' all weird on *me*." Sarah sits up the rest of the way, stretching her legs out in front of her. "You can't compare Jesse to these old actors, you know."

Leaning against the front of the couch, I stare at the cover of the *Frank Sinatra and Gene Kelly Collection*, touching the smooth surface of the box where the white sailor hats sit crooked on their heads. For one night, Jesse was my sailor. And he's fried everything in my brain.

Sarah moves to sit next to me and takes the box from my hands. "You'll find the right guy for you one day, Maddie. It's not something to get frazzled and depressed about."

"Says the girl with the perfect boyfriend who happens to be the lead in the next school play," I huff. "I, on the other hand, don't think I'll ever find a guy to fit my list of standards."

She huffs back. "You probably won't. The guy on my list has giant calf muscles because mine are huge and I'm self-conscious, black hair that's long in the front and super short on the sides, plays the guitar, drives a sports car, and would be happy eating Chinese takeout every night for the rest of his life."

I picture Ryan in his preppy clothes and clean-cut hairstyle. He drives a truck, like most every other guy at our school, and if I remember correctly, he isn't very musically talented.

"That doesn't sound like Ryan," I say. "At all."

"Right? He's not anything close to what I thought I wanted." She hugs her legs to her chest and rests her chin on her knees. "But he's wonderful."

We sit in silence as I let her declaration sink in. I mean, it's great and I'm happy for her, but I don't *think* I know what I want, I *know* what I want. And I don't understand how I can be happy with less.

Only two other girls from school come to our first night as an advertised club. I guess I shouldn't say *only*. It's a miracle anyone comes who doesn't have to be bribed. *An Affair to Remember* wins the vote, so it's a Cary Grant kind of night after all. Following pizza, ice cream, and the movie, I lead a discussion comparing modern actors with their predecessors, but I get a bunch of blank stares and one request to watch *The Princess Bride* at a future meeting. Rather than argue that's not exactly the type of classic movie I ever intend on highlighting, I give them the ole smile-and-nod and call it a night.

After Sarah and the two other girls leave, Angela and Tiffany pick out another movie. A new release with action like guns and explosions and guys without shirts spitting out one cheesy line after another. Total snoozefest.

I last about twenty minutes before I excuse myself for a bathroom break and peek in on Elise, who's passed out hugging the plush elephant Jesse gave her on her first day of kindergarten a few months ago. And I see a flash of my own future as an older sibling.

Will I be that thoughtful? I mean, sure I can be more thoughtful than an arrogant *boy*, but will I have any relationship with my sister or brother at all? For all I know, in a couple of years I'll be in another state, or at least another city. I'm going to miss most of the milestones, like their first day of school, first missing tooth, first crush. Rider and I know what it's like living under the same roof, playing together, throwing food at each other during dinner. This new little Brooks won't remember the one year of his or her life when I was still at home. Will I remember to check in with this child throughout their life? Will I even want to?

The alarm chirps softly as it does when someone opens a door, and I head down the secondary set of stairs that lets out near the kitchen to see who else is up. The house is quiet and dark except for a night-light above the stove and floodlights filtering through the fancy decorative window between the cabinets on the back wall.

My eyes catch sight of something outside as it whizzes past the window. It happens again and I barely make out a flash of red on the white surface. A baseball. Which means Jesse must be home from work.

I feel my way around the furniture in the next room and twist the blinds open. Jesse's only about ten feet out, illuminated in a yellow spotlight from the corner of the house. He winds up and pitches another ball toward the pool area, and my eyes follow it to a net, where it falls next to a few others. I sink sideways into an armchair and watch silently as Jesse brings the glove up toward his face, hikes up his left knee toward his stomach, stretches his right arm back, and hurls the last ball.

I'm a total creeper sitting here in the dark, like Jimmy Stewart in *Rear Window* spying on his neighbors across the courtyard of his apartment complex. But instead of a little yappy dog digging up evidence of a murder in a flower bed, I spy Jesse scrambling around the bushes for stray balls. He pulls out the hem of his shirt, exposing the last couple of abs, and loads about five or six worn baseballs in his makeshift pouch, dumping them in the patch of dirt where he started.

He wipes his shiny brow with his forearm, selects a ball, twists it until his fingers are in just the right position along the red stitching, and throws again. I'm transfixed. On him. On his arms. The muscles that tense and relax, tense and relax. The graceful, fluid movement as he winds up and follows through. The narrowed eyes and the teeth that bite his bottom lip in frustration. Determination. He reaches down and scratches just above his knee before throwing the next one.

What I wouldn't do to see those legs dance. Just once.

I'm quite tempted to let myself count that kiss, anyway.

CHAPTER NINETEEN

Since we're off from school the week of Thanksgiving, and because Ma's being especially sentimental and emotional and a little too pregnant for me to be around, I spend most of my time working and practicing at the playhouse. By Wednesday, the place is pretty much deserted, with everyone out of town or getting a head start on cooking. Traditionally, I'd be baking something with apples or pumpkin right about now, but if I don't get this triple time step down, I won't be able to keep my spot in the upcoming production of *Crazy for You*.

I didn't exactly blow anyone away in the dancing portion of my audition last weekend, but Mrs. Morales fought for me, and Mrs. Haskins, the director, said she admired my moxie and believed that with enough work and dance training, I could be one of the Follies Girls. It's not much of a speaking part, but I'm onstage for quite a few scenes.

One step closer to Broadway!

I'm practicing in the smallest dance room—without music because so far all it does is throw me off—when I hear a door shut down the hall. I know I locked myself in, so whoever it is either has a key, or they broke in. Nothing much here to steal, though, except a bunch of dusty props and a closet full of costumes.

Using the opportunity to get a drink of water and take off my shoes for a while, I mosey toward the closed door just as whoever's inside begins a tap warm-up. It's the same routine Mrs. Morales taught me, starting with shuffles then progressively adding flaps, leaps, digs, stamps, and other things I can't remember the names of. But this person goes past the part I know, and I don't recognize the complicated sounds.

I'm standing here, mesmerized, with my hand on the knob just as I was nearly a month ago, the first time I heard someone tapping away behind a closed door. It has to be the same person. She's incredible.

I must be taught by her.

I must be her best friend.

When the warm-up is over, I give a light knock and push open the door. The person's back is to me, but it's definitely a guy, which I wasn't expecting. I was hoping to have some rockin' female mentor, but I could work with a man . . . as long as we leave the door open and someone else is in the building.

I scan my eyes over his body and stop at his thighs. Suddenly I'm unable to breathe. I'd know those legs anywhere. I've dreamt about those legs.

"Jesse?"

He twists around to face me. It could be my imagination, but his cheeks look like they're turning a shade or two darker.

"When did you get here?" he asks, a mix of irritation and surprise in his voice.

"I've been here a couple hours. You didn't hear me practicing when you came in?"

He shakes his head. "And I didn't see any cars. I thought I was alone."

"Ah, yes. A car," I say through a sigh. "Still need one of those."

"Someone dropped you off?"

"Dad."

He nods, scratching at his leg just above his knee like he did when I watched him practice pitching. Again, it draws my attention.

Then the realization slams into me like a stage curtain dropping right on my head: Jesse Morales is standing in front of me in tight black pants. And tap shoes.

I have to sit down.

I find the nearest chair and collapse into it, trying not to act like a freak. It's just Jesse, dancing only for himself.

Such a waste.

I won't stand for it.

He spins a chair around and straddles it, pushing his sleeves up to his elbows and crossing his arms over the chair back. His eyes are trained on the floor, but I wait long enough and eventually they find their way to me.

"So," we both say at the same time.

"You still dance," I finish, and I'm proud how quickly I've composed myself.

He inhales and lets the breath out slowly. "I help out with choreography."

"Just choreography? I mean, you don't like to dance sometimes? Just to . . . dance?"

"Madison, I'm not going to *be* in the show, so don't even ask."

I swallow hard and try not to shrink away from his infinite tone. It's like I'm getting scolded, and I didn't even do anything wrong. Yet.

"Well, I heard you through the door, and this isn't the first time," I tell him. "You're good. You're beyond good—you're amazing."

Now I know his cheeks are darker. "This can never leave this room."

I agree to nothing, and he squirms in his seat until he can't handle my staring, and clicks across the room to fiddle with his iPod.

I don't know if I'm more dumbfounded that I may actually be about to witness Jesse dance or that he's capable of being embarrassed about something. And in front of *me*. The fact that he's still dancing and no one else knows . . . it's like I have power. A very special power that must be manipulated very, very, very carefully. I shall use this power for good. *My* good.

"Teach me what you know," I say from my chair because I'm afraid I still haven't regained the ability to stand.

He laughs and abandons his iPod without choosing a song.

"Why would I do that?" he asks.

As he walks oh so slowly toward me, my ears barely register any sound from his shoes.

Because if I never see you dance, I might possibly die.

"Because . . . you owe me?" It comes out as a question.

More laughter bounces off the mirrored walls as he continues his leisurely pace in my direction. He stops behind my chair, resting his hands on the plastic backrest. I keep my breathing as steady as possible, refusing to let him get to me. I can tell he's leaning down to me, and I swear if he starts to sing I really will fall over right here on this floor.

"Maddie," he says much too softly.

What was that I was just saying about me having power? And aren't I supposed to be mad at him for . . . something?

"Like I said before, I helped you. I don't owe you anything else."

And the spell is broken.

I jump up and rush down the hall to my practice room, grab my shoes, and march straight back to my chair. Jesse looks on as I stifle a whimper and shove my sore feet in my shoes again. We have to wear character shoes for the performance, which are practically high heels with taps, so that's what I have to practice in. They're killing me.

"I mean it," I say. "Stealing my first kiss and saying I should *thank* you is the most absurd thing I've ever heard. And you're going to make it up to me." I pause to see if he has a reaction, which he doesn't, outside of narrowing his eyes. "By giving me tap-dance lessons."

He crosses his arms over his chest. "I don't think s—"

"Oh, it's *happening*. And it's starting right now," I demand. "Unless you want your secret to get out. . . . I'm sure your jock friends would love resurrecting your old moniker, whatever it was they called you. Twinkle Toes, perhaps?" I probably wouldn't actually do that to him, but he doesn't need to know that. This must happen even if self-preservation is his sole motivation.

A scowl takes over his face as he runs a hand through his thick hair.

"Furthermore, I'm in this show that *your mother* helped me get in, and I'm not going to mess it up with inferior tapping."

He leaves me hanging for far too long before saying, "You know this means you'll actually have to talk to me again."

"Well, considering it's in the name of *making it up to me*, I'll allow it. I may even start carpooling with you again, you know, for convenience." Angela still takes me to school in the mornings, but my mom has been picking me up lately.

One of his eyebrows rises. "And we'd have to spend quite a bit of time together."

"I'll get over it."

The corner of his mouth pulls up. "And you'd have to take it seriously."

"I'll be the most willing and dedicated student you've ever had," I say, drawing an *X* over my heart.

Scratching his chin, he says, "What makes you think I'd be a good teacher?"

At this point, I don't even care what kind of teacher he'd make. I just want to see the boy move.

Clearing my throat, I ignore his question and muster the courage to ask one of my own. "Can you show me your time step?"

He sighs. "Which one?"

"Um . . . the first one?"

When he reaches the middle of the room, his feet fly. All the steps are there, I see them, I recognize them. Stomp, hop, step, flap, stamp, stomp, over and over, alternating feet. It's the most effortless movement I've ever seen from him. Like it's easier than walking.

His ego wins out, and his steps transition into a continuous flow of the most beautifully complex rhythms. He moves across the floor with such grace and strength, my brain doesn't understand how he could ever want to do anything but this.

I try to fight the thought, but this boy . . . he's getting closer to what I want.

"Say you'll dance with me," I softly plead when he finishes the impromptu demonstration.

He chugs half a bottle of water and tosses it into his open duffel bag. "How much do you already know?"

I give my shoelaces one last yank and stand just in front of him. I shuffle my right foot, out-in, out-in. "Shuffle." I do a similar movement, but instead of pulling my foot toward me at the second sound, I keep forward and put weight on it. "Flap."

After a deep inhale, he closes his eyes and mutters, "This is going to be so much work."

CHAPTER TWENTY

Now that we're talking again, I have my after-school driver back until the end of this year. In January, Jesse has practice with the baseball team after school, but Angela will be done with volleyball so she'll chauffeur me around until I'm able to afford my own set of wheels—a slowgoing effort. Hard to save much working part-time at $7.50 an hour.

I don't love being dependent on other people for rides. Even though it's handy that my current carpool driver is also my instructor for my super-secret dance lessons twice a week.

We pull out of the school parking lot and head in the opposite direction from the playhouse.

"Wait, where are we going?" I ask, my legs bouncing in anticipation of getting to practice.

"Miss O's" is all he says.

"Who?" I slouch in my seat, wondering why he didn't just drop me off first.

"It's a cupcake place."

"Cake?" I exclaim, my mood brightening. "This isn't some kind of trick, is it? You can't joke about cake with me."

"No tricks," he says through a laugh. "I have to pick up an order for my mom and bring it to the playhouse."

The small cupcakery, a cheerfully decorated space of pink and turquoise, is crammed in a busy shopping center not too far from the high school. The sweet aroma energizes me as soon as we walk in the door. I rush to the display case to ogle the miniature cakes swirled high with frosting and sprinkled with colored sugars or chocolate chips. I want them all.

"What's their best flavor?" I ask as he rings the bell on the counter.

"I usually get vanilla," Jesse says.

I scrunch my nose at him. "You would."

An employee comes out from the back, pulling an apron over her head. "What can I get y'all?"

"Just picking up an order for Sherri Morales."

I frown when the girl turns to find it. "You do realize I want one, right?"

He laughs. "I do now."

The girl slides the box of mini cupcakes onto the counter. "Anything else?"

"Do you have a yellow cupcake with chocolate on top?" Jesse asks.

I gape at him. That's exactly what I was scanning the case for but couldn't find. My absolute favorite.

She shakes her head. "No, but we have lemon poppy seed." She points to it, then to another. "Or maybe you'd like the chocolate with chocolate frosting?"

He shrugs. "Vanilla's fine."

I order red velvet and Jesse pays for both of ours.

"Thanks," I say. "I'll get the next one. Now that I know this place is here, we're coming back. And soon."

I hover my face over the plate to inhale the goodness as I head for the bar table along the front window.

Jesse takes the stool next to me and picks at the white icing of his cupcake with a plastic fork. "Sorry you won't get as much time to dance today. I know you need the practice."

"Oh, don't even!" I resist smacking him upside the head. No matter how true his words are, he better be joking. "We'll just have to make up the time the day after tomorrow." I take a bite of the moist red cake and suppress an embarrassing sound of enjoyment.

"Fine." He flits his hand in the air like he's tired of the subject.

"Do you think red velvet is really just chocolate cake with red food coloring?" I ask.

He glances at my plate before he says, "How should I know?" Abandoning his fork, he picks up his cupcake with his fingers. His mouth is open as wide as it can get, but the tower of icing heads straight for his nose.

"Just trying to make conversation. If you'd rather sit here in silence like we do on most of our rides home, fine by me." I swivel my stool at a slight angle away from him.

In my periphery I see the entire hunk of icing fall down to his plate. I risk a glance and laugh at him.

"Finally something he can't do."

"It just fell off."

"Elise could eat that with less of a mess." I snatch a napkin from the dispenser and hand it to him, motioning toward his upper lip.

He misses a glob on his nose, which shimmers with sugar crystals. "This is a sissy dessert, anyway."

"You poor cupcake-challenged boy." I grab another napkin and help him.

He jerks his head away, and I end up smearing the icing down his cheek.

"Would you just sit still?"

I swipe at the streak with a finger, accidentally grazing the corner of his mouth. Our eyes meet, and my mind jumps to Halloween, the last time we looked so closely at each other.

His cell phone rings, thankfully snapping me out of any swoony thoughts I had at the memory of our kiss. The kiss I keep trying not to count but can't forget.

He pulls it out of his pocket and answers. "Hey, Franklin. What's up?"

I nearly snort. "There's a person named Franklin?" I ask so only Jesse can hear.

He smiles and twists the phone away from his mouth. "Last name," he whispers to me before saying, "She dumped you? Oh, man, that's lame," to whoever Franklin is.

I try to tune out the tough-guy style of consoling and focus on enjoying the last few bites of cream cheese icing. Most of his words blend in with the easy listening background music, but I can't help hearing loud and clear when he says, "Girls are stupid, man. Not worth the effort."

My chewing slows and my body feels heavy. He keeps chattering on, oblivious to my inner crisis.

I tell myself he's just feeding that Franklin kid lines, but it had to be in his head to say it in the first place. I don't know if he really feels that way himself, or if he took the opportunity to send me a hint, but I do know he just said one of the most unromantic things I've ever heard in my life.

I work extra hard at practice, maybe to prove to myself and to him that I'm worth the time he's spending to train me. He doesn't seem to notice my determination, but my body sure does. By bedtime, I'm babying a new blister and massaging my calves to keep them from cramping. But I shall not whine. I'm that much closer to having dancers' legs.

I click off my paper lantern creation above my bed and collapse onto the feather pillows, my new mantra repeating in my head: *Boys are stupid. Not worth the effort.*

All boys except for one, who I can only dance with in my dreams.

I'm floating between awake and asleep when my phone vibrates from the nightstand.

Jesse: You're mad again.
Me: I'm asleep.
Jesse: Obviously.
Me: . . . ?

After a few minutes with no response, I hug my pillow, setting my mind on the ballet with Gene Kelly and Cyd Charisse in *Singin' in the Rain*. It's one of my favorite scenes visually, a wide expanse of pastel pinks and purples, with Gene contrasting in all black. And it's all in his character's head. He knows he can't have the girl, but in his dreams, he sees them together. He fights with everything he has to show her he can be what she needs.

The long white veil from the top of my dress catches the breeze and floats behind me like a cape. I circle him and it clings to his body. He twists around and uses it to guide me against him, spinning and wrapping us both in the fabric.

Dropping to one knee, he leans me down across his leg, eyes studying my face.

Mine study him too. Deep brown eyes, tiny scar on his cheek, lips that part and—

My phone buzzes. Again. I consider throwing it against the wall.

Jesse: Tell me what I did.

Me: Gee. Could you have said something offensive, I wonder? You think girls are what, now?

Jesse: I don't think you're stupid.

Me: What a relief. I think I'm trying to sleep.

Jesse: You know I was just saying what Franklin wanted to hear.

I roll my eyes, tapping a fingernail on the screen until I figure out what I want to say back.

Me: Then you should have said that PARTICULAR girl, not "girls," which is all-encompassing. I was sitting right there.

Jesse: I just had to use my dictionary app. This further proves you are not stupid.

I turn onto my side and pull the sheet up over my smile, as if he can see.

Jesse: So . . . we good?

And the smile's gone. The kiss is definitely not counting.

Me: Was that an apology?

Jesse: Yes.

Me: Well it sucked. Add it to the list of things you have to make up to me.

Jesse: There's a list? When will you decide I've appropriately rectified all of these wrongs?

Me: Excellent use of that dictionary app.

Jesse: Thank you.

Jesse: That wasn't an answer.

Me: I'll let you know when it happens.

Jesse: I'll take the use of "when" as optimism.

Me: Autocorrect. Should have been "if." Good night.

Jesse: Night.

Jesse: And I'm sorry.

I return my phone to the nightstand and burrow under the covers. My mind speeds through the same dance scene to pick up where I left off, with me in place of Cyd, of course. But when I get to the part with the dipping and the kissing, Gene's also replaced.

With Jesse.

CHAPTER TWENTY-ONE

Rica bursts through the door of the mock apartment onstage, in costume, and asks in a panic, "Are there M&M's in the greenroom?"

We're putting the finishing touches on the black box theatre before the opening of *Barefoot in the Park* tonight, and the prima donna is getting on everyone's last nerve. If Ryan gets through all three performances without wringing her neck, it will be a miracle.

I stop straightening a row of chairs and blink, my head cocked to the side as I try to figure out if I heard her right. "Uh, no. I don't think so."

"I need M&M's."

"I suppose you also want me to pick out all the blue ones, or something ridiculous?"

She puts her hands on her hips. "Like I want you touching anything I'm going to eat."

I flash her my teeth in a sarcastic smile and blink a few more times, with no intention of hunting down candy just for her. I may be in charge of the greenroom tonight as part of my extra credit, but I'm not a personal assistant to a movie star.

Mrs. Morales's voice calls out from the room entrance. "I'm about to let our audience take their seats. Rica, get back behind that door, and everyone else, get where you're supposed to be, please. Show starts in fifteen minutes."

Rica disappears and I head for the last row reserved for students in theatre classes and claim a seat beside a younger girl I don't know. We smile at each other, but I'm saved from having to start a conversation when Brian plops into the empty aisle seat on my other side and hands me one of the programs we just spent the last hour folding and stapling together.

"I know what you're thinking," I tell him.

"Yeah?" He unzips his navy hooded sweatshirt. "You're thinking about how annoying it is that when it's cold outside it's hot inside?"

"Well, now I am, but no." I point to the cast list on the program.

"Could have been us." He reaches toward me like he's about to pat my leg or something, then changes his mind.

"Should have been." I twist in my seat and wait until his eyes find mine. "Have I apologized recently? Because I'm so, so, so sorry. We had it, and I ruined it."

"Don't beat yourself up over it for my sake. I think Ryan would have gotten the part anyway. He's really good."

"You're better at the funny," I offer quietly, so no one overhears.

He looks away from me but smiles, biting a fingernail. "Did you watch any of their rehearsals?"

"No," I huff. "I don't even want to watch it now, but whatever."

"Just focus on Ryan. We're here for him, not her."

I sigh, crossing my arms. "I know, I know."

"And I brought him flowers for the curtain call," he says with a laugh. "Some really girly-looking pink and white ones."

"Oh, that's great!" I smile. "I should have gotten some for Sarah for directing."

"We can divide them up if you want."

"Are you sure?" I ask, and he nods. "Where are they?"

Brian looks around on the floor. "Shoot. Left 'em in my car." He stands and tugs his sweatshirt around him. "Be right back."

I thumb through the cream-colored pages of the program without really reading the ads, but my heart flutters when I spot a half-page promo for *Crazy for You* at the playhouse next month. I want to shout to everyone taking their seats around me that I'll actually be in that one. And maybe someone will bring *me* flowers.

"You look jealous," says a familiar voice.

Jesse's standing over me, dressed in a green shirt with the sleeves pushed up to his elbows, as usual, and thumbs hooked on the pockets of his distressed jeans. His dark hair spikes up every which way, and I wonder if he spent half an hour getting it to look that perfect or if he just ran a hand through it.

"I'm not jealous, I'm . . . disappointed. In myself." The program falls out of my hands and flutters to the floor, where I leave it. "And I'd rather not be here," I mutter.

"Me neither." Jesse sits next to me, settling in like he's planning to stay there for the whole performance.

"Brian was sitting there," I say.

"You want me to move?" He faces me as the houselights cut off, daring me to answer with that smug smile of his.

My mind takes me back to that dream where I was dancing with Gene and suddenly he turned into Jesse, and I'm thankful I'm sitting down. And I'm glad it's Jesse next to me and not Brian.

I shake my head. "So why are you here? I thought this wasn't your thing . . . anymore."

"Mom likes the support, or whatever."

"That sounds so sincere." I snort.

"Hey, I came, didn't I?"

Brian reappears as the music intro plays through the speakers, a mass of assorted flowers in hand. He looks from me to Jesse with his mouth hitched to the side, one of his cheeks puckering.

"That's my seat," Brian says.

"I told him that," I'm quick to say, so he doesn't think I had anything to do with it.

Jesse shrugs.

"Come on, man," Brian says, clearly annoyed. "Just go sit somewhere else."

"Nah, I'm good." Jesse rests a boot over the opposite knee. "If you wanted to sit by her so bad, you shouldn't have gotten up."

"Whoa," I say, turning to Jesse in surprise. "I'm flattered to be worth your time."

"Shut up," he fires back through a laugh.

Brian throws me one last glance for help, but all I can do is mirror his puckered expression, secretly thrilled two guys are practically fighting over who gets to sit next to me. He gives up and sidesteps past us to the end of the row, and Jesse crosses his arms and sinks deeper into his chair, satisfied.

"What are you doing tomorrow?" Jesse asks as the music plays on but the actual show has yet to start.

"I don't know," I answer, staring at a girl's wavy hair in front of me. "It's Saturday, so probably sleeping in. Why?"

"Feel like a bonus practice session?"

My eyes widen. "For realsies?"

His body shakes once as he swallows a laugh. "Yeah. For *realsies*. I'm free in the afternoon if you are."

I look at him and he's making this face I've never seen on him, eyes soft and almost . . . hopeful? Maybe he misses dancing more than he let on.

I can work with that.

"Sure. Tomorrow."

The stage lights brighten, and Rica once again bursts through the door to the living room of the tiny one-bedroom apartment, humming a melody, filling an empty paint bucket with invisible water for a bouquet of flowers.

I lean toward Jesse to comment on the set and our shoulders press together. He tilts his head down to hear me, and I find myself staring at his ear, my thoughts gone. His ear, of all things. We all have them, they're nothing special. I move even closer, hoping that if I lose focus on it, I'll remember what I was going to say, but I still haven't said a word and he turns to look at me without warning. Our cheeks brush against each other, and we pull away slowly. A tremor shoots down my spine to my toes.

Don't look at his lips, don't look at his lips. Look at his eyes . . . which are looking at my lips.

No.

I redirect my attention to the play and do my best to keep it there, laughing at all the right places—at Ryan's lines more so than Rica's—and occasionally glancing at Jesse for reactions, which he doesn't have many of. At intermission, Brian switches seats with the girl on my right, and I notice that every time I chat quietly with him about how weird it is to see Ryan in a suit, or laugh with Brian at the way Rica keeps drawling out "Paul" like "Pawl," Jesse gets fidgety. He uncrosses or crosses his arms, stretches out his legs, or rests his elbows on his knees to support his head in his hands.

"You look bored out of your mind," I whisper to Jesse.

He leans in close so no one else can hear, almost turning his head to the back wall. "Why did you bring me here? Next time, I'll decide what we do with our Friday night. The lead actress is awful."

He's lying—she's sickly talented—but I fight a smile and whisper, "Positively ghastly."

"You and your silly words. Do I need to open my dictionary app again?"

He reaches for his pocket as if to take out his phone, but I clutch his wrist.

"If you mess with your phone in the middle of this play I will smack you."

"Promise?" Twisting his arm over, he slides his hand into mine and gives it a quick squeeze.

I'm paralyzed with fear that he thinks I was trying to hold his hand, and that he won't let go. That he *will* let go.

Ugh, why is that kiss still haunting me?

His mouth is at my ear in an instant. "Do you want to get out of here?"

"Is something going on with y'all?" Brian asks in my other ear.

"No!" I whisper a little too loudly, making the girl in front of me shoot me a look. I steal my hand back and hide both of them in the big front pocket of my sweater.

Jesse stands, and I realize he doesn't know Brian said anything, or that it was him I was answering. That my mind was determining if I'd still get my extra credit if I left now.

"Your loss." Jesse leans down to add, "See you tomorrow."

He slips behind our row of seats. And maybe it's just from his body as he sneaks past, but I feel something brush against my hair, and I find myself hoping he touched it on purpose.

CHAPTER TWENTY-TWO

Me: Why is kissing so awesome?
Sarah: Did u kiss someone else? WHOOOO?
Me: No.
Sarah: Oh, ur still living off Jesse's kiss?
Me: It's all I have. But what has been sampled cannot be unsampled.
Sarah: LOL thought u weren't counting it???
Me: Ugh. I lied.
Me: WHY WAS IT SO AWESOME?

"No texting in the car," Jesse says, bopping the underside of my arm so my phone flies out of my hand and flops onto the floorboard.

"Rude!" I laugh and bend as far as I can, but it's closer to Jesse than it is to me. "And that only applies to the driver."

He turns into the parking lot of the playhouse.

"Maybe I should make you drive," he says. "Then I'll sit in the passenger seat and text away. See how it makes *you* feel."

"How should it make me feel?" I glance at him while undoing my seat belt, ready to make a dive for my phone.

But then he says, "Ignored."

I blink, waiting for him to laugh, which he doesn't. Confusion swirls with fear that he's going to see my last text to Sarah.

"My most humble apologies," I say, with exaggerated formality. "If you want to talk, talk. I'm sitting right here next to you just like I do every day."

He shuts off the ignition and stares at the dash. "Forget it," he finally says.

My phone chirps and I can see that the entire text conversation with Sarah is still open, the screen as bright as the surface of the sun. I hold my breath. *Don't look. Don't look.*

In slow motion, his arm extends, his hand opens, and he reaches for my phone near his feet. It's probable my brain will explode from the telepathy I'm screaming at him not to look. But if I verbalize it, he'll definitely loo—

He looks. His lips purse like he's organizing his thoughts. Another alert dings and I snatch it from him without warning, terrified to see the new message I know he saw:

Sarah: Maybe Jesse will kiss u again. R u w/ him now?

The endless possibilities of everything he could say hang in the silence between us, and I prepare myself for the onslaught of comments confirming I just successfully inflated his already giant head. Somehow he keeps himself from saying anything at all. There's no way he could be mad. We didn't text anything even remotely offensive.

Unless he's completely repelled by the idea of kissing me again. Maybe I really was awful compared to the other girls.

Oh, no. That's it.

I'm a repellent.

Without replying to Sarah, I turn off my phone and stow it in my backpack, which I sling over a shoulder as I slide out of the truck. Jesse's already at the front door, one arm raised high to hold it open for me. I duck underneath and into the musty cool air as Jesse's cell phone rings. Instead of the basic ringtone, the ominous two-note riff from *Jaws* breaks the silence of the hallway. Instinctively, I glance around us with a watchful eye as if there could really be a shark or something else sinister lurking about.

He answers, following me into our practice room and dropping his bag into a chair, and then he paces as he talks to who I assume is his dad. Jesse's words are clipped, irritated, his eyebrows pushed together.

"Yes, I'm going to the batting cages," he says into the phone.

I stop tying my tap shoes and stare at him, disappointment growing inside.

"No. I know. I'm working on it," he continues. "I'll be ready."

He hangs up without a good-bye and glances at me as I sit frozen, waiting for instructions.

"Well, get your shoes on already." He sinks into a chair and rolls up his jeans into cuffs before pulling off his boots.

"What was all that about?" I ask, straightening one of my purple socks with turquoise hearts on it.

No response.

"So this is what it feels like to be ignored," I tease. "I don't like it."

He tugs on his tap shoes and mutters, "Well, I'd like it if certain people did a little more ignoring." He stands, leaving his jeans partially rolled up, and starts some combination I'd never be able to identify.

"Certain people? Like your dad?"

All he does is stare at himself in the mirror, jaw set in a hard line. I take the tense silence as confirmation, and halfheartedly do a few drawbacks to get my feet loosened up.

"Why would you want your dad to ignore you? Isn't that the sort of thing you'd end up in therapy for when you're older?"

The corner of his mouth perks up.

"It can't be that bad," I prompt, eager for him to open up. Besides the fact that his dad strongly encouraged him to work at that restaurant to help with his Spanish, I don't know much about their relationship.

His shoes click an angry rhythm across the floor, and I struggle to hear his words.

"I guess it's mostly just annoying. He acts like I won't practice on my own. He's always on me about it. Every year, the closer it gets to the start of baseball season, the more I have to hear about it." Sweat's already beading along his hairline. "The more I have to listen to the same tired speech about how close he was to making it into the major leagues."

"Really? Wow." I think about Tiffany and her Olympian mother. "*Y'all* sure are athletic down here," I say, with emphasis on the *y'all* so he can see how well I'm adapting.

Jesse continues his steps without a glance my way, the sweat drops now making trails down his face. His moves are fluid, seamless, as he floats around the room. I'm not even dancing, but I'm feeling a little warm myself.

Keeping my eyes trained on his feet, I say, "So . . . you're complaining that he wants you to have the same baseball career that you already want for yourself?"

I want him to fight me on it. To tell me that *this* is what he wants, to take control of the stage. I want him to tell me that baseball can take a hike.

He stops after a stomp and meets my gaze. "That's not—you couldn't understand, Maddie."

"You've said that before." I rest a hand on my hip. "I'm sure your dad just wants to be involved. He's proud of you. That's what parents do."

"Sure."

I'm not letting him clam up now. "I'm guessing he doesn't know you're *here*? At the playhouse."

He snorts.

"You told him you were going to the batting cages? Won't he figure out you lied to him?"

"I didn't really lie. I'm going. Just not right this second." He reaches out to me as if inviting me to dance. "Are you ready to get started or what?"

Biting my lip, I stare at his outstretched hand without taking it. I'm not done watching him yet.

"Can I see something first?"

He retracts his hand and touches the ends of his hair, now a bit floppy. "Depends."

"Can you do that move where your leg is up in the air and you jump over it with the other one?"

"Where did you see that?"

It's not an uncommon dance move, but of course I'm picturing the way Gene does it. "I've seen Gene Kelly do it. I've tried but I don't really have enough power to get any height. It just looks like I'm tripping over the air."

He snickers before he says, "Who's Gene Kelly?"

My mouth falls open and an audible gasp escapes. "Tell me you're kidding!" I cry, closing the distance between us in a few hurried steps with no ideas what to do once I reach him besides maybe smacking him upside the head.

"Whoa," he says, backing away with his hands raised. "Kidding, kidding. Of course I know who he is."

I clutch my chest and loll my head back. "That nearly killed me."

I'm thankful we've both been spared my rant about how someone who dances like he does was influenced by Gene whether they realize it or not, and it's only proper to educate yourself on the key predecessors of your craft.

"What's your thing with him, anyway? I saw that stack of movies you lent Angela and he was in all of 'em."

My head snaps up, and I inhale sharply. "You watched them?"

"Uh, no." When my face falls, he quickly adds, "I mean, I've seen that one set in Paris, but it wasn't really—"

"Just stop right there, before you completely destroy my spirit."

Shaking my head, I rifle through my bag and take a drink from my water bottle before turning back to him. Jeans and a button-down aren't his usual practice attire, but I like it. It gives me a tingly sensation like we could just be walking down the street and he'd spontaneously break out in some elaborately choreographed number, and it would seem completely natural. And of course, I'd magically know the steps as well and I'd join in by the first chorus.

But clearly, he didn't intend on dancing quite so hard today, and I feel bad for getting him worked up about his dad. Almost. He's starting to sweat through his shirt, not that I particularly mind the look.

"And here," I say, tossing a towel to him. "Do something about all the wetness, please, before it flies onto me."

He wipes his forehead and flings the towel back at me. I dodge it and squeal at an embarrassingly high pitch.

"Afraid of a little sweat?" He rubs his hand along the back of his neck and rushes in my direction.

I run and duck by the table pushed against the wall, pulling a chair close to conceal me. Stupid move. Jesse straddles it and wipes the moisture from his hand all down my arm.

"Ugh. Thanks for that."

I stand, shoving his chair out of my way, and he hurls himself backward in a dramatic show and sprawls onto the floor flat on his back, arms spread wide.

"Can we be done? I'm tired."

"Uh . . ." I refrain from pointing out that I haven't even danced yet. I got to watch him and that's more than enough to fill up my Saturday evening. "Sure. We can call it a night."

He raises an arm, and when I stare at him, blankly, he waves his hand around like he wants me to help him up. I grasp his hand and tug until he's upright, but the momentum of him springing forward slams his chest against my shoulder and suddenly everything's slow motion.

Here we are again, hand in hand, pressed against each other. All that's missing is the sailor uniform. My eyes dart to his lips. It would be so easy for me to take them. For him to take mine. But I don't, and he doesn't.

This is reality. He's only helping me learn to dance to keep my mouth shut.

So it surprises me when he says, "Come to the batting cages with me."

And it surprises me even more when I say, "Okay."

By the time Jesse pays the cashier, the sun's already dipped below the horizon, painting the sky a vibrant, cloud-streaked blue. The cold front that chilled the air yesterday—I nearly believed it's actually December—is on its way out, leaving behind a wet warmth that steals my residual giddiness from seeing Jesse leap over his own leg, high in the air. He did it in the parking lot on the way to the car, boots and all. I clapped, he bowed, and neither of us said a word about it all the way here.

Jesse pays for a handful of tokens to run the machine, and he leads me to the supply area.

"You'll like this sport," he says. "You get to wear a helmet."

"Wait. I thought I was just watching you," I say, taking a step back from the shelf lined with blue plastic helmets. "I don't know how."

"I figured." He holds a scratched aluminum bat level in both hands, lifting it up and down like he's checking to see how heavy it is. "I'll teach you."

"I don't think so," I say in a rush. My stomach twists at the vision that pops into my head. "You're not going to stand all up on me with your hands covering mine, helping me swing."

His eyes widen before he bursts into laughter. "Your whole life is a movie, Maddie Brooks."

I tilt my head to the side, contemplating his declaration. "And?"

"And I'll *talk* you through it. No touching."

Well, I didn't mean there had to be no touching . . .

He tests the weight of another bat and hands it to me. "You should be able to swing this one okay. How does it feel?"

I slide my fingers along the length of it. "Cold."

"Not what I meant." He rolls his eyes with a smirk. "Hold it like you're getting ready to hit the ball."

"Hey, batter batter batter," I say in a manly voice as I grip tightly near the bottom of the bat and lift it behind me, knees bent, butt out. I may or may not be intentionally overdoing the posture a tiny bit.

Jesse blinks, no longer smiling. "This is going to be like the first dance lesson, isn't it? Just hit me in the head with the bat now and get it over with."

"Hey! I wasn't that bad." I aim the bat toward him like I really am thinking about it. "And watch me end up being some sort of baseball prodigy, and you can get famous for having discovered me."

He laughs at that, selecting a bat and helmet for himself. "I'll get famous on my own, *mi reina*. Now, pick out a helmet and let's see if we can uncover your hidden talent."

We head outside, and once we're caged in our own box, Jesse demonstrates a few practice swings. He explains the importance of keeping your eye on the ball and following through, and a whole bunch of other points that I'll never be able to keep straight.

He inserts the token for his first round, and I watch in awe as he smacks each ball. I shield my eyes from the bright artificial lights and try to follow their paths, occasionally glancing at his arms or legs as his muscles work to power the swings.

"Are these all home runs?" I ask, impressed.

"Hardly." He grunts through a swing, sweating all over again.

"Oh, do you not hit home runs? Are there, like, players that hit the home runs and some that are supposed to hit to other parts of the field? Which are you?"

"That's ridiculous," he mutters after another swing. The ball pops high into the air and hits the net ceiling. "Of course I can hit home ru— You know what? Let's hold the rest of the questions until I'm done, cool?"

I cast my eyes to the ground and scratch at an imaginary itch on my arm. I thought he'd be pleased I was trying to learn, but all I'm succeeding at is irritating him. What I do best.

When it's my turn, he runs over all his points again, with extra emphasis on keeping my eye on the ball. If I watch it approach, apparently my brain will magically help my arms position the bat to hit it.

What a joke.

"So, I have a question," Jesse says after my seventh swing.

The ball barely grazes the bat, and it flies up and backward into the net overhead, as almost all my attempts have done.

"I thought I was supposed to be concentrating?"

He ignores me. "But I don't want you to get mad."

"Sounds ominous." Swing and a miss. My left shoulder is already sore and both of my calves are burning. "Ugh, this game is the *worst!*"

"Is your mom pregnant?"

His random question slams into me like a kick to the gut. Dropping the tip of my bat to the concrete with a clang, I turn to look at him, but it shifts my position too much and the next ball smacks me right on the hip. Jesse's curse comes out louder than mine as he yanks me out of the way of the next one.

"Don't ever take your eye off the ball!" he snaps.

"And I thought we weren't supposed to ask questions while someone was batting!" I throw right back.

Hesitantly, I lift up the bottom of my shirt and tug the waist of my pants down to check the damage, and I watch as the hint of a bruise appears.

"Awesome," I say through gritted teeth. "My first sports injury."

"My fault," he admits. "That was stupid of me to ask like that. I don't know what I was thinking."

"She is," I say. "Pregnant. Why? How did you . . . ?"

My round runs out, and Jesse picks up one of the missed balls and leans against the chain-link fencing. "I saw her the other day. At the grocery store. And she looked . . . different from the last time I saw her."

The sting from my hip is slowly spreading throughout my body, making me numb. I'd been doing such a good job of not going anywhere with her in an effort to avoid the humiliation. It didn't occur to me that someone might recognize her apart from me. And I'm sort of surprised Angela didn't tell him. I asked her not to, but things slip sometimes.

"*You* go to the grocery store?"

He shrugs, tossing the ball from one hand to the other. "I wanted Oreos. We didn't have any."

"Oh. Well. There you have it," I bite. "Please refrain from sick jokes about how my parents are still going at it or how when we go back to visit people in Chicago now, everyone will think we moved down here so I could have a baby in a place no one knows me."

He shakes his head, his tone serious as he says, "I wouldn't."

"Good. Because I don't think I could take it." I let out a long sigh, removing my helmet and trying to do damage control on my hair.

"It'll be okay, you know," he adds. "Having a little kid around—it's actually pretty cool."

"Yeah?"

"Yeah."

I make myself meet his gaze and I feel strangely comforted. Not judged or pitied, but understood. Supported.

Like we finally just became friends. Real ones.

CHAPTER TWENTY-THREE

"Ouch!" Angela shrieks. "That's, like, the fourth time I've stabbed myself with this stupid needle. Is this old-fashioned-themed tree really necessary?"

"I'm going to pretend you did not just ask me that." I jab a sewing needle into a cranberry followed by a few pieces of popcorn, sliding them down the thread.

"I can't believe how different this place is, Mrs. Brooks," Angela says, glancing around at the floor and walls. "I was in here once when the last people lived here. It was old looking and smelly."

Ma laughs, rising from the couch at the beep of the microwave. "New floors, new coat of paint, cabinets, appliances. It's been stressful, but I'm trying to get as much done as I can before I get too big."

Ma shuffles around in the kitchen and rejoins us in the living room with a big bowl of fresh popcorn. She flips the

Bing Crosby album over—I insist on playing vinyl Christmas records during holiday decorating activities—then settles into the recliner, munching as she watches us work.

"Are you going to help, or just eat all our supplies?" I ask, with maybe a hint of irritation worked in.

Ma scarfs another handful. "Your baby brother is hungry."

Angela looks up from her task, keeping the needle far from her other hand. "You didn't tell me it was a boy!"

I clench, then unclench my jaw. "She just calls it a boy. She doesn't know."

"We want to be surprised." Ma folds her hands over her protruding bump. "Not that we weren't already surprised once by the little pomegranate. But everything I'm feeling this time around reminds me of when I was pregnant with Rider. Has to be a boy."

"T-M-I, Ma. Way, way, way too much information."

Angela mouths the word "pomegranate" to me with her eyebrows raised.

"She's tracking the baby's size on some website," I explain with a roll of my eyes. "Apparently, the kid's the length and weight of a pomegranate right about now."

"Huh." Angela resumes the cranberry threading, likely regretting ever setting foot in my house tonight.

How many other nearly-seventeen-year-olds have dealt with pregnant parents? How long do their friends stick around?

"So when will he *or she*," Angela adds with a glance my way, "make their grand entrance into the world?"

"Near the end of March," Mom answers.

There must be more interesting things to talk about than my mother's due date. I don't typically wish for disasters, but

I find myself picturing the tree spontaneously bursting into flames.

So that's a little dramatic. Maybe the record player will skip, effectively distracting everyone enough so I can change the subject.

Or I could just change it, anyway.

"So what do you want for Christmas, Angela?"

"Ouch!" She drops her string and sucks on the tip of her finger. "Well, I always ask for gift cards for clothes, but I also want to get my car wired so I can play my iPod through the speakers."

"That'll be cool," I say. "I'd want that too, you know, if I had a *car.*" I look pointedly at my mom, who has now nearly finished the entire bowl of popcorn in her lap.

"Oh, honey," Ma says, her voice oozing with sympathy. "I hope you're not expecting to get a car for Christmas."

"Expecting? No." I reach into the bag of cranberries and find a firm one. "Hoping? Always."

She sits up straighter, stretching out her back and scratching her side near the bottom of her belly. "We'd love to be able to get you a vehicle, but we just can't afford it right now."

"So where did all the money come from that fixed up this house?" I snap, immediately regretting it.

She shifts her eyes to Angela for a second to let me know I shouldn't talk to her like this in front of my friend. "Maddie," she says through a forced smile. "We had a budget to move down here, which we stayed well under by buying a foreclosure we could fix up ourselves. So that's what we did. Would you have preferred we leave it a dump with cat spray all down the hallway?"

I shake my head.

"I'm sorry, but we don't have the money for another car right now. And the baby will be here before we know it. We have to buy furniture, a stroller, car seats, millions of diapers—the list is huge. We got rid of everything baby-related when you were about five years old. We have to start over."

Start over. They're totally going to be starting over. From scratch. New furniture, new stroller. New child. The old gets shoved aside. No help getting a car for you. Doesn't matter what you were promised. The pomegranate trumps all.

"I'm so sorry, Madison."

"I get it," I say, tying off the end of my popcorn string and swagging it on the tree.

Outside the window, I see Dad's car pull up the drive. I'm in no mood for him to jump into this conversation right now.

I turn to Angela. "Hey, I have something to show you."

We leave Ma with Bing and close ourselves in my room.

"What was it you wanted to show me?"

"Nothing, really. I just needed to walk out of there before I got thoroughly depressed."

"Your room looks great." Angela spins in place, eyeing the vintage movie posters slowly taking over my walls. "Though I'm not sure it's healthy to surround yourself with your unattainable standards," she says through a sigh.

The white lights bordering the bigger posters cast a comforting glow. I click on the paper lantern to add to the ambience and plop down on my bed.

Hugging one of the decorative pillows, I lie back and sigh too.

She joins me on top of the bed, pulling a furry blanket over her legs. "Still looking for a guy who can match up?" she asks.

Instantly I see Jesse, dancing alongside me. With his help, I've gotten so much better. I've actually been able to keep up during rehearsals of *Crazy for You* over the past few weeks, and I even caught a nod of approval from Mrs. Haskins.

If only I could just get Jesse to own up to all of his talents, publicly. I mean, he's good enough to go to school for it. He could tour—we could tour together one day! In real shows. All over. My chest flutters.

"I'm working on it." I clear my throat and keep my voice light so she might think I'm joking rather than legitimately trying to gauge a reaction. "If your brother weren't so set on a career throwing baseballs around, I'd have a contender."

"Ugh, don't make me hurl." She makes a grunting noise that rumbles in her throat. "What about Brian?"

"What about him?" I snort, picturing the festive cherry-red sneakers he wore at school all of last week before we let out for break.

"Well, y'all are close, right?"

"I don't know if I'd say *close*, but we're friends."

Angela props herself up on the pile of pillows. "So you've forgiven him for basically causing that bet that made you the object of every grody boy's desire?"

I hesitate, focusing on the muffled Christmas music from down the hall. "I know not of what you speak."

She stares at the ceiling. "I think enough time has passed for me to be able to talk about . . . you know."

"I know . . . ?"

"About the kiss. You and my . . . brother," she coughs, which progresses into a gag.

I laugh uncomfortably. "Hey, I wasn't about to be the one to bring it up."

She picks at the chipping paint on her fingernails. "Well, it never turned into anything, so it doesn't really bother me anymore."

Her words make me itch. No, it never turned into anything, but after our adventure at the batting cages last weekend, I allowed myself to picture similar outings in the future. But besides a text the next day asking how my hip was feeling, I haven't heard from him.

"But it did?" I ask. "Bother you, I mean."

"Wouldn't it be weird if *your* brother kissed *me*?"

I shoot a scowl at her. "Yes. You're a sophomore and he's in college."

"Age differences aside. It would be weird, right?"

I can't even let myself picture the two of them going at it. "Yes. Weird."

"He *is* pretty cute, though."

"Stop."

"See?" She laughs and jabs me with her elbow, then resumes destroying her fingernails.

"I worked hard on those nails, and you're ruining them."

Holding her hands palms out, she says, "You did the right, I'm only picking at the left. The ones that were already ruined by my incompetence as a self-manicurist. But you're trying to steer me off topic. I was saying before, maybe Brian could be a contender," she says, digging her phone out of her back pocket. "He's into acting, so that's got to be a big one on your list."

Now I make a grunting noise.

"What else does he need to do?" she asks, scrolling through her phone. "Dance? Sing?"

"All of it." I stare up at the lights and let them blur as my focus shifts to my thoughts. "But I don't really see Brian that way."

"He's not ugly or anything," she says, as if I've offended her. After a few seconds, she holds the little screen in front of my face with a picture of Brian she must have found online. "See?"

He's standing next to Sarah and Ryan, posed with water guns and cheesing it up for the camera. They all look a little younger. Brian's light hair is tidier than he keeps it now, his freckles extra pronounced on his tan skin. It's not a bad picture.

"He might be worth hanging out with more," Angela adds, scrolling through the rest of his photo albums.

"You're not going to let this go, are you?"

"Oh, come on. What's it gonna hurt?"

Closing my eyes, I try to imagine Brian dancing alongside the river Seine, like in *An American in Paris*. Not the easiest image to recreate with someone who only ever wears glowing sneakers.

I groan as I fire off a text to Sarah.

Me: What are you and the boys doing Saturday?

"You guys are acting like it's twenty degrees," I tease the trio as we walk from Brian's car to the movie theatre. "Back home, it probably would have snowed at least once already. This is nothing. This is like a mild spring day."

"You're crazy. It's freezing." Ryan breathes into his hands, then hides them in his sleeves.

"I told you to bring a coat." Sarah's bundled inside her *The Nightmare Before Christmas* hoodie, a pink circle of her face the only part visible.

I adjust my yellow scarf above my bright green peacoat, thankful to finally have an excuse to break out my cool-weather fashions. I probably won't see my beloved snow anytime soon, but this is at least a step in the right direction.

"Which one do you guys want to see?" I ask when we approach the entrance, scanning the movie schedule and recognizing none of the titles.

"I already paid for the tickets online," Ryan says through chattering teeth. He hands his confirmation number to the girl in the box office and she slides four tickets through the slot. "I can feel the heat coming from inside. Let's *go*."

"Shut up already before I jack you in the face," Brian says, opening the door for us to file in.

So Brian doesn't like whiners either. That's one point for him. I raise my palm up for a high five. He simultaneously lifts an eyebrow and a corner of his mouth, and slaps my hand.

"I approved of the movie selection, don't worry," Sarah says to me. "There are plenty of hot guys."

"Oh, plenty of hot guys," Brian mimics in a high-pitched voice.

Sarah laughs, but I give his shoulder a playful shove. A wide smile lights up his face. It's a nice smile. No dimples, but the freckles add something extra.

"Movie starts in five minutes," Ryan says, handing out the tickets.

"Okay." Sarah moves away from him and links arms with me. "Y'all go get the popcorn and we'll meet you at the door. We're going to the bathroom."

"We are?" I ask.

She pulls me toward the guy who tears the tickets and on to the bathroom. We head straight for the mirrors, where Sarah removes her hood and fluffs her hair.

"I'm so glad you asked us to do something tonight, Mads," she says, swiping strawberry ChapStick on her lips.

"Me too." I take off my coat and fold it over my arm.

"Ry told me that Brian hasn't stopped talking about it all day."

"Really?" Now I fluff my hair, separating some of the curls to make it look fuller. I'm getting pretty good with the styling wand.

She washes her hands, then raises her voice over the *whir* of the dryer. "He's been anxious to hang out with you outside of school, but wasn't sure if you'd go for it."

"I didn't know that," I say, retying my scarf. "He could have just asked."

"Would you have said yes?" The dryer stops midsentence and her voice echoes off the tile walls.

I don't answer. Until Angela put the idea in my head, I don't know if I would have.

"And I have to say I'm a little surprised to see you flirting with him." She crosses her arms and leans against the counter.

I swallow hard, worried I've been doing something wrong.

"Because we all sort of thought you had a thing going on with Jesse."

My eyes widen, but I try to keep the physical reaction to a minimum. Nothing looks guiltier than enthusiastic denial. And he'd kill me if I snitched about our dancing practices.

"Nah," I say, playing it cool. "We're neighbors, so he takes me home. And starting in January, I'll be riding home with Angela instead."

"Hmmm. Okay," she says with skepticism. "He'll be happy about that."

"Jesse?"

"Brian. Duh."

She leads me out and we meet up with the boys, each with a popcorn tub tucked under an arm and a cup in each hand.

"A lemon-lime *pop* for you," Brian says, handing one of the cups to me.

Good memory. Another point.

"I like your hair like that," he adds.

And another point. This might turn out to be a fun double-date thing after all.

The previews are already playing, and it's obvious right away that we're going to have to split up. Sarah and Ryan head to the other side, and Brian leads me up toward the top. The very back row.

"I'm glad we don't have to sit with them," he whispers, taking the seat against the wall.

"Why?" My heart kicks into high gear as I imagine the sorts of things that typically go on in the back row of movie theatres on a Saturday night.

"All they're going to do is make out." He leans in close. "And it's loud. I stopped going to movies with them a long time ago."

"Oh, I'm sorry. We could have done something else."

"Well, it's fine now that you're here." He offers me a timid smile just as the lights dim the rest of the way, darkening his features.

I look around until I find the silhouettes of our friends a few rows down to the right. I should say "silhouette," because they're practically one figure.

"Told you," says a whisper at my neck.

The movie turns out to be one of those over-the-top super-hero films, but I'm somewhat satisfied by the romance story line, so it keeps my attention. Though not enough to help me forget that Brian and I are sharing the same armrest. Or that his leg stretched out and touched mine ten minutes ago and he hasn't moved it.

I peek down to the dark blob that is Sarah and Ryan, and suffer through a twinge in my chest that might be akin to jealousy. I risk a glance at Brian out of the corner of my eye and turn my face fully toward him when I see that he's looking at me.

I have to strain to hear his whisper, but I'm fairly sure he says, "Would it be weird if I said I really wanted to kiss you right now?"

My mind chooses this moment to replay Jesse's kiss, my introduction to the world of kissing. That swirly feeling where your head goes numb and your toes tingle.

I liked it. And I want it again.

"You're supposed to feel it out," I manage through wild panic and curiosity. "If the moment is right, it won't be weird."

He laughs under his breath. "I only asked if it would be weird if I said I wanted to kiss you."

"You're making it weird right now," I whisper back, joining his laughter.

"Well, you already had the first kiss you were waiting for, so I figured I'm allowed now."

The kiss I was waiting for . . . The soft glow of the orange lights overhead, the hay falling everywhere, the sailor suit. I'm not sure if it gets more perfect the more I relive it, or if it really was just the most romantic first kiss I could have dreamed up for myself. I think I'll have to count it.

Maybe I really am free to kiss whoever I want now.

My eyes dart to his lips. They're a little thinner than Jesse's but—no. I stop myself from comparing them. Jesse is not my boyfriend.

"So . . . what are you thinking?" Brian asks.

"I don't think it's weird," I say.

His mouth twists into a pleased smirk. "Good."

Given how anxious he was to make out back when we were rehearsing for the audition together, I expect him to just grab me and kiss me right away, but he doesn't. He clasps my hand resting on my leg and turns his attention to the screen.

A warm sensation spreads up my arm. No one's ever just sat and held on to my hand before, just to keep touching me. I'm not sure what to do. I lift my eyes back to the movie, but nothing registers. I hear nothing but my heart in my ears and see nothing but the image of our joined hands.

Then his grip tightens, and I know he's asking me to look at him. So I do. He studies me in the dim lighting, leaning toward me. My eyes lock on his mouth as it gets closer and closer to mine.

This is happening. I'm about to be kissed. By Brian.

I stomp down that voice inside that says, *Don't do it! He's not the one!* and close my eyes. His other hand rests on my shoulder and pulls me gently forward until we kiss.

Nothing. I feel nothing.

It's just two sets of warm lips smashed against each other.

Brian leans away and we both stare at each other. Did he also feel nothing?

He smiles, which relieves some of my tension, and whispers, "Should we try that again?"

I let out a small laugh and nod, closing my eyes and pushing away that stupid little voice again. Only this time it's saying, *He's not Jesse.*

I try to get into this one more, putting a hand behind his head and allowing him to deepen the kiss. But after a few seconds, his mouth stops moving, and we both open our eyes. I fight back laughter, but it comes out when I see him bite his lips.

He clears his throat. "That was weird, right?"

"Totally weird," I say, eyebrows scrunched together. "I'm so sorry."

He straightens in his seat. "No, *I'm* sorry! I shouldn't have forced it. I just thought—"

I squeeze his hand to stop him. "We both thought, Brian. It's fine. It really is."

We laugh together, and I gulp down my Sprite, cooling my insides from the anticipation that had nowhere to go.

"Please don't hold this against me," he says after a minute of staring blankly at the screen.

"I won't if you won't hold it against me."

"Friends?"

I give his hand another squeeze, not ready to let go just yet. "Absolutely."

CHAPTER TWENTY-FOUR

As expected, there were no car keys under my tree this year. I shouldn't have let myself dream that my parents were just trying to fool me. My last hope is my birthday in February, which was the original agreement anyway, and a chunk of money to *help* me with a vehicle, like they helped Rider with his Camaro.

But I thought it would be different for me. Not only did they move me across the country halfway through my high school career, but I'm also their only daughter and the only child living at home, though I realize this won't necessarily be the case much longer.

I *understand* it, but that doesn't mean I'm happy about it.

At all.

And watching Ma *ooh* and *aah* over every little thing Dad gave her—a fancy gliding chair, baby bath toys, and the diaper bag he saw her petting in the store, to name a few of their "necessities"—did nothing for me but cause my lip to curl in irritation.

Rider handled it all with maturity, but he made his fair share of remarks when we were alone. He especially liked to rub it in that he won't be around for babysitting and diaper duties.

I sort of wish he wasn't around today because he's decided to tag along with me to the New Year's Eve party tonight, even after I said I didn't need a brother-bodyguard. When I reminded him of the Halloween party disaster, he said that was exactly why he needed to come. Not really the response I was going for, because I know what's going to happen: I'm going to be the one who has to watch him extra closely to make sure he doesn't sneak off with any of my classmates for a midnight make-out session, not the other way around.

I finish curling my hair and go back to my bedroom to examine my appearance in the full-length mirror on my closet door. Black boots, leggings, long silver top, black sweater, red lips, and an extra teeny star drawn next to the usual one by my left eye. Not that I have anyone in particular to impress.

I turn to grab my coat from the doorknob and catch sight of my newest and most prized possession, proudly displayed on my dresser. A framed head shot of Mr. Gene Kelly, *autographed*.

A few days after Christmas, the girls and I held a special meeting of Teens for Classic Movies, which turned out to be just Angela, Tiffany, Sarah, and me—I guess we scared the other two potentials away last month. We watched *White Christmas* while feasting on sugar cookies and drinking through an entire box of hot chocolate mix, then exchanged our meager gifts. We had set the limit at ten bucks each, because, well, we're broke, but they all chipped in and had Mrs. Morales help them find a legit autographed picture, just for me.

"Maddie!" Rider calls from down the hall. "You ready to walk over to the party?"

"One minute!"

I take Gene's photo out of the frame and gently smooth my hand over the surface. Chills run through me at the realization that Gene touched this very piece of paper as he signed his name in blue ink next to his own smiling black-and-white face. My eyes well up and threaten to spill over, but not because of that. Because I don't know how I got so lucky to find a group of friends who actually *get* me.

The type of New Year's Eve party I want to host one day will be a classically formal affair like in the old movies. The girls will wear fancy dresses with long white gloves, the guys will wear tuxes, we'll drink pop out of champagne flutes, eat a delectable catered dinner served by a waitstaff, and everyone will dance! Or maybe a themed party, the kind of extravagant fling Jay Gatsby would throw, and we could do the Charleston out on the lawn until the wee hours of the morning.

I told Angela my ideas when she was in planning mode, but she looked at me like I was crazy and said no one would ever come to anything like that. Normal teenagers want to wear jeans and eat bagel pizza bites and taquitos. So it's Angela's own fault she's stuck in the kitchen all night heating up frozen snacks and keeping the chip bowls full while Sarah and I hang out with everyone else, listening to ski-trip stories and watching the festivities in New York on TV.

Sarah and I load our plates with another round of cookies and head back to the living room, when I catch sight of the one girl who could turn my holiday sour.

"Who invited her?" I ask Sarah quietly as we watch Rica waltz in the front door and breeze past us, heading straight for the kitchen.

"Oh. Yeah. About that." Sarah takes a sip of cider from her green plastic cup. "Ryan sort of told Rica about it—"

"And why would your otherwise flawless boyfriend do such a thing?"

"—accidentally. At the wrap party for *Barefoot in the Park* the other week."

We move a few steps to the side so we can see Rica filling her plates with veggies, chips, and dip.

"What do you mean, 'accidentally'? How does that sort of thing just come up *accidentally?*"

"I don't know. We were all talking about holiday plans and vacations and who was having New Year's parties. It just came out. Maybe she thought she was invited."

"She's going to spoil the festive mood," I say. "It's one thing to see her at school, but here in my happy place? I just can't forget that Rica practically drugged me to beat me at an audition and then made a big deal, in front of who knows how many people, that the only guy I've ever loved is *dead*! What if I really had a boyfriend who died in some tragically tragic way?"

"She thought you *did*," Sarah says, biting the head off a gingerbread man.

"Exactly." I eat the arms off my own.

"Though once upon a time I thought you did too," she reminds me.

"I'm sorry about that," I say, body tensing. "I just didn't know how to explain it without sounding insane. It was too soon."

She laughs and my worry melts. "I get you more than you think I do."

"I know." I smile, truly grateful I can be myself with her. "And you would never have used it against me like Rica did. I mean, they don't get much more vile than that."

"Word. I'm surprised she's never slipped me a strawberry just to watch me break out in hives."

"Now that would just be evil." I swallow the last of my eggnog and shudder at the strong kick of nutmeg that settled on the bottom. "Really, though, we shouldn't let her bother us so much. We can't let her win by ruining our New Year's."

"Oh, she bothers me plenty," Sarah snorts. "You didn't have to direct the play that the tricky little witch and my boyfriend were in together. And the *kissing*. Don't even get me started on how hard *that* was to watch day after day."

I rip the head off my cookie too, thinking of all those actors you hear about who fall in love with their costars and wreck seemingly perfect marriages. "You're a true professional."

She blinks a few times. "I suddenly feel the need to find Ryan and hug him." And with that, she disappears into the crowded room.

I spot Rider in the kitchen, surrounded by girls, piling a bunch of cookies on a plate. All the girls are laughing that fake *Don't you think I'm awesome?* laugh. If I'm forced to witness the puffing out of chests and the fluffing of feathers over my brother, I might go sit outside by the fire pit with the adults. At least he's not following me around like a hawk.

The sharp feedback from a microphone makes me jump, and I turn to see Jesse and Red setting up a karaoke machine in the living room, between the fireplace and the Christmas tree. A row of girls including Rica are crammed next to each other on the couch, reading through the song selection.

"Are you actually going to sing?" I ask when I reach Jesse. My heart trills at the possibility.

He laughs. "Uh . . . my relationship with this machine ends as soon as I plug it in."

"Oh, come on," I prod. "What's it going to take to get you behind a mic? Money? Liquor?"

I've inadvertently drawn the attention of half the room, and laughter rings out all around us. Rica pops up from the couch and stands maybe a foot away from Jesse, already trying to control the show.

"Jesse's a great singer," she announces to her audience, bubbly and peppy like she's eaten nothing but sugar cookies all day. "A few years ago, we sang together at a school function. We should sing a duet, Jesse! Or I can just sing harmonies! Which one do you want to do?"

My insides twist. He sang with *her*?

He shakes his head. "That was in sixth grade. Our whole class sang together. For Grandparents' Day. And it was required."

My mouth explodes in one of those laughs I roll my eyes at, but who could help it?

The tips of her cheeks darken. "Well, I was standing next to him," she continues, talking about him instead of with him. "He must have, like, perfect pitch or something. I swear he can do anything." She turns to him. "Come on, let's sing for everyone."

This whole scene she's making probably shouldn't surprise me, but it does.

"I *can* do anything," Jesse says, snapping one of the microphones into its stand. "But I'm not singing with you."

Red fumbles with the second microphone stand, biting back laughter.

"Why don't *you* sing something?" Jesse asks.

I assume he's suggesting Rica perform a solo, until I realize he's looking at me. I'm about to protest, insisting that I haven't had time to prepare anything, yet fully intending to give in if I find something on the song list worth performing. But Rica's not done with her audience.

"Maddie doesn't have the right voice for lead." Always concerned with appearance, she tucks a strand of her sleek raven hair behind an ear. "She's just an alto, a chorus-type. Don't embarrass the poor girl."

A few hesitant chuckles and murmurs reach my ears. I start to hug my stomach but force my arms to my sides. I will not let her get to me. She can't win.

I open my mouth to ask how she even knows I'm *just an alto* when she reads my mind.

"I was there," she says. "For your audition at the playhouse."

"How—"

"Open audition. I was in the back. I never miss a chance to scope out the competition." Her silver bracelet jingles as she adjusts her skirt. "But it was just as I thought from the first time I saw you try out for the school play." She pauses. "I'm not threatened by you."

As much as I'd like to laugh in her face, I'm suddenly self-conscious and my eyes automatically zip to Jesse, his left eyebrow slightly raised as he studies Rica.

Sarah's by my side in an instant. "The fact that you just had to make another big speech to put her down in front of everyone sure makes it sound like you *are* threatened."

I want to clap. How is this the same girl who Rica walked all over a mere handful of months ago? Maybe Sarah got used to telling Rica what to do when she directed the play. My chest swells with pride, and I've almost forgotten that all of this was inspired by ugly words about me.

"How dare you?" Rica says in irritation. "You're not allowed to talk to me like that."

Sarah noticeably shrinks back. *Come on*, I mentally encourage. *Don't let her win.* But the moment is over, Sarah's brief surge of gumption used up.

"I guess I'll go first, then," Rica says, taking the microphone and standing front and center near the fireplace. She looks to Jesse like he's in charge of the karaoke machine. "I'm going to sing—"

"Find it yourself," Jesse growls. And without warning, he grabs my hand and weaves me between our classmates, his teammates, my distracted brother and his fan club, through the kitchen, and past Angela, with her mouth agape, and out the back door into the night.

"Hop on," Jesse says over the engine of the four-wheeler.

I glance around, and besides the glow from the fire pit closer to the house, I can't see much. "Where are we going?"

"Just for a ride. I like riding at night, it's . . . relaxing."

"Okay. . . ." I straddle the seat behind him. "Still no helmet, huh? What if we plummet into a ravine or something?"

"We won't. Trust me."

"You're so sure of yourself all the time."

"Uh, I'm sure we're not going to plummet into a ravine because there are no ravines to plummet into. Satisfied?"

He takes off before I can answer, and I clamp my hands on his waist to keep from doing a backflip. We follow the worn path into tall grasses and through the woods until we reach the creek where I saw my first deer. Everything's brown and dead, so this ride is sneeze-free, and it's somewhat exhilarating pulling the chilled air into my lungs. I could stand it to be colder, but I'm pleased by the numbness of my cheeks and my watering eyes. Makes me feel alive.

We come to a stop and I remove my hands from Jesse's sides, following him in the light of the nearly full moon closer to the edge of the water. What was a mere trickle a few months ago is now a fast-moving stream.

I lower myself to the crispy grass next to him, empowered by the darkness and our inability to completely see each other. "You know, people are probably thinking we came out here so you could mend my wounded pride with your lips." He doesn't respond, so I hug my knees to my chest for something to do. "Make-out therapy," I add with a laugh to make sure he knows I'm joking—mostly.

He stretches his legs out, crossing one boot over the other. "Maybe we did," he says with what I hope is a hint of humor.

My stomach tightens, and my pulse pounds in my ears. I might be shaking. But I'm not the nervous type. I don't get anxious about stuff. What's happening to me?

"Seriously." I nudge him with my elbow to lighten the mood. "What—"

"I just wanted to talk to you," he says, too quietly for me to be sure if I heard him right. "Away from everyone else. When I'm not your chauffeur or dance teacher."

I search for his face in the bluish light and follow the line of his profile down the ridge of his nose, stopping at the pair of lips I remember all too well on mine.

"You want to t-talk?" I ask through chattering teeth, inwardly cursing my body for betraying me.

Leaves rustle in the woods off to the right and I gasp, reaching out for Jesse and pulling myself closer to him at the same time.

"Scared?" he whispers through a laugh, giving my arm a squeeze.

He rifles through a bag he brought with us and clicks on a flashlight. A pair of eyes glow green from the face of a giant, grayish rodent thing, maybe twenty feet away. I scoot a hair closer to Jesse, better lining him up between me and the creature.

"Possum," he says as if I should have known, stowing the flashlight back in the bag.

"Possum. Right." I keep an eye in its direction in case it charges us. "Aren't those mean?"

"They can be. But if you ignore it, it'll act like it's dead or sneak off. Don't worry. I won't let it drag you away."

"You're just my hero tonight, aren't you?" I relax my hold on his arm, and he surprises me by taking my hand again. I clear my throat to fill the silence. "Really, though, thank you for getting me out of there."

"Okay," he says in a rushed way like he's changing the subject, and I have no clue where it's going. He takes a deep breath before continuing. "I'm trying to say this without sounding stupid, so don't freak out or anything."

"Uh, I can't make any promises. I mean, you did bring me out into the middle of the forest in the middle of the night."

"Maddie," he says, clearly dismissing my nervous rambling. He twists his upper body to look at me, tugging my arm, so I do the same. "I keep thinking about that kiss."

"Kiss?" I repeat, even though my mind was already replaying it before he said anything.

"Ever since the hayride, every time I see you, I have no idea what to say, how to act. I always feel like I say the wrong things."

My eyes widen as my brain struggles to absorb his fast-flying words that make no sense. He can't really mean that he can't stop thinking about *me*. He just likes kissing; who doesn't? I liked it so much I tried kissing *Brian* just to feel that again. But it was nothing like Jesse's kiss. With Jesse it was . . . like dancing.

I swallow, which makes a sound I fear is louder than the possum, and my teeth resume their chattering. Maybe I'm getting sick. Yes, that must be it.

"W-well," I sputter, "you usually act like your normal, overconfident self. I wouldn't worry too much."

"Tell me you think about it, too." He pauses, and a few fireworks whistle in the distance. "That you think about me."

"Do I think about how you stole my first kiss?" I watch his eyes as they stare out over the water, and instantly regret bringing it up again. I kissed him back. He didn't steal anything.

"I kissed you because I wanted to. And because I thought maybe you did, too." His tone is a mix of sadness and defensiveness.

For once, I'm not sure what to say, so I don't say anything.

Reaching toward me with his free hand, he grazes a finger over the stars on my cheek. "The first day I saw you, you had one of these on. I didn't really get it."

"Oh. Well, this lady in one of my favorite movies wears one for a few scenes." I memorize the feel of his touch as he glides his finger along my jaw before placing his hand on the ground to hold himself up. "I don't know. I guess I've just always liked it."

"You and your old movies," he snickers. "Angela told me about that girly club y'all have going."

"We'd let you come, if you wanted. It's not like a girls-only thing. It just turned out that way." I sit up straighter, hopeful. "Do you like old movies at all?"

"Nah." He shakes his head and my shoulders fall slightly. "But I like that you like them."

The hand clasping mine tightens. For the first time, I notice that his hand is cold, and there's a slight tremble. I tug my sleeve down to cover us both before it registers that he might be just as nervous as I am. That jittery, shaky nervous I've maybe experienced a handful of times in my life when I've had too much caffeine or when I met two Tony Award winners at a benefit. Is this what it feels like . . . when you *like* someone . . . in real life?

"I think about you all the time," I finally admit, allowing myself to smile when I see a grin take over his pretty face.

Jesse's phone sings out from his pocket.

"Aagh," he grunts, digging it out.

He squints in the brightness from the screen, and my heart does a little flip watching the corner of his mouth hitch up. How is he so gorgeous, sitting here with me, in the dark, talking about kissing?

"Who is it?" I ask. "Are they wondering where we went?" I almost pull out my phone to check, but I want to live on this perfect, peaceful stage just a bit longer.

"No one."

And my stomach drops. "This isn't a very good start to . . . whatever this is"—I wave my hands between us—"if you're already lying to me."

Jesse rolls his eyes and turns the phone toward me. "Not lying. Alarm. I set it so we'd know when it's midnight."

"Oh," I say, looking up to the sky as if I might be able to see the New Year. "It's already here? I don't feel any different."

"That's because it's eleven fifty-nine." He laughs and rummages through the bag again. I can't quite make out what he's doing until the flame from a lighter appears and he touches something to it to catch.

"Sparklers!" I exclaim as they spit out bright white streaks of light.

We stand, each holding a sparkler out over the creek, hand in hand. I wave it through the air and watch the fire travel down the stick, then meet Jesse's gaze just before the flames fizzle out. He checks his phone before pocketing it again and takes a step toward me, our hips just brushing against each other.

"Five," he says. "Four."

"Three," I join in.

"Two," we whisper.

Fireworks and firecrackers *pop* and *boom*, near and far. Jesse tosses our burned-out sparklers to the ground and sneaks a hand around to my back, pulling me even closer. He touches his forehead to mine and I swallow, my chin slowly tugging itself up until our noses slide past each other. Until my lips find the pair they've been dreaming about.

Until a New Year has begun and I feel completely different.

CHAPTER TWENTY-FIVE

It's one thirty in the morning by the time I'm tired enough to try falling asleep. I planned on spending the night with Angela, but it wasn't really an option anymore after Jesse and I resurfaced from our adventure in the woods with dry, red lips long after the rest of the party guests had gone home, including Rider. Angela took one look at us and stalked upstairs. Jesse brought me home on the four-wheeler, and we may or may not have made out on the porch for ten more minutes before my dad flicked on the front light.

I curl up in my hot-pink flannel pj's under my comforter and an extra blanket, colder than usual from the nervous excitement still coursing through me. I've completely lost my mind. I didn't even brush my teeth. Didn't want to lose the taste of him, not while I'm still convincing myself it's real. That he might be *my Jesse* after all.

Cradling my phone in my hands, I stare at the black screen, waiting for a text, a call, something. Some sign I'm more than just a mouth to kiss.

My eyes are begging me to close them, and I nearly break down and text him myself, when the phone vibrates.

Jesse: Happy New Year.
Me: Yes it is.
Jesse: Feel different now?
Me: How did you know?
Jesse: Because I do.

My cheeks hurt from smiling so hard.

Me: I guess we should talk about what happened.

My phone buzzes with an incoming call.

"I didn't mean right now." I pull the comforter over my head for one more sound barrier.

"You want me to hang up?" Jesse says, matching my near whisper.

"No!"

"Good." He laughs, his breath sounding like wind through the phone, and I imagine he's hiding under his covers, too. "So what do you want to talk about?"

I swallow hard, hoping I'm not about to jinx anything. "You kissed me."

"I remember."

"So . . . what's that mean? Like, for tomorrow?"

"Today is tomorrow."

"Oh. Yeah. So what does it mean for us today? Right now?"

"Right now I know that you're adorable and funny and all I want to do is walk back across the street and kiss you again."

I sit up, the blankets tenting around me. "Really?"

"You have no idea."

I keep myself from babbling about how inexperienced I am in the kissing department, and from secretly fishing for compliments and reassurance that I caught on quickly. He wants to kiss me again, so I must have done something right. Jesse Morales found my kissing ability worthy of seconds.

"What are you doing tomorrow?" he asks through a yawn.

"You mean today."

"Yes, today." I can tell he's smiling now too. "What do you want to do?"

I don't even have to think about it. "I want to dance. With you."

The rest of the holiday break is filled with overeating, overdancing, and overkissing. Well, I doubt there's such a thing as overkissing. I hope I never get used to the floaty, dreamy way Jesse's kisses make me feel. I usually dread the first day back to school every January, but this year I'm coming back with a boyfriend I can hold hands with in the hallways, steal glances at in class, and slip notes to through the little vent in his locker. And it's winter so I can wear his letterman jacket and he can carry my books and it will be like that *Happy Days* show all over again.

Angela's been moody since the awkward conversation the other day when I finally told her about my feelings, so she's not much help when I face the onslaught of girls I offend just by walking through the school entrance. Apparently, the kiss at the Halloween party didn't warrant much backlash since nothing came of it—I'm a little suspicious of how often Jesse made out with girls, not that I really want to know—but now that he's officially off the market, I'm not exactly getting voted "Most Liked" girl in school. I mean, I knew he was popular, but girls I don't remember ever seeing before go out of their way to glare at me as I pass by, or to comment to each other on my state of unfortunate normalness, plenty loud enough for me to hear.

It's so ridiculous I can't even be annoyed. Jesse likes *me*. So. I win.

I haven't talked to Brian since the failed double date that pushed our relationship into the friend zone for all time, so I'm surprised when he takes the seat next to me in theatre class.

"How was the break?" he asks, no hint of negativity in his voice.

I kick my backpack under my chair for a distraction, mentally processing how in the span of just a couple weeks I could go from kissing him in the back of a movie theatre to having a legit boyfriend.

"Um. Good. It was good. Yours?" Oh, if I were a blusher, I'd be in so much trouble right now.

"Mine rocked," he says, fidgeting like he's anxious about something. "Get anything cool for Christmas?"

Maybe he's beating around the bush? Afraid to ask about Jesse?

"Well, I didn't get a car." I huff and he makes a sympathetic grunt. "Let's see. Got some classic DVDs I've been wanting. And some shoe money." I peek at his highlighter-yellow sneakers. "Though I doubt I'll be shopping where you go."

"You have to order these puppies," he says through a laugh. He clears his throat and his tone suddenly shifts. "I hear you had a boyfriend under your tree. You and Jesse, huh?"

I swallow and nod, powerless to stop the smile that takes over my face.

"Never saw that coming," he says with pure sarcasm.

I cross my arms. "I don't know why you and Sarah both seem to thi—"

He holds up his hand to stop me, smiling softly. "You don't have to defend yourself to me." His smile grows. "And actually . . . I wanted to talk to you about something. I—I sort of met someone."

I straighten and turn to fully face him. "What? Where? Who?"

"Her name's Kristi." He slides a hand through his coppery hair, long overdue for a trim. "I went to Colorado to visit my aunt and uncle with my family, you know, for Christmas, and me and my cousin drove up to Winter Park to go skiing for a couple days."

I'm simultaneously thrilled for him and worried. I don't see how meeting someone in another state has a good outcome. After I moved down here from Illinois, I couldn't even hang on to the friends I'd seen every day.

"We took a half-day class," he continues, "for people who haven't skied in a while and need a refresher, and there she was. She literally fell into my arms."

"And you gazed into each other's eyes and it was love at first sight," I tease in a dreamy voice.

He looks to the ground with a sheepish grin. "Anyway, we've talked every day since. She lives outside Dallas, so it shouldn't be too hard to see her on weekends."

Sarah and Ryan take the empty seats on the other side of Brian.

"So what are we talking about?" Sarah asks with a sly little wink directed to me.

"Brian was just telling me about . . . Kristi, was it?"

"Oh, blargh. Heard this story twice already," Sarah teases before abandoning us for a conversation with Ryan instead.

"So," I say, looking back at Brian. "You're serious about this? The long-distance thing?"

"Yeah, I think so. I mean, we really hit it off. She's so cool too. She's not into theatre or anything, but she's really good at art. She even drew the tattoo she's going to get on her eighteenth birthday. And she's some kind of lacrosse star. Have you ever seen a lacrosse game?" He peers at me out of the corner of his eye, and I shake my head. "It's hot."

Ryan calls over his shoulder, "It's hot." He turns back to Sarah, who punches him in the arm.

I don't like Brian like that, I don't, but I can't help feeling this protective thing grow between us. Like I don't have enough on my mind already.

He must see the skepticism on my face, because he says, "This isn't weird, is it? I mean, we're friends."

"We're definitely friends. Sealed with a kiss even."

We both laugh at that, and Mrs. Morales cuts us off by welcoming the class to a new semester. She looks energetic and ready for the New Year, sporting a classy ensemble of brown dress slacks and a fitted blouse, accented with the same chunky turquoise necklace she wore when I first met her in the street between our houses. Who knew back then that I'd be making out with her son a few short months later?

I fight my smile and force myself to pay attention to what she's saying.

"This spring, we're going to do a variety show," she announces. "A talent show of sorts, complete with prizes."

Excitement races through me, but most of the class groans and Rica's hand shoots straight up, the tips of her fingers wiggling. Mrs. Morales sighs but motions for her to speak.

"But we always do a big spring musical," Rica whines.

"Well, we're changing it up this year. Opening it to more students whose talents might not be within the world of musical theatre," she explains.

"That's a fabulous idea," I offer, and she winks at me.

Of course Rica doesn't want anyone's talent in the spotlight but her own. "Why can't we do the talent show separately?"

"For starters, there's a budget issue. Resources are—"

"My friend's high school is doing *Sweeney Todd* next month," Rica continues, sitting so close to the edge of her seat I find myself wishing she'd fall off and smash her shapely little nose on the floor. "You could talk to them about what they're doing to raise money. Like, you know how Sweeney kills people with his razor and the lady downstairs makes meat pies out of the bodies? Well, they're going to sell these tiny pies at intermission along w—"

"Thank you, Rica." Mrs. Morales stops her, not a second too soon. "I'm well informed about what the other schools nearby are working on."

Brian leans close to me and whispers, "That musical sounds *awesome*. We should do it next year."

I scrunch up my face. "It sounds abhorrent."

He rolls his eyes and bumps my leg with his knee. "Don't be so stuck up."

Brian and I are lost in our own joke world for only a minute, but it's enough that I miss the office assistant slipping into the room and pulling Mrs. Morales aside. They chat briefly, and then Mrs. Morales leaves her by the door and approaches . . . me?

"Maddie," she says quietly, her voice smooth, calm. "Will you take your things with you and go with Miss Foley to the office?"

My pulse pounds in my ears as my mind runs through various scenarios. Am I in trouble? Not likely. Did something happen to Rider? To Ma? Dad?

I open my mouth to ask what this is about, but Brian speaks up first.

"Should I go with her?" Brian asks, and his concern sends an extra wave of anxiety through me.

Mrs. Morales must've nodded or something, because in an instant Brian has his backpack on and he hoists mine over a shoulder and we're sweeping out the door in a fog.

"What's going on?" I ask once we're in the hallway.

"Everything's okay," Miss Foley's quick to say, but I don't relax. She leads us toward the front of the school. "I've got your father on the office phone. This way."

"What? Why?" I ask in a panic. "What's going on?"

"You just need to talk with him, sweetheart."

Brian shifts my bag to his other shoulder and clasps my hand. I squeeze it like I'll disappear if I don't hold on to something. I don't know what's going on, but at this moment I'm so grateful for his friendship.

CHAPTER TWENTY-SIX

Mom went into premature labor. Doctors are doing what they can to stop it. Everything will be fine.

Everything will be fine.

Brian offers to give me a ride to the hospital, and I don't hesitate. The drive is short, but it feels like an eternity with all the doubt clawing through my head.

Fear.

What if Ma's life is in danger?

Anger.

Don't they know what causes pregnancy in the first place?

Worry.

What about the baby?

Anger.

They're so old!

Fear.

What am I going to do if she dies? If they both die . . . ?

There's so much I want to say to my parents, want to yell. It's all bubbling and mixing together in my stomach, leaving a sour taste in my mouth.

But the sourness dissolves into sympathy as soon as I see my mom asleep in the hospital bed, connected to tubes and flashing monitors and machines that beep. Dad leaves the room so we can be alone and I take slow steps toward her until I'm close enough to grab her hand, but I don't want to wake her. My eyes study everything about her, from her messy hair to the extra creases near her eyes. I've never noticed before how naked her ears look without the small diamond studs Dad gave her that she always wears.

Suddenly I'm worried about the earrings. Where are they? Did someone take them off her?

In a tizzy, I scan the bedside table for them, simultaneously searching my recent memories to figure out if she's even had them on lately. But I've been so annoyed with all the pregnancy stuff I didn't want to know about—heightened sense of smell, nose-bleeds, bigger boobs—that I've spent most of my time at home *not* looking at her. Not even being in the same room with her.

What if something happens to her and I've missed all that time by being angry just because they're having a baby at an unusual age? What if—

"Oh. Maddie. You didn't have to come here." Ma's voice is quiet. She reaches a hand out for me, then winces at the tug from the IV in her arm.

I clasp her hand, and she squeezes with more strength than I thought she'd have right now. All my acting experience fails me as I try to stay strong for her. I would hate for her to think of the worry on my face as a reflection of how she looks.

"How are you feeling?" I finally manage to ask.

"Much better now." She presses a button on a clunky remote and the head of the bed buzzes as it lifts her into an almost sitting position. The machine hooked up to her beeps, but she ignores it.

Too many sounds. Too many blinkies. Too many wires.

"Dad said you're going to have to be on bed rest or something?"

"They just want me to take it easy, so I'll have to stay home and relax. I can still walk around when I need to; it's not like I'm going to need a bedpan or anything. Yet, at least," she adds with a laugh that I struggle to return.

I stare at the gray floor and try to imagine lying in bed for two months. Not being able to go anywhere, getting up only to pee or eat meals. I shudder.

"I may need to borrow from your extensive movie collection," she says. "So all your boyfriends can sing to me while you're at school and your dad's at work."

"Of course you can watch them." Despite the smile on my face, my bottom lip trembles. "You paid for most of them, anyway." I glance at the ceiling to keep my eyes from welling over.

"Hey," she says, pulling me closer, "none of that. I'm fine, the baby's fine."

"Why did this happen? What's wrong?"

"Nothing's wrong. They're not always sure why things like this happen, sweetheart. Maybe he was just a little anxious to get here, that's all. But they stopped it in time, and he can cook in there a while longer."

"Did you find out for sure it's a boy?" I ask, tears dripping down my cheeks through silent laughter at my own ridiculousness.

She shakes her head, then shifts away from me so there's space on the edge of the bed. "Come here."

Careful not to disconnect her from any tubes or cords, I finagle myself to lie next to her and rest my head on her shoulder. As soon as both of her arms are around me, the tears really start to flow.

"I'm sorry," I say, barely audible.

"Shhh," she coos like the wonderful mother she's always been to me.

Suddenly I'm six years old, being pacified after a nightmare or during a thunderstorm, or when Dad's out of town and my little brain doesn't understand why I can't see him.

I'm basically whimpering into her neck. "I've been such a brat. So horrible to you. And Dad. I don't know how you even put up with me ignoring you like I have. That's not me. It's not us, not the way we are."

Stroking my arm, she says, "It hasn't been easy, I'm not going to lie, but I understand. I really do. You're already dealing with being a teenager, which isn't always a walk in the park. Then we uproot you to a new state, new school, where you have to make new friends. You started a job, you got a part in a musical you have to practice for nearly every day. Then there's the new boyfriend." I can feel her smile at that. "Throw a pregnant mom into the mix . . ."

"And you get one certifiable hot mess," I finish, sniffling and swiping at my eyes.

She laughs. "Ah, but you're *my* hot mess. And I love you."

"I love you, too," I choke out.

"My girls," Dad's voice calls from behind me. He leans down and kisses each of us on the head. "Everyone all right here?"

"We're perfect," Ma answers, taking her turn to kiss my forehead.

There's a brief moment of silence where I imagine them exchanging a look. Maybe I've earned back the one that says *We have such a great kid, why can't everyone be more like her?* I hope so.

"You have a visitor," Dad says.

"What?" Ma asks, tensing and reaching for her hair.

"Not you," he says, then lays a hand on my shoulder. "Jesse's in the waiting room. He said he could take you home when you're ready."

Jesse. I completely forgot to text him to let him know where I'd be when he got out of practice. Tingles spread through me at the thought of him finding me anyway.

"I'm going to stay here with your mom tonight," Dad says.

"You'll be okay without us?" Ma asks me as I slide off the bed and wrap my arms around Dad's middle. "Maybe you could stay with Angela? I can call Sherri and see if it's okay."

"I'm sure it'll be fine," I say. "I'll take care of it. You just rest."

They promise they'll be home tomorrow and remind me I can call to check in anytime. After a final round of hugs, reassurances, and I-love-yous, I grab my backpack and turn to leave.

"I like that boy," I hear Dad say to Ma before the door closes. "Very respectful."

Some girls might not appreciate parental approval of their boyfriends, but I find myself stretching taller, proud that my dad trusts my judgment.

I find Jesse with his butt balanced on the outer edge of his chair, head leaning back on the top of the backrest, staring at the ceiling, hands folded over his stomach, legs spread wide, one of them bouncing like crazy. He's exchanged his cleats for sneakers, but it occurs to me this is the first time I've seen him in baseball attire. It's not an official uniform, though he looks awfully adorable wearing white socks streaked with clay and pulled up to his knees, dark blue athletic shorts that give me a glimpse of his bare thighs, which have been hiding since warmer weather, and a white, long-sleeve T-shirt with "Fernwood Panthers Varsity Baseball" printed in blue across the chest.

I walk over to him and kick the shoe of his bouncing leg. "Nervous about something?"

He startles and springs to his feet before pulling me into a hug and resting his head on top of mine.

"You okay?" he asks in my ear.

"I'm okay." His shirt's damp against my face, and I inhale the lingering odor of sweat. "Smells like you had a good practice."

"It was fine." His laugh blows a breeze through my hair. "How's your mom? Your dad told me a little bit, but I felt weird asking too many questions." He takes a step back to look at me.

"I think everything's fine now." My eyebrows tense. "How did you know I was here, anyway?"

Jesse clears his throat and links arms with me, turning us toward the exit. "Brian called me."

"Oh. Wow." I realize I never said good-bye to Brian. I don't even remember when he left. "That was nice of him."

"He also said you were zombie-ish and thought I might want to come up here to be with you."

I laugh. Zombie-ish. "Of course he did."

Jesse opens the passenger door of his truck and I climb in, letting my bag thud to the floorboard.

He slides his hands around my waist and leans against my seat. "You tell me what you want to do. We can go somewhere to eat, go home, drive around. What do you need?"

My heart warms as I stare into his green eyes. "Home, maybe? I don't know. I'm not sure I could eat anything right now. Oh, but you're probably starving, aren't you? We can go somewhere if you want."

"Don't worry about me, I'll find something at the house."

I take a deep breath and slouch into the seat back. "I'm really glad you came here for me." My chin threatens to quiver and I close my eyes tightly, as if shutting out one of the senses will keep me from falling apart.

He doesn't reply, only touches his lips to my temple ever so gently, then closes the door.

CHAPTER TWENTY-SEVEN

Angela's in her room doing homework, Elise has been tucked in and kissed by all of us, Mrs. Morales is in the TV room catching up on the soap operas she recorded today, and Mr. Morales left this morning for the Middle East or somewhere on a business trip. Jesse reheats dinner for himself, and I stare out the kitchen window into the blackness of the backyard.

My mind zips back to the night I first learned I was getting a sibling, and how good I felt jumping out my shock on the trampoline. I can't see it, but I know it's out there, waiting for me, calling to me.

"Mind if I go jump while you eat?" I ask Jesse as I head for the door.

He laughs. "Want me to turn the lights on for you?"

I shake my head. "I think the moon's bright enough."

"Okay." He sits at the breakfast table with a plate of an unidentifiable cheesy, spicy-smelling mess. Another one of his mom's cooking experiments. "I'll come find you when I'm done."

Take your time, I almost tell him. The promise of being alone for even just a few minutes rushes me out the door, across the flagstone, through the grass, and up the cold miniature ladder. I hear the crinkle of dead leaves break apart under my feet as I begin to bounce, and soon there's nearly a pile of them in the middle. I make it a game, trying to manipulate which way the leaves go with my jumps, but they dance around me as they please. I dance with them, flying high, kicking, doing splits in the air, bouncing off my back over and over until I can't push myself upright.

Exhausted, I lie among the leaves and catch my breath, my hair fanning all around me. I stare up between the silhouettes of the tree branches to the hundreds of tiny dots of light that sparkle against the black sky. My eyes water and my throat stings but I focus on the stars and force my worry aside.

She's going to be fine. The baby will be fine.

We'll all be fine.

A tear slips down the side of my face despite my inner pep talk, just as someone comes outside through the back door. Footsteps grow closer, and soon Jesse's crawling toward me on his hands and knees. He flips over onto his back in a practiced, springy motion and lays his head on my stomach like it's a pillow. Little fluttering things awaken underneath him, and I relish the electricity that spreads through me and dries the tears I'm thankful it's too dark for him to see.

"When Angela and I were little," Jesse says through a yawn, "we'd shine flashlights at the stars. We swore it made them brighter."

I giggle, picturing a miniature Jesse lying out here on the trampoline with a flashlight aimed at the sky. I reach for his hair, but stop myself just before my fingers dive in. It feels like something I should be allowed to do now, especially since I can kiss him anytime I want, but it's so new.

"The sky doesn't look like this back home," I say as I start slow, brushing a palm over the ends of his hair. "We always lived too close to the city. I could only ever really see the brightest few."

"I'll miss nights like this when I live in a big city," he says, taking me off guard. We haven't really discussed future plans yet. "One day."

"Where do you want to go?"

"Some of the guys want to go to the University of Texas, which is in Austin, so I'm considering trying to play for them, or maybe the Aggies. I'm also thinking about LSU or North Carolina. This season I should be able to line some things up, talk to some scouts. See what my options are."

"I have an option for you," I say, getting a bit braver with his hair and lightly massaging his scalp. "You could study theatre. With me."

"Uh, don't think so." He laughs. "That's not gonna get me on a pro team."

I don't feel like igniting an argument tonight, so I drop it, indulging him with his professional baseball fantasy. "Fine, fine. What team do you want to play for?"

An owl hoots from somewhere in the trees as he considers my question.

"It's not really something you choose, but if I played for the Astros I could live close to my family. Though it might be fun to go somewhere really far away, like Boston."

Pretty far from here, but relatively close to New York, where I hope to be.

"Boston. Is that the Red Sox?"

He turns his head toward me, the movement tickling my stomach. "I'm surprised you know that."

"It's one of the few I do know," I admit. "In Chicago we have the White Sox, right? Well, I remember getting confused when I first heard about the Red Sox. I thought Chicago's team had to change their name for some reason, so I imagined that the person who washed the uniforms accidentally put something red in with all their white socks. Only when I got older and learned how to do laundry myself did I figure out it would have only made them pink anyway."

Jesse laughs so hard he starts coughing and has to sit up. When he composes himself, he leans over me, balancing on his elbows on either side of my head.

"Just when I thought you couldn't get any cuter."

I start to smile but he crushes his mouth to mine. All my emotions from the day fill my head in a rush and I grab his hair by the fistful, yanking him down to me so hard he falls onto my chest, nearly knocking the wind out of me. But he's still not close enough.

He slides a hand down my torso and hooks it on my waist, then pulls me against him, leaning back at the same time until we're both on our sides, facing each other. The stretchy fabric underneath bounces us gently. I palm his neck and pull him closer, our lips parting again and again, the lengths of our bodies pressed together. He slips his ankle between my calves, and I shiver as his fingers make contact with the bare skin just above my jeans. I expect his hand to wander, exploring my back, but he moves to comb his fingers through my long hair.

"I like that boy. Very respectful."

And my mind ruins everything when I remember I'm spending the night here, and now I'm wondering if my parents were thinking straight enough to realize they suggested I sleep under the same roof as my new boyfriend.

Feigning the need to come up for air, I let my kisses travel toward his cheek, then to his scar. I touch it lightly with a fingertip. "How'd you get that?" I ask in a whisper so as not to disrupt the calm of the night.

"Chicken pox," he answers quietly. "I was six and remember being very itchy."

"Aww, poor little thing."

I hug him for a moment before rolling myself onto my back and releasing a few breathy laughs. Lying side by side, my head resting on Jesse's arm, we listen to the quiet of the night, watching a series of fast-moving clouds hide the moon.

In my sleepy haze, I think about the two sides of Jesse. The confident jock with a fan club and dreams of a sports career, next to the secret dancer who moves with strength and grace and doesn't share it with anyone. Except me.

I smile in the darkness, thankful to be in on his most guarded secret. Happy he chooses to dance with *me*.

* * *

After a few texts back and forth with Dad to say good night, I trudge upstairs and get ready for bed, then open the door to Angela's room, relieved to see she's still awake. I didn't want her thinking I slept in another room and snuck in just before the alarm went off in the morning or something. Though seeing her after she knows I just kissed Jesse is only slightly less awkward.

"Hey," she says from her usual side of the bed, flipping through an issue of *People*.

"Hey. What's the latest?" I ask, nodding toward the magazine.

"Nothing I believe," she says, tossing it aside.

"Then why read it?"

She shrugs. "Better than homework."

I slide into bed next to her and adjust the pillow so it's as flat as possible. "I always forget to bring my memory-foam pillow over here. I don't know how you sleep on these awful things."

"Did you brush your teeth?" Angela randomly asks. "Because I wouldn't want any of Jesse's cooties crawling over here."

"Cooties?" I let a cautious laugh escape. "I brushed. We're good."

She clicks off the lamp and settles into the sheets. My eyes adjust to the pale blue of the plug-in night-light near the door and I stare at the posters on her walls. Young new actors and musicians I'm unfamiliar with keep watch over us, their "sexy" smiles taking on a more sinister if not perverted vibe in the dimness. I much prefer my classic posters over these, but I shiver when I think of sleeping in my own house alone all night, knowing my parents are at the hospital with the beeps and the blinks.

"So, I've been wondering," I begin, too curious to fall asleep yet. "Are *we* good? You and me?"

"What do you mean?"

"With Jesse and everything. I know you were really against it. I mean, you even encouraged me to go on a date with *Brian*. Epic disaster."

"Hey! Y'all are still friends, so don't blame me for the kiss of nothingness."

"I don't, I don't. I guess it was just weird that you were trying to play cupid all of a sudden."

She grunts.

"What?"

"Well . . . I haven't been totally honest with you."

"What do you mean?" My brows scrunch together as I turn my head to look at her, even though I can't see much in the weak light but a mass where her hair is.

She sucks in a deep breath and squeaks the air out between her lips. "Okay . . . yes, it's kind of weird that my friend is dating my brother, but I'm not as completely scandalized by it as I thought I'd be. And that whole thing last month, me trying to steer you away from him, that was more about Dad than me."

"Uh, why would your dad want me to date Brian?" But as soon as the words come out of my mouth, I know exactly where she's going.

Angela flips over to face me, talking low as if someone might overhear. "Dad's done more than a little hinting around, to both me and Jesse, for years now. Always telling us how we need to embrace our heritage, and I totally do, you know. He's always halfway teased Jesse about how he needs to find a nice Latina who knows how to take care of him."

"Which I'm definitely not." My lips push out in a scowl. He can't just assume I won't be a good wife.

Not that I'm thinking about marriage. At all. It hasn't even been a week.

In my head I see Gabby, the girl Jesse brought to homecoming. The family friend Jesse used to hang out with as a "favor" to his dad. The naïve side of me thought maybe he meant "hang out" as in show her around, take her to dances, entertain her, or keep her out of trouble. But really, his dad was hoping there would be more.

But . . . I'm not the only person in this house right now who is not Latina.

"What about your mom?"

"Her maiden name is Applegate. I think that's Scottish, maybe? I don't know, but her family's lived in Michigan for, like, ever."

I have to force myself to keep my volume down. "If he's okay with marrying your mom, why is he freaking out about who his son's going to end up with? Especially now. He's only seventeen."

"He's not freaking out," she assures me with urgency. "He likes you, he really does. You have nothing to worry about there, honestly. I'm telling you this so you can see what Jesse's dealing with in his head. It's not, like, the law of the land, but it's a subtle pressure that's been built up for years, so it's there."

"And now it's in my head too." Here I was so worried about finding someone to meet my standards, I didn't consider that I might fall short of someone else's.

"Don't worry about it. Jesse likes you a *lot* or he wouldn't have made it so official."

I don't even want to know about the plethora of "unofficial" girls before me. One more thing to fret over.

"So, do you feel pressure too? How come you never talk about any particular guys?" I ask, hoping this might be the moment she finally opens up about the tensions with Red. I don't want to put any words in her mouth, so I refrain from mentioning him yet.

"It's more pressure I put on myself. I want to make Dad happy, and I see how excited he gets when I speak to him in Spanish. I like when he takes me to Mexico to visit his family, and they teach me family traditions and recipes. When it's time for me to go to college, I'll be proud to go where he went." She pauses. "There's a whole invisible list of things he wants for his kids and I've always seen myself as the one to check those off, you know?"

Truth is, I don't know. I don't know anything. I don't have a specific culture like hers to latch on to and pass down. I don't understand the inner battle between wanting something and feeling obligated to want something else. Or someone.

I close my eyes and muster the courage to just flat-out ask, "So you like Red but you feel like you shouldn't?"

She hesitates. "Who said anything about Red?"

"I'm not totally blind."

Angela's hands cover her face. "Oh, this is so embarrassing."

"Why? It's me!" I say in my best comforting voice. "You can talk to me about anything. I should have asked you sooner, but I wasn't sure."

She brings her arms back under the covers, pulling the quilt around her until only her head sticks out at the top, like she's suddenly freezing. "I've been crushing on him for two years. I thought it would go away as I got into high school and met new guys, but it's just getting worse and I have no idea why. It's just Red. My brother's best friend!"

An image of this dark-haired beauty and the bulky blond holding hands pops into my mind. It would be so adorable I can hardly stand it.

"Judging by the way Tiffany acts around him, I'm guessing you haven't told her how you feel?"

A sigh. "There's no reason to. I'm never going to make a move, so who am I to stop her from flirting with him?" Her tone says she's still trying to convince herself this is a healthy idea.

"So what's holding you back from making a move the most? The fact that he's Jesse's best friend or that he doesn't match up to your invisible checklist?"

She ponders this a moment. "Probably mostly fear that he'd never look at me that way. You hear what he calls me: 'kid.' That's all I am to him."

"Impossible."

Another sigh.

"Think about what would make *Angela* happy," I say, hoping it's not too much to ask that she make this monumental decision tonight, and that I may have helped.

I reach for her hand and give it a squeeze, and when she squeezes back I realize I really did help. Her mood swings last semester had to stem from all of this; she just didn't think she had anyone to talk to about it.

And maybe I can help even more. Next time I get Red alone, we're going to have some words.

CHAPTER TWENTY-EIGHT

It kills me to admit it's taking a lot longer to catch on to this tap-dancing thing than I imagined. Some of the numbers I have to memorize are super long, and I'm the youngest and least experienced of the cast, so it's up to me to work my tail off to keep up. I haven't verbally expressed any of my concerns to anyone, for obvious anti-whining reasons, but I'm starting to question how much the dancing-and-singing path is for me. As much as I love musicals, I never thought I'd say that I miss climbing inside a character's head and poring over my lines. I miss acting.

I've been practicing nearly every day in January, and Jesse's helping me as much as his preseason baseball schedule allows, but I know he's frustrated with me, which makes me frustrated with him. And today he's withholding kisses, saying I need to focus. So I made up a game of my own with motivation worked into the reward: I get a kiss for every step I perfect. But we've been at it for over an hour, and I've only earned about two.

"My lips are lonely," Jesse says to the rhythm his feet tap out, once again showing me a tricky part from the last act near the end. "Think you can get it this time? For meeee?" He draws out the last word in singsong.

My heart taps out a dance of its own at the strong sound of it. "Sing! Please!"

"Nope."

"Come on, it's just me. I want to hear you belt out some big musical number. Or maybe a jazzy standard. You're probably a crooner, aren't you? Like Dean Martin. I could totally see that smooth, buttery voice coming out of you." I take in a deep breath and exhale slowly, batting my lashes and adding some sugar to my voice. "Please?"

He laughs, resting a hip against the ballet bar along the wall and crossing his arms. "I haven't seen any dancing from you worthy of a song."

"Rude!" I laugh and spread my arms wide, starting the combination with extra enthusiasm. Besides the extra flap I accidentally added somewhere in the middle, I'm pretty proud of myself. I turn my hands palm up as if to say "Ta-da!" but Jesse only cocks his head.

"So, it's not worthy of a song," I say, "but I'm getting better, right?"

"Yes, better." He scratches his temple.

"But?" I ask, afraid he's about to be too honest with me.

He exhales and wipes the sweat from his hairline. "You were behind the beat in a few spots."

"Which spots?"

He bites his lip. "Most of them."

"*Most* of them?"

"Okay, all of them."

"All of them? The whole—"

"The whole sequence is dragging." His head is still tilted to the side but his expression is blank. "You're too much in your head. You don't feel it."

I clench my teeth together, inhaling through my nose.

"Sometimes you don't shift your weight quickly enough, and it makes you lean forward too much. Looks like you're about to fall."

"Oh, is that all?" I ask, not without sarcasm.

"Well, I guess while we're talking about it, sometimes you get the heel drops confused on your Eleanor Powell."

"Which one was the Eleanor Powell again?"

"You do realize opening night is tomorrow?" he asks.

In an instant, my eyes sting and my throat tightens. "You're being so mean," I whisper through my quivering bottom lip.

"Maddie, I'm not saying it to be mean. I just—"

"*You've* just been dancing your entire life and all of this comes *so* easily for you, and you don't understand how it can be so hard for me to learn!" I explode. And I don't stop there. "Well, guess what? I don't know why it's so hard for me to learn either. There's like a disconnect between what my brain knows I need to do and what my feet actually perform."

"Where is this coming from?" He reaches for my shoulder, but I swat him away.

"And you want to know what else *I* don't understand," I

continue, ignoring his question, "is why even though everyone knows we're together now, they still can't know about *this*?" I wave my hands wildly to indicate the dance room as well as the playhouse as a whole.

"They don't need to know," he spits out hurriedly, taking a step toward me. "Why can't it just be our thing?"

"I was fine with that at first, but it's just a cop-out," I huff. It's like the plug on the drain has been pulled and my irritation's gushing out. "You don't want your friends to look down on you for dancing. You're so scared of what people will think, it's ridiculous."

"No, I'm not!" Lies.

"But it shouldn't matter, because you're talented, Jesse. Like *really* amazing."

"Like you said, I've danced my whole life. Mom put Angela and me in classes almost as soon as we could walk. Angela just didn't take to it like I did. But then I grew up. My goals changed."

"If you love something so much, why can't you be who you are *all* the time, not half in public and half in secret?"

"What makes you think I love dancing so much? I—"

"Don't act like I'm stupid. I caught you practicing, more than once. You wouldn't keep up with it if you didn't really love it. If it wasn't in you deep down." I step closer but don't touch him in case it causes me to lose my train of thought. "Just own up to it. Be your whole self, all the time."

Backing away from me, he pulls down a chair from the stack and sinks into it. "You don't understand because you can't understand," he says softly.

"Then tell me so I can." I sit on the ground near his feet, my shoes clinking the floor as I stretch out my sore legs. "I want to know about you. All of it. The good, the bad."

"And the ugly?"

"Hey, he does know about old movies," I mutter in monotone.

He guzzles a bottle of water before his mouth perks up in a partial smile. "I know Clint Eastwood, anyway. Proud of me?"

"Absolutely, but you're changing the subject." I cross my arms.

I wait patiently for him to open up, but he only leans forward, resting his elbows on his knees, and looks me in the eye.

"Please, just let it go," he says, so close I can see the ring of amber in his green irises. "We've got to get you ready for tomorrow. I think if we work on getting each . . ."

He keeps yammering on about how I dance too much in my head and that once the moves really click, my feet will do them without me forcing it, but I'm not completely listening. I can't stop thinking about getting him to admit to the world that he's not just a baseball player, he's a dancer too. That it's possible he can be both.

I have to get him on a real stage again. I won't rest until it happens.

Opening night of *Crazy for You* is both a dream and a nightmare, all rolled into a big blur. A Jesse-less blur, as he's playing a preseason tournament. I'm disappointed he's missing my first real musical debut, but I'm not sure our budding relationship can handle much more of the coach/student dynamic. He takes perfectionism to a new level, enough so I can hear his voice loud and clear in my head, running through all my flaws. A voice that's so irritated with me by curtain call, I don't want to talk to the real Jesse when I get home because I'm afraid I won't be able to separate the two.

I take my place second to the end in the line of chorus girls, and the curtain cinches up into the rafters. The audience stands, applauding and cheering wildly. I scan their faces as the lights shine on them, but no one's looking at me except for the few who breeze their eyes over the cast as a whole. No one is here for my first performance on the community theatre stage.

Ma's home in bed as usual, Dad's taking care of her, Angela and Tiffany had to serve dinner at some booster club banquet, and Sarah has a tennis thing all weekend, so Ryan went along to watch with her family. I'm supposed to call Dad for a ride home when it's over. The glamorous life of a song-and-dance girl.

I take a few steps back and to the side to make way for the stars of the show, and I might as well be offstage. I keep the plastic smile just in case someone happens to be looking, but all I can think is how much I wish this were closing night rather than opening night. Then I could switch gears and start working on the talent show piece.

The curtain finally hides us and my smile dissolves into a yawn. I massage my cheeks, working up to my temples as I dodge giant sections of the set backstage on my way to the dressing room, where I change behind a partition in a very crowded and loud room of cast members shouting their congratulations and late-night dinner invitations. I'm sort of included in one group's invite, but I decline because I can tell it's an afterthought. Besides, I haven't done the best job of trying to make friends here. It's safer to imagine what they think of my substandard skills rather than hear it firsthand.

When I finally make it out of the room with all my junk, Mrs. Morales places a hand on my shoulder as she passes by.

"Maddie, you did a fantastic job! I'm so proud of you!" I can't tell if she believes her words or if she's just being nice.

My eyebrows fly up, and I manage to squeak, "Oh, wow. Thanks."

"See you tomorrow," she turns back to say. "Please be here no later than four thirty. We need to run through a few scenes we hiccuped on tonight."

I watch her disappear into her office just as an excited voice calls my name from down the hallway. I turn to find Brian waving a bouquet of fat red and pink daisies in the air. He pulls me into a hug as soon as he reaches me.

His touch effectively melts the bitter ice that's been forming around my heart the whole night. A friend actually came to support me.

"You were amazing up there!" he says.

I pull away from him but have a hard time meeting his eye. "Are you joking?" I choke out. "The door to the car prop closed on my dress and tore a hole in it, I confused my heel drops on the Eleanor Powell just like"—I stop myself from mentioning Jesse and our practices—"just like I always do, and if you looked closely enough you would have noticed I wasn't even singing because I couldn't concentrate on moving my feet and my mouth at the same time. I was an epic failure."

He laughs and cups a hand over my shoulder. "I'm not sure if anyone ever told you this, but the audience doesn't really notice the little mistakes. You're not supposed to point them out."

I try to laugh but it comes out a little blubbery because I'm suddenly holding back a sob. "Yeah, but if you *did* see my mistakes and I said nothing about them, then you'd think I thought I was wonderful, and I can't let you think that because it's so far from the truth."

"You girls and your complicated minds." Brian leads me to a less crowded space closer to the exit door at the end of the hall. "To me, you *were* wonderful. So chill."

My eyes water, and everything around me gets fuzzy. "But I did *not* think I was wonderful," I continue in a higher pitch. I don't even care if I sound whiny at this point; I just need to get it out. "I thought I was terrible and I had a miserably stressful time and I want it all to be over."

He takes a step back, likely frightened of my blatant honesty, and tucks the stems of the flowers under an arm. "You really didn't have any fun?"

I shrug and lean against the wall and calm my breathing so I can speak coherently. "Yes and no. I mean, I've always wanted to do a musical, so tonight was partly a dream come true. Back at my old school, I'd get so mad that my teacher didn't like them. We always did straight plays, and I'd beg him to let us do just one musical, but no. Now I feel like I should thank him for saving me from premature disappointment and humiliation. I'm not sure I could have handled this before."

"Why not?"

I shake my head. "Because I didn't have the friends I do now."
He smiles and squeezes my shoulder.

"I don't know, I guess I thought this void inside me would be filled. That musical theatre was part of my ultimate destiny. But I feel let down. Betrayed."

"Betrayed by your *ultimate* destiny. Leave it to you never to feel anything halfway."

I dab at my eye with my sleeve and search for a distraction. "Are those for me?" I ask, nodding at the flowers.

"Oh! Yes!" He hurriedly hands the bouquet to me and relieves me of my bag. "Sarah picked them out. They're from all of us—me and Sarah and Ryan. They're sorry they couldn't make it, by the way."

"Sarah's only apologized a dozen times."

"And now you have a dozen flowers."

"They're perfect," I say, fingering the bright petals.

He switches my bag to his other hand and digs a set of keys out of his pocket. "So, is someone bringing you home, or do you need a lift?"

"I was just about to call my dad to have him pick me up, but if you don't mind . . ."

Brian convinces me to tell my dad I have a ride, and I follow him through the parking lot and down a couple blocks to the overflow parking, hopping over the occasional puddle and lamenting that it's not frozen so I can slide across it. Here it is almost February and I haven't seen so much as a flurry.

A black Chevy truck *chirps* to my left. I glance around, but no one else is near it.

"After you," Brian says, opening the passenger door and tossing in my bag.

"Whose truck is this?" I ask, stepping on the running board and settling in my seat.

"Mine!" He shuts me in and walks around to climb in the driver's side. "My dad just bought a new truck, a big Dodge diesel, so he passed this down to me."

An abundance of vehicles. How nice for them.

"What about your car?"

"Selling it," he says, without any emotional attachment. "Interested?"

I perk up. "Uh, yeah!" Then I deflate just as quickly. "But considering I don't have much saved and there won't be a lot of help from my parents, it's not feasible." I cross my arms over my stomach and let out a huff of air while Brian makes a contemplative grunting noise.

We begin the drive in silence, but I realize quickly it's only an opportunity for my brain to replay everything I did wrong tonight. I see every shuffle I did instead of a flap, how I turned left when everyone else turned right. And again I hear Jesse barking instructions at me.

Jesse.

I dig my phone out of my bag, thrilled to see he sent me a text about two hours ago.

Jesse: Sorry I'm missing your big night. Hope you're having fun. You'll do GREAT! And we're killing it out here, in case you were wondering. ;)
Me: It was . . . an experience. Happy baseballing!

"So how's Kristi?" I ask Brian, pocketing my phone but keeping my smile.

"Good," he says. I catch a glimpse of his grin by the light of a passing car. "I'm actually driving up to Dallas to see her for the day tomorrow."

"Whoa. Your parents don't care?"

"No. They met her and her family when we were in Colorado. My mom's a little *too* excited about it all, honestly."

"Uh-oh. Parental approval," I tease, remembering how my dad said he liked Jesse, though it didn't bother me. "It's been known to cause adverse reactions."

He laughs from his gut as he makes the turn onto my street. "Nah. My mom's opinion actually means a lot to me."

As I stare at the side of his face, pondering his genuine confession, it occurs to me that maybe we're too much alike. Maybe that's why the kiss was such an awkward disaster. We make good friends, but anything more just feels off.

He pulls into my driveway and I slide down from the truck. "Thanks for the ride."

"No problem," he says, still behind the wheel.

"And the flowers," I add, cradling them under my arm and reaching for my bag. "See you Monday."

I'm about to close the door when he says, "Hey, wait. I was thinking . . . about my Camry. If you want it—"

"I really don't see how I can afford it, though. I don't make a whole lot."

"I know." He nods, his floppy hair dipping toward his eyes. "But my parents said I could do what I wanted with it, so I was thinking maybe we could work something out you can handle. Relaxed payments, you know?"

"Are you kidding me right now?"

"I mean, if you want it. I'm not trying to force you into a car payment here."

"Of course I want it!" I blurt out with a little hop, my bag slipping off my shoulder. "I just want to make sure you understand exactly how *relaxed* these payments are going to be."

"It's no big deal. I mean, I can't get that much for it anyway. My mom drove it for years before I got it. It doesn't matter to me if I get paid for it up front or over the next year or so."

"Is this really happening? You're totally serious?" Hope swells inside my chest. A car. My very own car. One that can take me places as I blast music that *I* want to listen to, windows down with the heater on my feet.

He laughs and shifts his truck into reverse. "But don't think you can cheat me," he teases, complete with wagging finger. "I'll be keeping strict records."

"No cheating. Promise." I cross the bouquet of flowers over my heart as an oath. "Can I get it tomorrow?" I ask, rising up on my toes like a giddy child.

"I'm going to Dallas tomorrow. Sunday?"

"Oh, right. Sunday!"

We say our good nights and as he drives away, I repeat "Sunday, Sunday, I'm getting a car on Sunday" under my breath all the way up to the house. I dig the house key out of my bag, but the front door swings open. My eyes scan Dad's outfit of business shirt and flannel pajama pants before I catch the panic on his face.

"Good," he says, his shoulders noticeably relaxing but still a bit tight for this late at night. "You're home."

"What's wrong?" I ask in a rush, every sore muscle in my own body tensing.

"Baby's coming." He grabs the keys from the hook on the wall and drags a suitcase down the front steps.

"But it's still way too early. Are you sure it's not just a fake-out like last time?" I ask, looking through the doorway for a sign of Ma, but I don't see her.

"No." He starts the car, loads the suitcase, and walks briskly back to me, frozen in place on the porch. "Her water broke. It's time."

CHAPTER TWENTY-NINE

A boy. Just like Ma thought. They're calling him Christopher James Brooks. Christopher after Dad's father, James after Ma's. She confesses they considered letting me name him, but realized I would have gone with Gene Kelly Brooks—this is likely—and didn't think a modern boy would appreciate the name itself, or that it came from his teen sister.

In my new Camry—Dad made me practice driving near our house practically all day Sunday as a refresher—I follow Dad up to the hospital Monday morning before school. My heart skips with anticipation of seeing my brother for the first time—only my parents have been allowed in the NICU so far. Rider wanted to come into town right away, but they talked him into holding off at least until Friday so he wouldn't miss any school.

I'm led through a maze of swinging doors, past nurses' stations, and I'm handed a sterile robe to put on over my clothes before entering the room Christopher's in. Ma beckons me over to his incubator to see four pounds of a skinny body, eyelids fluttering, legs kicking in irritation at all the tubes and wires stuck to him. He needs help breathing, but hopefully not for too long, and he'll have to stay in the incubator until he can hold a good temperature. The doctor says he's strong, and encourages my parents that he'll catch up in no time.

With a gloved hand, I worm my pinkie under the tiniest fingers I've ever seen, and he grips onto it with more muscle than I thought possible.

"Talk to him," Ma says from just behind me, her hand resting gently on my back. "Let him know who you are."

"Can he really hear me?" I ask, studying his funny ears, still a bit smashed against his head.

"Of course."

I speak softly so as not to overwhelm him if he can, in fact, hear me. "Hey, Chris. It's Maddie. Your sister." My breath catches on the word "sister," and I work to convince my head that this little thing is related to me. I'm more than Rider's sister now. There are three of us.

"Isn't he perfect?" Ma asks through a sigh.

I nod. "It's so weird that he was inside you, and now he's right here. We can see him and touch him, like he's a real person."

"He is a real person." She laughs softly. "And it's not too weird for me yet. I did just push—"

"Whoa," I say, nudging her with my hip. "You can stop. I get it."

She nudges me back. "Want to know what *is* weird, though?"

"What?" I ask, not taking my eyes off the new fingers holding mine.

Ma moves her hand to my shoulder and pulls me against her. "That you and Rider were each inside me at one time too, and here you are, practically full grown. I mean, Rider's taller than me now, so it's a little harder to comprehend that he's the same baby I brought home from the hospital nineteen years ago." She pauses, and one of Christopher's machines goes through some sort of dance. "Nineteen years."

The crack in her voice makes me recall all my initial thoughts when I found out they were having another baby. Here they were about to be empty nesters, smooth sailing until retirement, which can't be that far away because they're old, and now they have to raise a child all over again.

But this time, at least for the first couple of years, she'll have my help.

"He's going to be okay, right?" I ask as Christopher tightens his grip, demanding my full attention.

"He has us as a family," she says, hugging me even closer to her and kissing the top of my head. "He's going to be just fine."

Looking at him now, so small and pink, I'm thankful my parents were smart enough not to give me the responsibility of naming a human. Because he is real. Totally and completely, a real person.

In the school parking lot, Jesse sits on the tailgate of his truck, swinging his legs, clad in the usual jeans and boots. I begin to press on the brake as I approach him and roll down my window, but it's not until I come to a complete stop behind his truck that he actually looks at me.

His brows scrunch together and his jaw tightens in a hard line. "Isn't that what's-his-name's car? Why are you driving it?"

"It *was* Brian's." I don't let his obvious distaste beat down my smile. "But I bought it."

"You bought it?"

"Well, I'm in the *process* of buying it, Mr. Technical."

"With what?"

"Money." I prop my elbow in the window and rest my head against my fist. "He's cutting me a good deal. Isn't it great? I have my own car!"

He slides down from his perch. "Is this the surprise you couldn't wait to show me?"

Now my smile withers. "Maybe."

His eyes scan the length of the car with a near scowl and suddenly my pride in the detail job my dad paid for yesterday is gone. Did they miss a spot? Is there a scratch I don't know about? My shiny blue miracle is getting dimmer in my mind as my excitement fizzles. Did I make a mistake?

"You're not happy for me," I say as a statement. "You know I need my own car. I can't keep mooching off everyone, including you. I'm tired of being that girl who needs a ride everywhere."

"I know. I'm glad you finally have a car, I am." He bites the corner of his bottom lip. "I just liked that you needed me to drive you places."

I blink. "As adorable as that is, baseball is about to take over your life. You can't always be ready to answer my call for spontaneous cupcake runs."

His face goes sour, but I don't see that what I said was untrue. After slipping an arm through a strap of his backpack, he closes the tailgate with a *squeak* and a *clank*. "We're gonna be late. You should find a parking spot."

"What just happened?" I ask, suddenly nervous. "What did you get upset about?"

"You should hear your attitude when the word 'baseball' comes out of your mouth."

"I don't have an attitude," I say, replaying what I said in my mind. "I just wanted you to be excited that I needed my own car and now I have one. You're getting busier, and I'll be at the hospital a lot until Christopher can come home."

He lifts his eyes to meet mine. "How is he?"

I brighten, thankful for this change of subject. "He's pretty awesome. I can't believe I already love him as much as I do."

Jesse smiles. My foot relaxes on the brake, and the car starts to coast forward.

"I guess I'm going to find a parking spot," I say in a rush.

"Hey, wait," he calls before I get too far. "I . . . was wondering if you'd come watch my practice today after school."

I stop the car and look back at him. "Your baseball practice?"

He rolls his eyes, forgoing the opportunity to say something smart, which makes me think I really did a number on his mood.

"It's okay for people to come watch?" I ask.

"Uh, yeah. You can sit in the bleachers. The ball field is behind the football stadium. I'll already be out there when your last class lets out."

"Oh. Well, you didn't come see my show last weekend, so . . . ," I say, playing hard to get.

"Not my fault," he defends, voice gruff. "And I'm going to see it this weekend. Look, you don't have to come, I know it's beneath you. I just thought it'd be cool if you wanted to."

Now my mouth drops open at his tone. I can't help analyzing the way he said it would be cool if I *wanted* to. I don't really *want* to sit around for an hour or whatever watching boys swing bats and throw balls, but now it feels like I'm going to be in trouble if I don't. Besides, he's watched me work on my mediocre dance moves more times than I can count. I suppose I could take one for the team, as they say.

I offer what I aim to be an enticing smile, imagining all my tingly and gushy feelings about him in hopes that he can sense them. "Can't wait."

Angela never mentioned that she was going to watch the guys practice, but I spot her up toward the top of the bleachers, all the way at the end, near the outfield.

"How can you even see the action from way up here?" I ask, sitting next to her. The chill from the metal quickly seeps through my jeans, and goose bumps travel down my legs.

"I figure Red won't notice me this far away." Angela looks up from her phone and adjusts her bright yellow scarf to cover her ears. "I'm surprised to see you here. Aren't you afraid of encouraging his career of 'throwing baseballs'?" she teases, with air quotes.

"Yeah, well, he asked, and it's my turn to do something for him, right?"

"Mmmhmm. What a dutiful girlfriend you are."

I squint toward the pitcher's mound to watch Jesse chunk a ball crazy fast over home plate. The batter swings and misses. I think.

"Seriously, can we move closer?" I ask. "I can hardly tell who's who down there."

"But—"

"So what if Red notices you?" I say, standing and rubbing my hands together, thoroughly loving that the current cold front is actually capable of making me shiver. "Might do everyone some good," I mutter.

With a huff, she gathers her tote bag, and we start down the steps.

"That looks like Red coming up to bat," I say, slowing when we're about halfway down. "He's supposed to be some sort of slugger, right?"

"Uh, right," she says through a laugh. "*Slugger.* You're hilarious."

"What?" I turn on her. "Is that not the correct terminology?"

"It might be. It just sounds funny when you say it like that."

"Gee, thanks."

I pick up the pace, glancing up every few steps to watch Jesse pitch. The windup, the leg hike, the hurling forward of his body. Have to say, there's something strong and attractive about it. Skilled. Red swings, and with a loud *ping* the ball goes flying into the outfield, where someone hustles to catch it.

Angela lets out a breathy whistle as we settle ourselves on an empty row behind a few parents.

Jesse fires another pitch for Red—I guess they aren't playing a mock game—and this time there are two *pings*, one almost immediately after the first. Jesse's hands fly up to his head, and he drops to his knees, then falls the rest of the way onto his side, curling into a fetal position.

I can't breathe. Can't move.

I'm reminded of that scene in *Take Me Out to the Ball Game* when Frank Sinatra's character deliberately konks out Gene's character by pitching a ball at his head during a pregame gag. It was so fakey in the movie, I didn't think anything like it could ever actually happen in real life, though I'm sure a line drive to the head from the strongest guy in school is much more serious than if someone is only throwing it.

What if his skull is cracked? What if he's . . .

Angela yanks my arm and suddenly I'm on my feet and we're both yelling "Jesse!" as we race down the rest of the stairs toward the field. I keep my eyes on him the whole time we're running, thankful to see he's rubbing his feet together, so I can be certain that he's not: 1) dead, 2) knocked out, or 3) paralyzed.

We approach cautiously, keeping behind the coaches hovering over him as they consult with each other in serious tones about who's dealt with this situation before, and who's taking him to the hospital, and who's going to tell his mother. Once in a while I hear a little groan escape his mouth, and all I want to do is crawl down there next to him and kiss him and make it better. I try to position myself to see his face so I can get an idea of how much pain he's in, but after I manage to catch eyes with him for a split second, he shuts his eyes and groans again.

Red paces near the pitcher's mound, hands laced together on top of his helmet, making his elbows stick out like wings. I can just make out the faint string of curses he's muttering.

"Were you trying to *kill* him?" Angela nearly screams, shooting past me and slamming herself into Red. She shoves him with everything she's got, then beats on his massive chest a couple times for good measure. He barely sways backward.

"Oh, right, I was trying to kill your brother."

"You're such an insensitive jerk," she sneers, pulling the crowd's attention off Jesse and toward their impromptu soap opera.

"It was an *accident*, Angela. I'm sorry, okay?" He clutches her arms and holds her away from him as she continues to slap at him. "Get. Off. Me."

She stops flailing, and they give each other that look. That slow-motion-only-in-the-movies look that's filled with loathing and want and anger that usually precludes a major kiss. They don't kiss, but the look lasts a moment too long for me to believe he only sees her as a "kid."

Jesse's helped to his feet and led to a bench, and I follow, feeling completely useless. The muscles in my forehead start to throb, and I rub the tension away.

He's walking. He's going to be fine.

"Everybody back to practice," one of the coaches says. "Franklin! On the mound. Warm up."

The players scatter and I offer to sit with Jesse and wait for Angela to come back with their mom so we can go to the hospital, a place I'm becoming entirely too familiar with. As if I weren't already worried enough about my new baby brother, I've got to add a boyfriend with a head injury to the list.

I scoot close enough for Jesse to lean against me if he wants, but he presses his back into the chain-link fence just behind us instead, tilting his head back a little and breathing heavy through his mouth. I reach for his hand, but he doesn't exactly hold on to me, which makes me feel even more useless.

"Where did it hit you?" I ask, studying the right side of his head where I thought he grabbed when it happened. The knot is already the size of half a golf ball. "Oh. Ouch. What can I do?"

"Nothing," he mumbles. "I'm fine."

A sputter of laughter nervously bubbles from my lips. "Well, this just gives new meaning to your hardheadedness, doesn't it?"

He closes his eyes and grunts in a way I can't decipher. Was it what I said, or is he really in that much pain? Sure he's conscious and everything right now, but what's happening inside that expanding lump?

"You'd never take a line drive to the head onstage," I say, not without bitterness. Sports are stupid and dangerous and it takes all my effort not to tell him so.

Jesse palms either side of his face, smashing his cheeks in until his lips look like a fish's mouth.

"Stop, you're going to hurt yourself," I say, reaching for his hands.

"No, *you* stop," he growls.

I gasp, straightening and pulling away from him.

"You have to stop telling me that what I'm doing is wrong. I don't dance onstage anymore; get over it. How many times do I have to tell you that baseball is what I want to do?"

I swallow the tightness in my throat, but it only grows. "Even after something like this?" I manage to get out.

"You get hurt sometimes; it's part of it," he says, and I can hear the eye roll in his voice. "I've got my dad pulling me one way, you pulling me the other. I can't fight you both, and I can't make both of you happy. And it's making me crazy."

"But I just want—"

"I know what you want. I'm not him."

My mouth hangs open like he just slapped my face.

"That's not even what I was going to say!" I don't mean to raise my voice, but he knows me better than to think I'd walk away now. "I was trying to say that I just wanted you to be honest with yourself. With your friends, your dad. I hate that you feel like you have to hide things because of how other people will react."

"Wake up, Madison."

My stomach drops at the sound of my full name spitting off his tongue.

"This is real life. People tear each other down for things they don't understand. It's easier to only show the parts of you they can handle."

"But it's not really you," I huff, tugging on my own hair in frustration. "You wouldn't even be saying any of this if you weren't concussing or whatever right now."

"It *is* me. It's just not what *you* want me to be." He takes a deep breath and grips the edge of the bench. "It was like pulling teeth to even get you to come to one of my practices. I can't be with someone who doesn't like who I am."

I take in a shaky breath of my own, gathering courage to say, "I do like who you are, Jesse. I just don't think I should be the only one who knows all of you. So what if the kids on the base-ball team laugh at you? Let them be jealous and miserable with their lives while you're happy with yours. Your *real* friends, the ones who matter, the ones who might actually grow up to be decent human beings, they'd support you no matter what you did." I take one last shot in the dark. "You could do both."

"I don't want to do both," he snaps, then winces, gingerly touching his head. "Not only do I like baseball and want to make it my career, but I also don't care about performing anymore. All of your best-prepared speeches and movie quotes aren't going to change me. You say you want me to be *all* of me all the time, but you only want to see half of me. The half *you* like. And it's stupid. It hurts. You either like all of me or you don't." He pauses to take a few breaths. "The end."

Nothing. I'm out of words. My hopes, my daydreams, slaughtered in a gutter somewhere. He's only breaking up with performing, but somehow it feels like he's breaking up with—

"I don't think *this*"—he motions weakly between us—"is working anymore."

—*me.*

He doesn't look at me.

Coward.

And I can't look away. It's as if this is the last time I'm ever going to see him this close. If only I was on his other side so I could see the scar, the one like Gene's.

In the worst timing of all bad timings, I spot Angela and Mrs. Morales rushing over, my window for fighting closing quickly. There's so much I want to say that everything jumbles together in my head and nothing comes out but a strained *squeak*, and I have to stop myself before I erupt into Niagara Falls.

My heartbeat pounds in my ears, turning all extra noises into a dull roar as Mrs. Morales whisks him away and Angela probably asks if I'm coming, and I have no idea what kind of expression I'm wearing or what I say or don't say. I don't even know how much time passes before I'm aware that I'm staring at the ground while baseball practice carries on around me, business as usual. The whole team has probably figured out what happened by now, and they're laughing among themselves about the girl who tried too desperately to hang on to the Baseball King, only to be left alone on a cold metal bench.

Like a wounded sloth, I mope through the mostly empty parking lot to my car and collapse onto the seat, the car rocking forward and back underneath me. I hug the steering wheel and smash my forehead into my arms and finally let out big, blubbering, scarf-soaking sobs. Maybe I can float home on the river of my tears.

CHAPTER THIRTY

Jesse was lucky, according to Angela—he won't return my texts, though, and I'm too chicken to call. He had to stay at the hospital overnight just to be safe, but thankfully there weren't any fractures or hematomas or anything life threatening, just a mild concussion. Not that I've stopped worrying about him. Or us. Doctor's orders, he didn't come to school the rest of the week, and Angela can't get any information out of him, so the longer I'm left to stew over everything he said to me, the more I'm convinced he hates me.

The end came so fast, and I was too distracted by concern over his injury to be able now to clearly recall our entire conversation, but I think he basically told me that I ruined my first relationship because I wanted him to dance. Which feels epically stupid now, because *I* don't even want to dance anymore.

If Jesse came to watch one of my final performances of *Crazy for You*, I missed him. I'm sure he didn't, though, seeing as how he hates me and all.

Sarah and Ryan finally got a chance to come to a show, so did Angela and Tiffany, and my parents each came a night while the other stayed at the hospital with Christopher.

Rider even surprises me by escorting Ma to closing night. After the depressing week I've had, it feels reassuring to be supported.

"Tap dancing, huh?" Rider asks, carrying all my junk to the car after the show. "And singing at the same time? I didn't know you could do that."

I smile at his rare half-compliment. "I'm sure you noticed I can't do it very well."

"All three of my kids can do anything if they put their mind to it," Ma jumps in, squeezing my hand.

"Three," Rider mumbles, shaking his head and tossing my bag into the trunk of his Camaro. "Unreal."

"I'm so proud of you!" Ma continues. "You were so good! Oh, I wish I had time to make you a cake."

"You're trying to make me blush, and it's not going to work!" I laugh. "No, really, thanks, but I'm hereby proclaiming that tonight was my first and last closing night of a musical production."

"What are you saying?" Ma gasps, turning me to face her. "This was your dream. To be like Judy Garland and Ginger Rogers and all those people on your bedroom walls. It was like you were one of them up there tonight. I had tears in my eyes."

"You're easy," I say, tears welling in my own eyes. "And it *was* a dream come true up there, and I'm thankful for it."

I pause, remembering the work Jesse and I put into my training. All the secret hours we had together that he can't take away from me. Thanks to him, for this tiny moment in my life, I did get to feel like one of my heroes. And I'll never forget it. "It's just not for me. I have to be realistic about my shortcomings, and focus on improving my strengths."

"You're so weird." Rider laughs, pulling the passenger seat forward for me.

"Well, your dad and I support you in whatever you want to do, you know that." Ma kisses the top of my head before I squeeze into the backseat. "But I do think you're too critical of yourself."

"Can we just drop it?" I groan. "It's over."

It's all over.

"You really don't want to go to the wrap party with the rest of the cast?" Ma asks, closing the door after settling in the front seat. "I'm sure they'll be wondering where you are."

I shake my head even though no one can see me crammed back here. "I told them I was spending time with my family tonight."

On the drive to the hospital, Mom asks Rider all about school and girls and if he's keeping up with his laundry. I only half listen to his answers, my brain still running through all my mistakes from the show as I keep talking myself into believing I'm making the right decision, leaving one of my loves behind. Wondering what Jesse would have seen onstage if he had come like he promised. If he would have been proud or embarrassed. Or indifferent.

Rider drops Ma off at the door, and we coast to find a parking spot. When he helps me out of the back, he cups a hand on my shoulder and looks me in the eye, our faces illuminated by the buzzing light overhead. I'm usually not this close to him, so I haven't thought about it much before, but we sort of have the same hazel eyes. His lashes are thicker than mine, though. So unfair.

"What's going on with you?" he asks, with real concern scrunching his brows.

"Meaning?" For a distraction, I pull out my phone from my pocket and check for texts. None.

"This whole weekend, you've been, I don't know, bummed about something. And now you're all, 'I'll never dance again!'" He rolls his head in a circle and places the back of his hand on his forehead.

I clear my throat, staring back at my phone's blank screen, waiting for it to do something and pull me away from this intervention. "I've just been worried about Christopher."

"I don't think that's it. You know Christopher's doing good," he says. "Does it have anything to do with that guy? The one with the girl's name?"

Don't smile. "Jesse."

"Ma told me a few weeks ago that you two were together."

"She did?" My shoulders fall. And here I thought I was keeping him in the dark. Didn't want to give him the satisfaction of knowing he'd been right when he predicted the whole thing.

"Like we didn't all see that coming," he teases. "But then I saw him tonight, sneaking out as soon as the show was over."

Heart flying, I narrow my eyes at Rider to gauge his honesty. "He was there?"

He gives a quick nod and a grunt. "What did he do?"

I can't believe Jesse came.

"Nothing," I say.

"Obviously, something happened." He crosses his arms. "I saw it in his face, and I see it in yours. Do I need to have a chat with the kid? How badly should he suffer?"

I let myself smile. I'm so used to Rider not living at home, I've mostly forgotten what it's like to have a big brother on my side. "Thanks, but I don't need you to do anything." I shut the car door and push on it with my side until it clicks. "I'm the one who did all the damage; I'm the one who gets to do all the suffering."

"You and your dramatics." After locking the car, he guides me through the parking lot toward the hospital entrance. "Well, even though I'm a few hours away, you know I'm available for ass-kicking at any moment. Just call me."

Without even fully meaning to, I stop just outside the sliding doors and wrap my arms around Rider.

He pats me on the back a couple times and I mumble into his shirt, "Thanks."

We aren't usually the most affectionate siblings, but with Christopher coming early, Jesse dumping me, the residual stress from the musical, and my future now up in the air, I'm feeling more than a bit emotionally compromised. Having my whole family here, loving each other, fills me with a hope I didn't realize was missing.

Never in a million years did I expect to be eager to flash around pictures of my baby brother at school, but Monday at lunch I can't help myself from sharing with Angela and Tiffany. Plus, it keeps me from my thoughts about Jesse. Besides the agonizing forty minutes in English class when we sit two feet from each other and it hurts me to look at him—he does say hello and asks me how I'm doing every day, so that's something—I'm out of the Jesse loop. I miss our carpooling, the late-night phone calls. The kissing.

"Whoa, he's seriously itty-bitty," Tiffany says while inhaling a bag of ranch Doritos. "How early was he?"

"Almost two months." I return my phone to my backpack before any nosy onlookers learn more about me than necessary.

"That's crazy." Angela dips a piece of soft pretzel into mustard. "He's gonna be okay?"

I smile as I wind the cap back on my bottle of Sprite. "He's doing great. Should get to come home in the next few weeks."

"Well, we're super excited about the new mini-Brooks," Tiffany says, licking the spices off her fingers before tightening her ponytail, "but we do have something very important to discuss."

My stomach clenches at her serious tone. "We do?"

She nods. "A certain person's seventeenth birthday is right around the corner." Her pointer finger circles in my direction. "*What* are we going to do about it?"

"Oh, no. We don't—"

"That's right!" Angela squeaks. "Party! What color scheme do you want? I'm thinking yellow! And maybe pink, since it is Valentine's Day too. Unless that's too themed for you. You're probably tired of the birthday-Valentine's combo by now, aren't you?"

"I like pink more than yellow," I say, "but really, we don't need to have a party for me. Especially since it's on Valentine's Day. I'm sure you guys have better plans." They stare at me blankly. "Like dates?"

Tiffany lets a stream of purple mineral water dribble out of her mouth instead of a full-on spew, which would have landed on my face. "And where might these magical dates come from? You go to the same school we do."

"You both had dates to homecoming," I argue. "I'm just saying, I don't want you to feel obligated to forgo any potential romantic escapades for my sake."

Angela chews on her pretzel. "Romantic escapades. I don't think I've ever had a romantic escapade in my life." She rests her head in her hand. "Sometimes I don't think I ever will."

Tiffany raises her water bottle. "May the three of us find ourselves on romantic escapades sooner rather than later."

As Angela and I tap our drinks to hers and take a swig, I rack my brain for a subject change before we all tailspin into depression.

"Are either of you going to do the talent show in a few weeks? I hear first prize is five hundred bucks or something."

"Right," Tiffany says. "What would I do? Set up a volleyball net onstage and show off my spikes?"

"Who's spiking what now?" Red asks, plopping down next to Tiffany, across from me and Angela. "Ladies," he says, then nods to Angela. "Hey, kid."

I feel her body tense before she slaps a palm on the table, face fuming. "Stop it! Either stop calling me that, or stop talking to me altogether."

My mouth falls open, and I catch eyes with Tiffany, who's also surprised at the outburst.

Red raises his eyebrows. "You sure have been popping off a lot lately. I told you, what happened with Jesse was an accident. He's not even upset about it, so you shouldn't be either."

I can't help what comes out of my mouth. "Wow, you really are thick."

Angela jabs my side with her elbow. I give her a look that says *What? I thought you were letting him have it! This is your chance! Tell hiiiim!*

Nothing.

"I think it just got too awkward in here for me," Tiffany says with uncomfortable laughter, grabbing her tray and looking to Angela. "I'm going to my advisory period. See y'all."

Angela glances from Tiffany to Red to me, then to her half-eaten lunch. She follows Tiffany without another word.

"You really are pathetic, you know that?" I begin.

"I don't know what you're talking about." He takes a sip of his Dr Pepper, careful not to look me in the eye. He's *so* not an actor.

Kids start filtering out of the cafeteria. I'm running out of time.

"I think you're scared."

"I ain't scared of nothing," Red says, turning on his Southern charms. He shuffles the chicken tenders on his plate.

"You are," I insist, tossing my food back into my lunch box. "The possibility of a real and happy relationship is right there, and you're just—"

"Right where?" This playing dumb thing is the opposite of endearing.

"It's right in front of you!" I resist reaching across the table to smack the top of his head. "Please tell me you're not as stupid as I think you might actually be."

He presses his lips together and glances at the passing students carrying their trays to the trash. "I can't."

I fold my arms over my lunch box, waiting for him to elaborate.

"I know who you're talking about, and of course I've thought about it." He adjusts the collar on his blue polo shirt. "But I've known her my whole life."

"And that's bad, why?"

"I don't know how to make the switch. She's always just been Jesse's little sister, and all of the sudden I'm supposed to make out with her. Won't it be weird?"

Now I'm looking around to see who's within earshot. Thankfully the room is nearly cleared out. "It won't be weird if you like her."

"I do, I just . . ." He shakes his head and stands, gathering his trash and turning to leave. "Jesse would beat the crap out of me."

"He would not. Look, all I'm saying is . . . my best friend deserves to know the guy she likes actually cares about her."

"Maddie." His Adam's apple bobs. "I appreciate you trying to help me here"—he throws an arm casually over my shoulders—"but don't you think maybe you should work at repairing your own broken relationship before you start playing cupid? I mean, I know Valentine's Day is coming up and all, but—"

"I don't know why I even bother." I smack him on top of the head and leave him alone by the trash cans.

CHAPTER THIRTY-ONE

It's never really bothered me that my birthday's on Valentine's Day. It's like a double party—double the gifts, double the cards, and double the candy. And I've never cared that I didn't have a valentine.

But this year, no amount of conversation hearts can sweeten my mood. I had my valentine all lined up, and I couldn't even hang on to him for more than a month. Whatever. The varsity baseball team is out of town, so I wouldn't have gotten to see Jesse today anyway. Though a "Happy Birthday" text would have been nice. Unless he forgot.

And now I'm just depressed. I hurt him. I was the problem. Me. Anything I say to him now to try to get him back will just sound like a load. No. I need to figure me out first. Me first, boys second.

At least my family still loves me, even after the attitude I gave them throughout most of Ma's pregnancy. Rider's missing—he called, though, which was nice—but Christopher is home and getting stronger every day, and it's good to have the family at home to celebrate with me. Dad whipped up his famous lasagna—the only thing he knows how to make—and Ma taught herself how to make cake balls—a miniature kitchen disaster, but still tasty. Presents include a one hundred dollar gas card, a sterling-silver star charm on a dainty chain necklace, and an authentic vintage poster of *Desk Set*, one of my favorite Katharine Hepburn and Spencer Tracy films.

"Birthday girl." Dad sticks one of the gift bows to the top of my head as he clears the table and throws the wrapping paper into the trash. "One more year and you'll be an adult!"

"Oh, no," Ma says, reaching for another cake ball. "We're not talking about that."

There's a knock on the door, so soft I almost don't hear it.

Ma perks up in her chair. "Well, I wonder who *that* could be," she says, as if she somehow knows exactly who it could be.

My heart swells with hope that Jesse is standing on my porch, arms full of flowers and a sign that says I'M AN IDIOT. I'M SORRY. I LOVE YOU. BE MINE.

I scramble from the table and dash for the door, hiding my disappointment from Angela that her brother is nowhere to be seen. Hello. He's playing baseball.

And I'm working on me.

"Happy birthday, beautiful!" Angela exclaims, tossing a handful of paper confetti high into the air over our heads. "And look." She points next to her left eye to a glittery red star outlined in black. "We match!"

"Love it!" I brush confetti off my shoulders and take the bow out of my hair. "Do you want to come in? We were just gorging ourselves on cake-ball experiments."

"Nope," she says, rising to her toes in excitement. "I've come to take you *out*."

"Out? Where?"

"I can't tell you that. It'll ruin the surprise," she pouts. "But we need to go, like, now. They're waiting." She claps a hand over her mouth. "I've said too much already! Get your purse, and let's go!"

"Well . . ." I glance back at my parents in the dining room, smiling and chatting with each other. "I was sort of hanging out with my family. Let me ask if they mind—" I pause at the devious smile that creeps across her face. "They already know?"

She hops down the steps and heads toward her bright yellow Beetle. "Your chariot awaits!"

"The playhouse?"

We pull into a reserved front-row spot in an otherwise full parking lot.

"What's going on here tonight?" I ask, getting out of the car and straightening my sweater. A few stray circles of confetti fall to the ground. "I've worked here every day after school this week, and I never heard one peep about a Valentine's Day event."

She holds the front door of the playhouse open for me. "Valentine's shmalentines."

"Happy birthday, Maddie!" shout the combined voices of Tiffany, Sarah, Ryan, and Brian, all with stars on their cheeks.

"You guys are so cute!" I hug each of them, refusing to let my eyes water, because that would be silly. I don't need Jesse here. I have the best friends in the world, and I'm going to be fine.

"Maddie!" Elise bounds between Tiffany and Sarah, a hot-pink feather boa in her hands. "It's your birthday so you have to wear this!"

"Aww, I would love to!" I bend down for her to wrap it around my neck.

"Now you're ready," Elise says, grabbing my hand.

"For?"

The boys open the main double doors to the theatre, and the place is packed. I recognize a few kids from school on the aisle, but there are a lot of adults, mostly couples, I notice. The smell of fresh popcorn hits my nose and makes my mouth water. Brian hands me a red-and-white-striped bag, popcorn still warm inside.

"What's going on?"

Angela bends down to Elise. "Run and go sit with Mom."

Elise hugs my legs before she scampers off, and Angela points to the stage, leading our group down the aisle to our row in the middle of the middle, my favorite seat anywhere. In front of the curtain, the giant white pull-down screen used to project announcements before a show displays a graphic with shimmery stars and pink curly font that says *Happy 17th Birthday, Maddie!*

I gape at the full house and whisper, "Surely all these people aren't here for me. I don't know most of them!"

"Think of it as a little private viewing party," Tiffany says, pouring a bag of M&M's over her popcorn. "Some Valentine's

Day fun for some of our friends, and maybe their friends, and maybe their parents and some of their parents' friends," she adds with a laugh.

"But if it weren't also your birthday, this wouldn't be happening." Angela reaches across me for the box of Milk Duds that Sarah's holding hostage.

"I don't even know what to say," I say through an exhale, staring up at my name on the gigantic screen. "What happens next?"

The house lights dim, and there's a frantic shuffling throughout the theatre as people open their candy wrappers and shift in their seats, preparing to be entertained. The graphic on the screen disappears, replaced by MGM's roaring lion logo, and as a very familiar string melody plays through the speakers all around me, my heart sprouts wings. The screen changes. Three black umbrellas hide three figures in rain slickers. One by one, names appear in yellow overtop the umbrellas: *Gene Kelly, Donald O'Connor, Debbie Reynolds.*

They pivot, and they sing. In the rain.

I can't hold in the tears this time. I'm sitting in the middle of a packed theatre, watching one of my favorite movies of all time on a huge screen, with surround sound. And popcorn.

I sense Angela staring at me just before she nudges me in the arm. "You said it was tragic you'd never get to see any of your favorite movies on the big screen."

This thought runs through my head every day, but I don't remember telling her in those words. But I did tell—

"I have a confession to make," she whispers close to my ear as the opening number continues. "As much as I'd like to take credit for all of this, it wasn't my idea. It was Jesse's."

My eyes flood, throat tight. "Why would he do all of this for me?" I swipe my cheek with the back of my hand. "He doesn't want me anymore."

"I don't think that's true," she says, giving my arm a reassuring pat. "He's just a baby sometimes. He's under a lot of pressure, and I don't think he knows how to handle it."

"Clearly," I bite through a trembling bottom lip.

"Just give him time." She slips her hand into mine and squeezes. "I think you both just need to take some time. Know what I mean?"

I nod, thinking about how time changes things. How it's changed me since I got here, barely six months ago. I've grown to love our small cozy house, and I've gained a new brother who I would already do anything for. I'm closer to my parents and somehow closer to my big brother, even being several hours away. I've finally found the set of friends I believe I was always meant to find. The kind of friends who would paint stars on their faces and organize a private Valentine's-birthday viewing of *Singin' in the Rain*.

I may be a little confused about my future, but I've got time to figure it out. Time. I just need to give it time.

"Yes," I say, clenching her hand in return before reaching into my bag of popcorn. "I know what you mean."

As the movie plays on, I find myself watching the audience just as much as the screen, relishing their reactions, their expressions that prove they're invested in the story, in the characters. They laugh at all the right places, and even some places I didn't realize were funny. Sharing this movie with them, it's like I'm seeing everything in a new perspective. So many people seem turned off by the idea of older movies, so much so they don't even give them a chance, but I always knew the heart and the comedy of the classics could translate, and I'm seeing it in this audience. Right here, right now. I've never had a better birthday present.

The screen goes black, the crowd applauds, and I sit in awe of it all and do the one thing I've been thinking about doing all night. I pull my phone out of my pocket and open a new text message to Jesse.

Me: Thank you. So much.

Angela pulls into my driveway at half past eleven and I'm happy to see my parents remembered to leave on the porch light. As much as I like our actual house now, it still freaks me out being outside in the woods in the middle of the night.

"Thanks for tonight, Angela," I say, grabbing my purse from the floor and pulling my coat tighter around me. "Best night of my life. Seriously. Gene on the big screen. I can't believe it."

And I can't believe it was Jesse's idea. I'm still so excited, I might not sleep tonight.

"Yay!" She claps a couple times, and I can see her face beam in the glow from the dashboard. "I'm so happy you were surprised!"

"Totally surprised." I lean in to hug her. "Sets the bar pretty high for your birthday this summer, but I'm sure Tiffany and I can come up with something stellar."

"Oh, we can just do a pool party or something easy. I have, like, zero hobbies to pull inspiration from."

"Pshhh," I hiss. "We'll just have to see."

We air-kiss our good-byes and I sprint to the porch and up the steps. I hear Angela's tires meet the gravel of their driveway across the street as I approach the door with the key, and my foot knocks something over. A box.

A box of yellow cake mix. And next to it, a tub of chocolate icing.

My eyebrows pull together as my mouth flips into a smile. I pick them up, and my heart races when I find messy writing on the front of the box in thick black marker:

Maddie, I don't know how to bake,
but I know you like yellow cake.
I didn't mean for that to rhyme.
Happy birthday. From, Jesse

CHAPTER THIRTY-TWO

Part of me hoped things would go back to the way they were between Jesse and me. I don't think it's unreasonable, considering the movie night he set up for my birthday and the cake mix he left at my door with the note. I thought maybe if I gave it time, like Angela suggested, it would make him ache for me the way I'm aching for him. But over the following couple of weeks, nothing's different. We're cordial, and he still smiles and occasionally jokes around like we're old pals, but it's like he's deep in thought all the time.

I am too. Wondering what I could have done differently, could have said. But I only ever said what I was feeling. I never lied about anything.

It's like Jesse's permanently infiltrated my brain, and I'm forever doomed to be reminded of him everywhere I look. A hunting sticker of a deer head on the back window of someone's vehicle reminds me of the baby deer he was so sweet to show me that morning. Any old-fashioned truck, no matter the color or condition, brings me back to our carpool days and all the wasted opportunities to get to know him on a deeper level. Kids zipping down the street on four-wheelers remind me of our adventures through the woods, which of course make me think of sparklers and midnight and kissing.

His stupid amazing kissing.

Makes it hard to focus on getting *me* straightened out when all I can think about is how much I miss *us*.

But today's practice for the talent competition is too important for me to be distracted by Jesse's ghost. It's our first rehearsal in costume and our last before the performance tonight. I have to be on top of my game along with everyone else, though Brian's also a bit scattered because Kristi's driving in from Dallas to watch.

We're performing a few scenes from the Marilyn Monroe movie *Some Like It Hot*, about two musicians in 1929 who witness a massacre, then dress in drag and join an all-women's jazz band to escape mobsters who want to kill them. Sarah masterfully arranged highlights from the first few scenes where the guys pretend to be girls, board the train with the band to head to Florida for a gig, and get to know Marilyn's character, the band's singer, Sugar Kane—the character I get to play. Sarah's directing us and playing the small role of Sweet Sue, the bandleader. Ryan plays the more serious guy, Tony Curtis's character, Joe or "Josephine," and Brian naturally gets to play Jack Lemmon's hysterical character, Jerry, who's supposed to go by "Geraldine" but changes it to "Daphne" at the last minute.

The boys are in my bedroom helping each other fasten and stuff their bras—they refuse to accept help—and Sarah and I are waiting in the living room, fully dressed in short blond wigs and black dresses with fringe. Instead of the standard star near my eye, today I've drawn a mole on my chin to better channel Marilyn. I may or may not have also stuffed my bra.

"Okay. We need to talk," Sarah says, setting her clipboard of notes on the coffee table. "I can't handle the moping anymore."

I strum the ukulele we borrowed from the playhouse's prop closet. "What's that from?"

"It's not a quote, it's from me. About you. What's going on? Are you still hung up on Jesse?"

I stuff the ukulele in its case and shift on the couch, careful not to tangle any of the fringe on my dress. "I didn't realize I was moping . . ." *Outwardly.*

"Well, you're not your normal chipper self. It just doesn't seem like you to hang on to it for so long. Look at all that stuff that happened with Rica that you let bounce off you. You're tough."

I reach for my glass and take a sip of water, stalling for time as I try to figure out what to say. "It's not him *exactly*. It's more some of the things he said. Some of it stuck with me. I've just had a lot on my mind." I run a finger along the rim of my cup. "I didn't mean for it to show."

"What did he say?" she asks, carefully scratching the side of her head through her wig.

"That he'll never be what I want him to be." I take a deep breath. "That he knows what I want, and he's not him."

"Yikes." Her eyes widen. "What does that even mean?"

"He was upset I was pushing him to be what he used to be." I return my cup to the side table. "A dancer."

Sarah makes a contemplative noise.

"I wanted him to embrace all of his interests, to be proud of all of them, and he called me out for only liking half of him." My throat burns with the threat of emotional overflow, but I swallow it away.

"Is that legit? Do you think you only liked half of him?"

I'm too afraid to answer, because that's probably exactly what I did. And that sounds horrible and selfish and stupid.

"Well, you don't want to dance anymore, right?" She pauses and I nod. "So why is it so hard for you to get that Jesse doesn't want to either?"

Gee, she's really twisting the knife. But I deserve it. "I get that he says he doesn't want to pursue it. I just had a hard time accepting it because of his skill level. He's incredible."

"Well, you might be some crazy-good volleyball player, but because you're not interested in it, you don't play."

This stumps me. I've never given a second thought to volleyball. I've never even played. I assume that because I don't care about it, I wouldn't be any good, but what she says makes sense. I could be awesome at it, at anything I've never tried. Anyone could.

A memory pops to mind . . . something Jesse said before we were together. *"Just because you're good at something doesn't mean that it's what you should be doing."*

Or that you *want* to do it.

I let my head fall back against the couch. "I really am a dope, aren't I?"

Why did I ever think I could force my ideals onto him? I

can't make Jesse dance in front of people any more than he can make me take up softball. How many times did he try to tell me he didn't want to perform anymore and I wouldn't take it seriously? I kept rationalizing it in my head, blaming his negative attitude about it on his dad and what the other kids would say. But it wasn't any of that making up his mind; it was always him.

I only saw what I wanted to see.

The boys strut in with hands on their hips, wearing stockings and dresses and coats and wigs and dainty hats and *high heels*. Absolute perfection.

I buckle over in laughter, but Sarah stands and exclaims, "We're gonna win this whole thing!"

Jesse's nearly the first person I see when I get to the school's theatre. He's dressed in all black, wearing a headset and pointing people where to go. We catch eyes, and he smiles, offering a little wave. I bite my lip and wave back. I have so much to tell him. I hope we get a chance to talk tonight.

He disappears as Sarah pushes me, the boys, and our props to one of the dressing rooms, already crammed with kids and costumes and glitter and instruments and vocalists warming up their voices, not all of them pleasing to the ears. After we stow our empty instrument cases and a huge roll of paper with the outside of a passenger train car painted on it, the click of hot-pink high heels catches our attention.

"Well, look at this room brimming with raw talent just waiting to be discovered," Rica says, crossing her skinny arms over her shimmery pink dress.

"Please," Brian fires back. "Are you expecting to get your big break tonight? It's a high school talent show, not open mic night at some famous bar in Nashville."

"Guess I know something y'all don't know. No surprise there." She tosses me a nasty smirk and turns to leave. "Good luck."

"*Good luck*?" Sarah hisses once Rica's out of earshot. "How many times do we need to say 'Break a leg' to cancel that out?"

I breathe slowly, in and out, finding my calm. "We can't let her in our heads. Ever. She doesn't deserve space there."

"Right, right." Sarah nods, hiking up her stockings. "Ugh, she's just so toxic."

I adjust my stockings as well. Sugar Kane is supposed to get caught sneaking alcohol, so I secure a small plastic flask in the band around my thigh. We go on later in the show, but I don't want to forget one of my character's only two props.

We're able to catch the first half of the show in the audience, over to the side where the performers rotate and watch. A few of the memorable acts include a pair of guys from my Spanish class who do some lasso tricks, Rica performing "Popular" from the Broadway musical *Wicked*—I hate to admit it, but she really is good and could possibly win this thing even though she's a *terrible person*—and the biggest surprise of all, Red's juggling act. He starts with a trio of baseballs and eventually ends up with five, then switches to wooden bats! The crowd eats up his showmanship, and I find myself thoroughly impressed by the whole thing. It's a shame he's so stupid when it comes to girls.

When it's nearly our turn, we gather all our props—I triple-check my flask is still secure—and wait in the dark wings, watching the profiles of the singing act before us. I'm lost in a pre-performance trance when I feel a hand slide into my right one from behind. The familiar size and the calluses on the palm make my breath catch in my throat.

A warm whisper on the back of my neck. "Break a leg, *mi reina.*"

I close my eyes and smile through gritted teeth, refusing to get emotional. I can't do this now. I'll find him after the show. Tell him I'm sorry. That I want to make things right.

He's gone just as quickly as he came, and suddenly it's our turn. A pair of stage hands unroll our paper train across the stage, securing the ends onto music stands. Ryan and Brian shimmy onstage in their heels first, and before anything even comes out of their mouths, the audience is roaring. And we nail it. All of it. The timing, the blocking, the delivery. Better than we rehearsed. Better than I ever dreamed.

We exit the stage to fervent applause, and as we quietly hug each other but inwardly freak out about what we just did, I'm filled with a sense of accomplishment. When I was in *Crazy for You*, I never felt like anyone really saw me, like I contributed at all. I was too burdened by my inferior dancing to enjoy any of it. This time, I know this applause belongs, in part, to me.

A tingle worms its way through my body. A revelation. A truth I've known but needed a boost to believe.

I can act. And I love it. The characters. The lines. The stories to tell. That's what I want to do. That's what I'm good at.

I look at Sarah and the boys.

That's what *we're* good at.

We store our props in the dressing room and find some empty seats to watch the rest of the show, but I hardly know what's happening. My mind is still whirling, reviewing our performance and wishing we had the opportunity to do it again. I can't remember the last time I had so much fun onstage.

The competition ends, and Mrs. Morales steps into the spotlight. "Let's hear it one more time for the students of Fernwood High!" The audience cheers wildly. "While our judges come to their decision, we've got a special treat for your entertainment. Please welcome Jesse Morales, with musical accompaniment by Shauna Riggs, Donna Lufkin, Jeffrey Pratt, Colter Light, and Michael Sparks from the Fernwood High Orchestra!"

Wait, WHAT?

With the clapping and dimness of the theatre, my head is so clouded. I have to rub my eyes to make sure everything's working right.

I turn to Sarah. "Did she say Jesse? As in—"

She nods and nudges me to look at the stage as a few colored lights paint a soft glow on the sparse set. A set that I recognize immediately. A three-tiered wooden platform sits upstage to the right, with a chair and a small table strewn with newspaper to the left. An open sheet of newspaper is spread on the middle of the floor. It's from *Summer Stock.* My favorite scene.

Jesse's carefree whistle fills the theatre as he walks slowly across the stage, hands in his pockets, and I'm likely one of only two people in this building who know the words that melody represents. It's the song "You Wonderful You." He continues whistling, starting on the tapping, and it's only then that I realize he's wearing the outfit too: tight yellow polo shirt and blue pants with the cuffs rolled up, exposing his ankles.

I think I'm having a heart attack.

The kids from the orchestra take over for his whistling with their horns and a few strings, and he's flying through the routine, exactly how Gene does it, incorporating the noises of a squeaky floorboard—a sound effect by someone offstage—and the shuffle of newspaper along with the taps. He does the whole number, even picking up the newspaper at the end, reading it and walking offstage, whistling again. It's perfect. He's perfect.

Why is he trying to kill me?

The audience goes mad, standing on their feet and clapping so much that Jesse has to come out and take a bow. I'm sad my mom planned to leave to feed Christopher just after my performance, because she missed one epically epic surprise with my name on it.

Eyes wide and unfocused, I'm still sitting numb in my chair when Mrs. Morales announces my name along with Brian's, Ryan's, and Sarah's as the first-prize winners. There's an acceptance, Brian makes a speech I don't hear, and the next thing I know, I'm standing in the middle of the middle of the theatre as people around me cluster in groups to chat and filter outside.

And there's Jesse, still in his yellow shirt, though the tap shoes are gone. A sheepish grin dances on his face.

"Before you say anything," he begins, "this isn't some big announcement that I'm jumping back on the stage. I'm not. I just wanted you to know that I'm not ashamed of this part of me."

I swallow, taking a beat to compose myself. "So . . . you don't care if the guys make fun of you for this?"

He shakes his head. "First of all, did you notice the standing ovation? That's not something I'm going to forget after a few jabs." He laughs it off, but I know he loves the attention. "But also, you sort of opened my eyes to something."

"*I* did?" My hand finds my chest and rests there, heartbeat running wild.

"My real friends aren't going to care what I do."

My eyes spill over, and happy laughter sputters out of my mouth.

"Whoa," Jesse says, taking a step toward me. "Why are you crying?"

The happy laughter twists into near sobs, which I fight with all my strength to control. "I'm so sorry. It was wrong of me to try to change you like that. You were right, about everything."

He reaches for my hands, and I anchor to his like a lifeline.

"I thought I knew what I wanted," I continue, "and instead of seeing it in you all along, I annoyed you with my whining until you couldn't take it anymore." I swipe at my nose. "I can't stand whiners, and I totally was one."

He wraps his arms around me, and I blubber onto his shoulder.

"I'm so, so sorry," I keep on, in case the message hasn't gotten through. "I love who you are and what you can do, and I think you're amazing. And I miss you."

His head rests on top of mine as he says, "All of that, right back at ya."

After a few minutes of holding each other, we sit in the still-crowded auditorium, but he keeps an arm around me, so I snuggle against him.

"How did you know that was my favorite dance?" I finally ask.

He kisses my temple. "It wasn't that hard to figure out."

"You're incredible. I hope someone filmed that, because if not, you'll be doing it again."

Now he kisses my forehead and holds it longer. "I took care of it."

"You're amazing. Did I say that already?"

"Well, I think you're pretty amazing too. You were incredible up there tonight."

"Thanks." I smile, nestling closer to his side. "And I'm sorry, if I didn't say that already too. If you want to be a baseball star, that's what I want too."

I feel him exhale underneath me. "You want to know what kept me in dance as long as I stayed with it?" I nod. "Girls in leotards."

"Get out." I slap his arm.

"Seriously. I got to hang out with a room full of them every day, dance close to them, lift them. I mean, you get to touch girls pretty much everywhere. Why wouldn't I want to do that?"

"Ugh, you're such a guy," I scoff, though I can't stop smiling.

"But when I started showing potential with baseball, my dad wouldn't let it go. Then I grew to love it, and Dad talked me into quitting performing—"

"But you still dance on your own."

"Yeah. It's a great workout, so I like keeping up with it. It would be a waste to just let everything go that I spent years learning. But training and preparing for shows, it takes too much time away from baseball. As much as I might get annoyed with my dad for his micromanaging, it's still what I want for myself."

I let this sink in. "I know I didn't see much of your practice before you got beamed, but from what I could tell, you're just as good at that as you are at dancing. I think you're going to go far; I really believe that."

He hooks a finger under my chin and tilts my face up to look at him. "Thank you for saying that."

He presses his lips to mine and I lose all awareness of where I am. Oh, how I've missed this. The floating, the spinning, the chills. When we surface, I lean over the armrest between us and snuggle back down against his chest. I know we can't sit here all night, but just a little bit longer. I need to soak it in. Believe it's happening.

"It's about time you two kissed and made up." Tiffany's voice cuts through my daze, echoing through the near empty theatre. "Speaking of kissing, did y'all see the lips on that guy who was helping you with music, Jesse? The taller guy on the end. I don't know what that instrument is called. One of the horns."

"Oh." Jesse clears his throat and crosses an ankle at the knee, relaxing deeper into the chair. "Sorry. He doesn't like girls."

"Ugh, figures." Tiffany rests her fists on her hips. "What about the guy next to him. He wasn't too bad looking."

"Colter," Jesse says, amused. "I'll introduce you."

"Sweet, thanks! Great job with the tappity-tapping, by the way. Super hot." She flips back her ponytail from in front of her. "Okay, I'm outta here. Congrats on the win, Maddie. Y'all were awesome!"

As we watch her nearly skip down the aisle, Brian and a short, ginger-headed girl make their way toward us.

"Hey, we're about to leave," Brian says, "but I wanted you to meet Kristi."

"Oh!" I spring to my feet and extend my hand, but she flings her arms around my neck.

"It's so good to finally meet you," she says in a thick and adorable Southern drawl. "Y'all did *so* good tonight!"

"Thanks!" I say, returning the hug. "I'm so glad to meet you too."

"I've never seen that movie, but I'm dying to now!"

"We'll watch it tomorrow," Brian says, reaching for her hand to pull her close, ears flaming red. He's completely smitten, and it's adorable. "I borrowed the DVD from Maddie to practice."

My work here is done.

After I introduce her to Jesse, Kristi and Brian leave to get frozen yogurt with Sarah and Ryan to celebrate. I decline the invite in favor of staying with Jesse alone just a little longer. I'm hoping there's a way we can ride home together.

When we sit back down, I clear my throat and muster the courage to ask the heavy question I'm not completely sure I want an answer to. "So, I need to know something."

He leans into me. "Anything."

"I need to know you don't feel pressure to be with someone like . . . Gabby. I'm not going to cause problems for you or anything, am I?" I hold perfectly still, waiting for his response.

"You're worried about my dad." He nods, understanding, but then the nod evolves into a shake. "Don't be. Ever. Please. He gets it. He fell in love with my mom, didn't he?" The corner of his mouth perks in its cute little way.

He said love and didn't flinch. My insides warm.

"I'm proud of where I come from," he continues, "but it's only a part of who I am. I have to be my own person, and know what I want for myself. And what I want is to be with you."

My cheeks hurt from grinning like a fool. "That's what I want too."

"Oh, you haven't left yet." Mrs. Morales approaches us fast. "You kids did so good, I can't stop smiling!"

We stand and Mrs. Morales pulls her son into her arms.

"I'm so glad you decided to do a talent show instead of a big spring musical," I say.

"Me too, me too. Listen," she says, switching to serious mode. "I've been looking for you. I've already got the rest of your team in my office. Mr. and Mrs. Campbell want to meet with y'all."

My pulse races as I brace myself for clarification. Anytime someone calls you to their office, it's an automatic sinking feeling. "Who?"

"They're talent scouts. They work for an agency downtown. I've known them for years; they're completely legitimate. Anyway, they thought the four of you really put together something special."

Talent scouts! This has to be the thing Rica was being so cryptic about. I'm surprised she didn't make a huge deal about it to throw everyone off their game. But then she'd lose her advantage of being the only one who knew how important our performances were tonight.

"Whoa. Who else do they want to talk to?" I ask.

"A few from the orchestra and Rica."

Of course. I can only console myself with the hope that one day she'll get the wake-up call that forces her to change the way she treats people.

"And Jesse," she adds, beaming at him.

Jesse raises his hands and shakes his head. "No way; this was a one-time thing. Unless they're also baseball scouts, I'm going to pass."

She nods, her smile breaking only a fraction. "I told them that's what you'd say. Just know, they said they were extremely impressed and you did the famous number proud. And I'm proud too, of course." She places a hand on his shoulder before turning back to me. "So, can you be in my office in a few minutes?"

"Yes, ma'am! Thank you so much!" I call as she scurries back the way she came.

Jaw slack, I turn to Jesse, whose smile is wider than I've ever seen. "This could be good, right?"

He laughs. "My little Marilyn." He lifts me into a hug, twirling me in a circle, and my wig falls to the floor.

I snatch it and comb my fingers through my real hair, matted and sweaty. "Ugh, I'm sorry you have to see me like this. I feel disgusting."

He shushes me with a finger to my lips. "You're beautiful."

"You are." I smile a stupidly giddy smile and bury my face in his neck. "Have I mentioned how sorry I am?"

"Stop it." He palms the back of my head and makes me look at him. "No more apologizing. We're good, all right?"

And because I've missed his lips so, I lean forward until we're touching, ever so softly. "All right."

Clasping my hand, he leads me to the side aisle to make our way to his mom's office for my meeting. I'm buzzing with anticipation, no idea what they're going to say. Do they come right out and offer something? Representation? Classes?

We make it to the front hallway and a flash of yellow catches my eye. I look up to the doorway just in time to spot Angela leaving with . . . *Red*? And they're holding hands! I'm about to squeal when I realize Jesse didn't see, and I decide to save that discussion for later. But this smile isn't going away any time soon. This whole day is proof that time changes things. You just have to have the patience to see it through.

"You know," I say, tugging on his hand, "I still haven't heard you sing."

"You will." He flashes me that smirk I haven't seen in so long. "We've got plenty of time."

"Yeah." My insides tingle. "We do."

When the door to the office comes into sight, Jesse slows our pace, neither of us ready to split up just yet.

"So, I've got a home game next weekend," he says.

"Yeah? Are you pitching?"

"Of course." He pretends to polish the fingernails of his free hand on his shirt. "I was sort of hoping you might want to come watch."

I let go of his hand and slide mine around his waist, pressing myself closer against the side of his body. He drapes his arm over my shoulder, and nothing's ever felt so perfect, so right.

I stretch up on my toes and kiss the tiny scar on his cheek. "Can't wait."

THANK YOU:

God, for life and love and journeys and dreams.

Josh, for taking the journey with me, and supporting my dreams. Layla, for showing me what love really is. Mom, for introducing me to classic movies at an early age, dancing with me in the living room, and singing with me at the top of your lungs. Dad, for giving me the signed head shot of Gene Kelly when I was in high school. Looking at it every day since gave me inspiration and courage to write this story. Grandma Rosie, for making my dress up clothes, and for the seemingly crazy yet brilliant ideas you share with me. My sweet in-laws—I will never cease to be thankful for your love and support.

Marietta Zacker, for your expert agenting skills. I can't imagine walking this publishing path with anyone else. Sarah Shumway, for helping me whip this story into shape while keeping the heart safe. Laura Whitaker and the Bloomsbury team. Y'all are simply wonderful.

Katie M. Stout, Kristi Chestnutt, and Kim Franklin, my critique pals of wonder. I will be forever thankful I found my Ks! Lauren Magaziner, you know what you did and you know how thankful I am for it! Maria Cari Soto, the best beta reader ever. Jennifer Haight, for letting me tag along to high school plays and musicals. Christin Baker, for allowing me to pick your brain. Madalyn, for sharing your youthful insights and wisdom. Kristin Thetford, for cheering me on via Gchat until three in the morning when I reached The End. The Lufkin Six, for the advice, support, and encouragement. The YAHous, for accepting me with open arms. The lovely ladies from the Class of 2k14 and everyone in OneFour KidLit, for one exciting debut year! Boni's Dance and Performing Arts Studio, for the tap classes!

Author, writing, and blogging friends: Amy Finnegan, Mandy Hubbard, Joy Preble, Christina Mandelski, Dahlia Adler, Sharon Morse, Jessica Capelle, Kirsten Squires, Mari Ferrer, Katy Upperman, Jesselle from The Lifelong Bookworm, Jamie from The Perpetual Page-Turner, Jana from That Artsy Reader Girl, Kate from Ex Libris, Ginger from GReads!, and Hazel from Stay Bookish. Thank you for the book love, reviews, and tweets. Feeling supported means more than I can say!

Gene Kelly, for changing entertainment history and for continuing to inspire even after you left us. This accomplishment in my writing career would not exist without you, and for that I can never thank you enough.

Kristin Rae is the author of the If Only title *Wish You Were Italian* and was brought up on classic movies and often daydreams that her life is one big musical number. A former figure-skating coach, LEGO merchandiser, and photographer, she's now happy to create stories while pretending to ignore the carton of gelato in the freezer. Kristin lives in Houston, Texas, with her husband, daughter, and their two boxers.

www.kristinrae.com
@kristincreative